"Tell me wha ~~snatching th~~ **tossing it ove** ~~one of~~ **very grown-up looking shoulders.**

When exactly had the Cade Montgomery she'd grown up with transformed into a fully adult man? Had she been in some sort of trance for the past decade or so?

Yes, she had. It was called grief. She'd hoped and prayed its dark cloud would lift one day. She'd just never imagined that when it finally did, she'd come so completely unglued.

"I appreciate the offer, but I've got everything under control," she lied. Then she reached for the towel to grab it back.

Cade caught her wrist just before her fingertips made contact with the soft cotton, and for a second, it was like the old days back in middle school when he and Ethan would tease her and play keep-away with her pom poms, tossing them back and forth to each other over her head. She squirmed, laughing as she struggled against his grasp and poked at Cade's ribs with her free hand.

"Cade, please. You are *such* a child."

Her throat went dry, and she tried to convince herself she was only imagining it—this strange, delicious swirl of sensation. But then Cade's eyes darkened a shade or two until his irises were as brooding and dangerous as the sky over Bishop Falls during one of its legendary Texas thunderstorms. He felt it, too, didn't he?

Whatever this was, it was real. And it was wrong.

So very wrong.

Dear Reader,

Welcome back to Bishop Falls, Texas, home of the legendary high school state football champions, the Bishop Bulldogs! Now that the Bulldogs have their long-awaited championship, things in Bishop Falls should be smooth sailing. Or so everyone thinks...

Bailey Davis, town darling and owner of the local coffee shop, Huddle Up, has a secret. On the night of the championship ring ceremony, that secret begins to unravel in a spectacular fashion.

Quarterbacks coach Cade Montgomery has been Bailey's best friend since they were kids. Growing up, Cade, Bailey and Bailey's late husband, Ethan, were inseparable. Four years have passed since Ethan's heartbreaking death, but the town still has Bailey up on her good girl, devoted wife pedestal. Ethan will always be a local hero, after all.

But Cade's feelings for Bailey have begun to change. He might just know her better than anyone else, secrets and all. He also knows no one in Bishop Falls is ready to see her give her heart to anyone who isn't Ethan...and even Cade himself might not be ready for that.

What follows that surprising night of the ring ceremony is filled with angst, humor and even more secrets. I couldn't wait to write Bailey and Cade's story. Even when I was writing the first book in this series, *The Perfect Pass*, I kept thinking about Bailey and Cade and how they needed to end up together. I hope you enjoy the ride as much as I did.

Happy reading!

Teri

THEIR SECRET PLAYBOOK

TERI WILSON

SPECIAL EDITION

MIX
Paper | Supporting responsible forestry
FSC® C021394
www.fsc.org

Harlequin®
SPECIAL
EDITION™

Recycling programs for this product may not exist in your area.

ISBN-13: 978-1-335-18037-7

Their Secret Playbook

Harlequin Enterprises ULC
22 Adelaide St. West, 41st Floor
Toronto, Ontario M5H 4E3, Canada
www.Harlequin.com

HarperCollins Publishers
Macken House, 39/40 Mayor Street Upper,
Dublin 1, D01 C9W8, Ireland
www.HarperCollins.com

Printed in Lithuania

New York Times bestselling author **Teri Wilson** writes heartwarming, feel-good contemporary romance with a touch of whimsy. Four of Teri's books have been adapted into Hallmark Channel movies, including fan favorite *Unleashing Mr. Darcy*. Teri is a recipient of the prestigious RITA® Award for Excellence in Romantic Fiction and a recent inductee into the San Antonio Women's Hall of Fame. When not writing, Teri enjoys spreading doggy joy with her Cavalier King Charles spaniel, Charm, a registered therapy dog.

Books by Teri Wilson

Harlequin Special Edition

Texas Forever After

The Perfect Pass

Comfort Paws

Dog Days of Summer
Fa-La-La-La Faking It
Bluebonnet Season

Love, Unveiled

Her Man of Honor
Faking a Fairy Tale

Lovestruck, Vermont

Baby Lessons
A Firehouse Christmas Baby
The Trouble with Picket Fences

Furever Yours

How to Rescue a Family
A Double Dose of Happiness

The Fortunes of Texas: Secrets of Fortune's Gold Ranch

A Fortune's Secret

Visit the Author Profile page
at Harlequin.com for more titles.

Texas forever.

XOXO

Chapter One

If football had a golden rule, it would be this: never, *ever* drop the ball.

Like most people who'd grown up in Bishop Falls, Texas, Bailey Davis learned that lesson at an early age. So early, in fact, that her very first childhood memory was the sensation of being tossed in the air, giggling like mad as her mother implored her father to not "fumble the baby." Unbeknownst to Bailey at the time, that particular memory had been steeped in foreshadowing, because now—more than twenty-five years later—the entire population of Bishop Falls had taken it upon themselves to make sure *no one* fumbled the baby.

These days, the warning was a tad more metaphorical. Bailey was no longer an actual baby, but to anyone who knew her story, she was considered the angel of Bishop Falls—the tender-hearted, devoted young widow of the town's most beloved football hero. A hometown icon to be protected at all costs.

Heaven help the poor, misguided soul who fumbled Bailey Davis's heart.

Her gaze flitted toward Cade Montgomery, who was standing with the rest of their friend group at Huddle Up, the coffee shop Bailey owned and operated on Bulldog

Avenue in the heart of downtown Bishop Falls. She ran her dish towel over the same pristine spot she'd been wiping down for the past several minutes and then blinked as she realized she'd been staring.

Bailey had been doing that a lot lately—not staring so much as daydreaming, particularly when Cade was anywhere in the immediate vicinity. Honestly, she wasn't sure what was wrong with her. Sometimes she thought she was on the verge of having an honest-to-goodness breakdown of sorts. She was long overdue for one, she supposed. Still, it was disconcerting, and the Cade part wasn't even her most worrisome symptom.

Right on cue, she heard a thump from the back room of the coffee shop. Bailey froze, and when a mournful wail followed the thump, she coughed to try and cover it up. Cade was the only one who seemed to notice, thank goodness. His smoky gray eyes snapped in her direction, and she wiggled her fingertips in a little wave to indicate she was fine. *Everything* was fine. His gaze lingered a beat, his mouth tipping into a tender half smile before he turned back to their friends Jackson Knight and Calla Dunne.

Bailey went back to scrubbing the imaginary spot on the counter with renewed fervor.

She needed to get everyone out of here before her dirty little secret busted out of the back room and swished to the bar, demanding a saucer of steamed milk. Under normal circumstances, Huddle Up would've closed hours ago. Tonight's circumstances, however, were anything but normal.

"Thanks so much for having us here, Bailey." Cade, who was the quarterbacks coach of the newly christened

Texas state high-school champions, the Bishop Falls Bull-dogs, grinned at her from across the counter as he abandoned the conversation he'd been having to come chat with her. His massive championship ring glittered like a disco ball on the ring finger of his right hand. "I can't imagine a better place for the after-party, you know?"

Cade cast a meaningful glance at the portrait of Ethan Dunne that hung in a place of prominence just above the shiny chrome espresso machine that had been Bailey's pride and joy since she opened the coffee house shortly after her graduation from Bishop Falls High. He grinned, eyes softening in a way that never failed to make her heart clench.

Stop, Bailey told herself as her pulse started to gallop like a runaway horse. *Cade is just a friend—one of your best friends.* More importantly, he'd also been like a brother to Ethan. Back in high school, the three of them had been as thick as thieves. The Three Musketeers.

"Ethan would've really gotten a kick out of today," Cade said, and his smile turned bittersweet. The dimple in his left cheek that Bailey liked so much went into hiding again.

She swallowed hard. "He sure would've."

Like so many other small Texas towns, everything in Bishop Falls revolved around the high-school football team. Ethan had been a star player during senior year, and Bailey had been the head cheerleader. For the longest time, those innocent days had felt like yesterday. Lately, though, they'd begun to take on a hazy, dreamlike quality—like she was flipping through an old photo album instead of revisiting her own cherished memories. So much had changed since Ethan and Cade were co-captains on the team…and so much had been left behind. In a single, horrifying instant, all their hopes and dreams had shattered into pieces. Bailey had moved heaven and earth to hold everything together in the aftermath. She'd handled the subsequent years with a strength and grace that she hadn't even known she possessed. She'd had to.

For Ethan.

Cade's forehead creased as he toyed with the enormous ring on his finger, and he frowned down at it like it didn't quite belong there. Bailey knew exactly what direction his thoughts were spinning. Unlike everyone else at this after-party, he'd already moved on from the celebratory ring ceremony that had taken place earlier today in the high-school cafetorium. The Bulldogs had waited fourteen long years for another state championship, and they'd finally done it. The town would be celebrating for days, weeks, *months*. But from the moment Principal Dean slipped that ring onto Cade's finger, he'd been thinking about Ethan and the state championship that would've been theirs, if not for one bad tackle that had changed everything. Bailey knew Cade well enough to recognize when the past snuck up on him. Maybe because it did the same to her, most often when she least expected it to.

Sure enough, a muscle in his jaw flexed as he slid his hand off the counter, out of sight. "Everyone's about to head out. I'm sure you're more than ready to get this place closed up for the night."

Translation: the hardcore celebrants were moving on from Huddle Up and headed toward the town green, where they'd sit under the historic water tower and sip champagne out of plastic Bulldogs cups until the wee hours of the morning. At least that's what Bailey heard happened whenever the team had something big to celebrate. No one ever bothered to invite her to the afterparty's after-party. She was too pure of heart for that sort of revelry.

Don't fumble the baby!

If they only knew.

"Tell me what I can do to help," Cade said, snatching the dish towel away from her and tossing it over one of his very muscular, very grown-up-looking shoulders.

When exactly had the Cade Montgomery she'd grown up with transformed into a fully adult man? Had she been in some sort of trance for the past decade or so?

Yes, she had. It was called grief. She'd hoped and prayed the dark cloud would lift one day. She'd just never imagined that when it finally did, she'd come so completely unglued.

"I appreciate the offer, but I've got everything under control," she lied. Then she reached for the towel to grab it back.

Cade caught her wrist just before her fingertips made contact with the soft cotton, and for a second, it was like the old days back in middle school, when he and Ethan would tease her and play keep-away with her pompoms, tossing them back and forth to each other over her head. She squirmed, laughing as she struggled against his grasp and poked at Cade's ribs with her free hand.

"Cade, seriously," she squealed, giving him a wholly ineffectual swat. "You are *such* a child."

A flood of giggles escaped her, and she could feel Cade's warm breath against her cheek as he chuckled along, dangling the dish towel just above her head. Then their laughter lingered a heartbeat too long, fading into a silence that felt thicker than it should have. Their eyes met, and the playful spark between them was replaced with an electricity Bailey felt all the way down to her toes.

Her throat went dry, and she tried to convince herself she was only imagining it—this strange, delicious swirl of sensation. But then Cade's eyes darkened a shade or two until his irises were as brooding and dangerous as the sky over Bishop Falls during one of its legendary Texas thunderstorms. He felt it, too, didn't he?

Whatever this was, it was real. And it was wrong.

So very wrong.

"What are you two up to?" Jackson Knight, head coach of the Bulldogs, let out a laugh as he glanced back and forth between them.

Bailey had been so wrapped up in Cade and his crinkly eyes and his warm, comforting presence that she hadn't even realized Jackson had wandered over to them. And, oh, look—Calla was right beside him, because, of course, she was. She and Jackson had fallen hard for each other during football season. Bailey was genuinely thrilled for them. Calla was her best friend in the entire world.

She also happened to be Ethan's younger sister.

"What do you mean?" Bailey blurted and sprang away from Cade so fast that she slammed into the countertop. Good. Maybe that little jolt would knock some sense into her. "We're not doing anything."

"Are you okay, Bails?" Cade reached for her, eyeing her hip where it had just bumped into the hard wood. "Let me get you some ice."

"I don't need any ice." She wiggled out of his reach, cheeks burning as Jackson and Calla watched their exchange with curious interest. "I'm fine. I'm not a delicate little doll, you know."

"Sorry." Cade held up his hands and shot her a wounded look. "Just trying to help."

Great, she'd made things even more awkward. Could this night just end already so she could curl up in bed with a book? Alone, as per usual.

"I appreciate it, but I'm fine." She crossed her arms and tried her best to ignore the throb near her hipbone. Tomorrow, she'd probably have a whopper of a bruise.

"Yeah, you said that already." Cade tilted his head and regarded her through narrowed eyes.

That broody look was back again, and before Bailey realized what was happening, they seemed to be engaged in some sort of staring contest. Not the kind from their middle-school days, though—a new, different kind that made her feel like her knees had turned to water.

"Jackson's right. You two are up to something," Calla said. Her nose scrunched the way it always did when she was hot on the trail of a story.

Ugh, why did Bailey's best friend have to be a reporter for the local paper? She was far too perceptive for her own good.

Bailey blinked, willingly forfeiting the saucy staring contest in the interest of getting Cade—and everyone else—out of her coffee shop.

She beamed at Calla. "We're really not. In fact, Cade was just leaving." Bailey's gaze darted back to him and her smile instantly wobbled off her face. She *really* wished he'd stop doing that smoldering thing he had going on at the moment. It made it impossible for her to think straight. "He said so a few seconds ago. Right?"

"Right," he said. The corners of his lips twitched ever so slightly.

Not that Bailey was looking at his mouth or anything.

"You're sure you're okay?" Calla asked. "Because I could stay and—"

Another thump came from the back room, and this time, Bailey wasn't the only one who noticed.

Calla paused, inclining her ear toward the door that led to the storage area. "What was that?"

"What do you mean? What was what?" Bailey asked a little too quickly.

Goodness, she was the worst liar on the planet. Maybe she really was as pure of heart as everyone around here thought she was.

"I definitely heard something." Calla rested a hand on Jackson's chest, and Bailey's heart gave a little pull. They were so sweet together. If Bailey didn't know better, she might've mistaken the tug on her heartstrings as envy. "Did you?"

Jackson arched an eyebrow. "Maybe? It sort of sounded like something might've fallen off a shelf back there."

"I'm sure that's what it was. I got a big supply delivery earlier today, and with the party and everything, I haven't had a chance to unpack and organize things yet." Bailey took a deep breath. The lies were really beginning to pile up. "Which is why y'all should get going! I have so much to do around here, and look, everyone's already left to head over to the town green. You guys shut the place down."

She gestured at the empty coffee shop, praying they'd take the hint and go. When she turned back to her friends, her attention snagged on Ethan's portrait and her throat went thick. She wasn't even sure why.

"We'll get out of your hair," Calla said gently, wrapping Bailey in a hug. Her voice lowered to a whisper just before she let go. "Thank you for hosting the afterparty. It's almost like my brother was right here with us. He always wanted one of those silly state-champ rings."

Calla liked to pretend she still hated football, but Bailey knew better. Everyone did. Since Jackson came to town and took over as head coach of the Bulldogs, a lot had changed. There was nothing silly about how badly everyone had wanted the Bulldogs to win State. At long last, they had.

"He sure did," Bailey murmured, and for some reason, she found herself going out of her way to avoid looking at Cade.

After another round of goodbyes, the trio finally headed for the door. Bailey twisted the dish towel until she'd practically tied it into a knot as she waited for their silhouettes to disappear from view. When the coast was finally clear, she sprinted to the back room and pushed the door open.

Bailey's furry little hostage made an immediate escape, weaving around her legs with a rumbling purr. She scooped the kitty into her arms and pressed her face into the cat's plush, warm fur. *Hostage* was such an ugly word, and it didn't *technically* apply to this scenario. Not completely, anyway.

At least that's what Bailey told herself as—once again—she pushed away the thought of returning the world's sweetest feline to her rightful owner. She still had time to do the right thing, and she would…eventually.

Probably.

Guilt pricked her consciousness. *Look at yourself. You've somehow gone from town sweetheart to illicit kitten thief, and you don't even feel bad about it. You should be ashamed.*

Bailey *was* ashamed…

She just wasn't quite as ashamed as she was lonely, that's all.

"I'm taking you back first thing tomorrow," she whispered against Bluebell's chocolate-colored face. It was a lie, and they both knew it. The thirteen cans of gourmet cat food neatly lined up alongside the coffee beans for Huddle Up's signature Bulldog Brew spoke for themselves.

Bailey squeezed her eyes closed and let herself revel in the feel of a warm heart beating against her own. What would Ethan think if he could see her now? What would Cade think? And why on earth did she suddenly seem to care so much about the opinion of her dead husband's best friend?

Her thoughts were a mess right now—so much so that when she opened her eyes again, she thought she saw Cade standing just a few feet away, watching her with those piercing gray eyes of his, as if her loneliness had carried him straight back to her just like it had seemed to lure Bluebell to Huddle Up's doorstep.

But then he spoke, and she knew he wasn't a figment of her imagination at all.

"Bailey?" He took a step closer as a look of stunned disbelief etched itself onto his handsome features, and

Bailey no longer needed to wonder what he might think if he could see her now. A crooked smile tipped his lips, and she could suddenly read his mind as clear as day.

"That cat looks awfully familiar," he said in a voice laced with teasing charm.

He knew exactly what she'd done, and miraculously, he wasn't judging her. There wasn't a trace of pity in his gaze, either, and Bailey's gratitude was so immense that her knees nearly buckled. There wasn't a single person in Bishop Falls who didn't feel sorry for Bailey Davis. Sometimes she got so sick of it that she wanted to scream. If she hadn't had an armful of stolen cat right then, she might've kissed him smack on the lips.

There you go again, thinking about kissing Cade Montgomery.

Town angel? What a joke.

Chapter Two

Cade Montgomery crossed his arms and stood quietly for a beat, trying to wrap his head around what he'd just stumbled upon.

Surely, it wasn't what it looked like. It *couldn't* be what it looked like. Because what it looked like was that Bailey Davis—sweet, kind, good Bailey Davis—was the nefarious person responsible for the profusion of missing-cat posters that had been plastered all over Bishop Falls for the past four weeks.

Or had it been five? Cade wasn't altogether sure. All he knew was that the lost cat had been the subject of multiple articles in the *Lone Star Gazette*, at least two crime-blotter updates on the local television news and a substantial portion of the town's gossip train, which had been churning full steam ahead since the day the kitten disappeared.

Such was life in rural Texas. The fact that the missing cat belonged to the town's mayor, a self-proclaimed cat lady, didn't help. Everyone this side of Oklahoma had heard about her lost kitten. Around town, theories abounded regarding the cat's whereabouts, and the speculation seemed to get more outlandish the longer the feline was missing. The last Cade heard, the rumor du jour involved an alien abduction.

Cade had never bought in to that one, and apparently he'd been correct. Because the kitten was right here, safely within the confines of the earth's atmosphere, blinking its bright blue eyes at him. As cats went, this one was awfully cute. Abduction-worthy, for sure. If Cade had been a space alien, he'd have been sorely tempted.

"What are you doing here?" Bailey asked crisply, as if the cat in question was thoroughly invisible and he hadn't just asked why you couldn't swing a stick in Bishop Falls without hitting a missing-cat poster with its exact face printed on it.

Nice try, but Cade wasn't giving up that easily.

He tilted his head. "You didn't answer my question, Bails."

He couldn't stop the smile that blossomed on his lips. The thought of Bailey doing something as out of character as stealing a cat was even more comical than it was impossible to believe. Not that pet thievery was particularly amusing... Not really.

This was just the most bizarre turn of events he could possibly imagine, that's all.

"Why does that cat look so familiar?" he repeated.

"Maybe Bluebell just has one of those faces," Bailey said quickly. Her cheeks flamed as pink as the little bows that decorated her Huddle Up apron. The print featured footballs topped with carnation-pink ribbons, tied into bows. If that specific combination didn't sum up Bailey in a nutshell, nothing else could. "Bluebell is a Ragdoll kitten. Ragdolls all have a common look."

Cade had no idea what a Ragdoll kitten was. A breed, he supposed?

Bailey clutched the cat closer to her chin. "You still haven't answered *my* question. What are you doing here? I thought you were going to the after-party."

So this was it? She expected him to pretend that she hadn't turned into a literal cat burglar sometime in the past four weeks?

"I was worried about you," he said, and then he cleared his throat and looked away. The admission made him feel uncharacteristically bare. Vulnerable, even.

Cade knew he spent far more time thinking about his best friend's widow than he should—especially lately. But the second he averted his gaze, his eyes landed on Ethan's portrait. He swallowed hard and refocused on Bailey.

I was worried about you.

How much was she reading into that simple statement? Cade wished he knew.

Bailey stared at him for a moment that stretched just a little too long. Then she walked past him toward the front door, flipped the lock into place and pulled the shade down so no one could see inside—presumably to hide the cat, not him. Although, if anyone in Bishop Falls knew how he truly felt about Bailey Davis, they'd no doubt think he didn't belong at Huddle Up after hours any more than Mayor Pearl's kitten did.

Bailey's shoulders sagged when she spun back around to face him. "You shouldn't have come back."

She set the kitten on the floor. It slunk toward Cade, waving its chocolate-brown tail and mewing sweetly. He could see why she'd called it a Ragdoll. It looked like one—soft, floppy and utterly adorable.

Nothing at all like the animal Cade spent most of his time with—Bishop, the slobbery bulldog mascot of Bishop High School's football team. Bishop belonged to Jackson, Cade's best friend and boss, which meant Cade spent a good amount of time with the dog. Enough time that the bottom hem of the khaki pants and sneakers he wore to work at the high school were typically covered in drool by the time he got home every night.

The kitten rubbed against his leg, and he scooped it up with one hand. The little thing was as light as a feather.

"Bluebell, huh?" he asked. "That's her name?"

"Yes," Bailey said, but she didn't quite meet his gaze.

She'd always been the worst liar in the world. A memory flickered in Cade's mind of Ethan trying to teach her how to bluff in Texas Hold'em back in high school. *It's no use, bro,* Cade had said with a shake of his head. *Your girl's too wholesome to fib to anyone's face like that.*

He'd meant it as a compliment, but Bailey had taken it as a personal challenge. She'd spent the rest of the night targeting him in a series of ill-fated bluffs that made her blow through her stacks of quarters and dimes in record speed. Cade had ended up with enough of her pocket change to fund an entire semester of postfootball-practice vending-machine purchases.

She'd obviously never gotten any better at subterfuge. It was nice to know that some things never changed...

Even after almost everything Cade ever knew and counted on had.

He glanced at the cat's pink collar, barely visible through the thick piles of fluff, and arched an eyebrow at Bailey. *Busted.* "If her name is Bluebell, then why does her tag say 'Baby'?"

"Fine," Bailey huffed as she wadded her dish towel into a ball and threw it at his face. The cat in his arms didn't even flinch as it came hurtling toward them. Cade had never seen such a laid-back feline in his life. "You win. She's the mayor's cat and I've been keeping her in hiding and calling her by a new name like I'm the evil main character in a baby-snatching Lifetime movie."

Cade bit back a smile. "A baby-snatching Lifetime movie? That's a thing?"

"Very much a thing." Bailey crossed her arms. "Is that really what you want to talk about right now? Made-for-television suspense movies and their subgenres?"

"I have so many questions…about *a lot,* Bails. We can circle back to the TV thing, though." He walked slowly toward her as he scratched the sweet cat under the chin. The animal purred up a storm, and it vibrated through Cade's chest with a pleasant hum. That's what he told himself, anyway, because he refused to believe that the soft thrum of his senses had anything to do with Bailey…or the thrill of how she'd just managed to catch him so off guard when he'd thought there were no surprises left between them, save for the one he fully intended to take to his grave.

Guys weren't supposed to develop feelings for their dead best friends' widows. He may as well have set fire to each and every clause of the bro code.

"It's not what you think," Bailey said, swallowing hard enough for Cade to trace the movement up and down the graceful column of her throat.

Heaven help him, he wanted to bury his face in her

dark hair and place his lips against the tender curve that ran from her ear to her shoulder. He wanted it so much that he could practically feel the eyes on Ethan's portrait burning a hole in the back of his head.

Cade gently placed the Ragdoll on the floor, lest she burst into flames. Collateral damage.

"How do you know what I'm thinking?" he countered. *Please,* please *don't know*.

"I guess I don't, but you're looking at me in a strange way right now. If you're thinking that I put on a ski mask and snuck into Mayor Pearl's house and stole Baby, I didn't." She bit her bottom lip, like his opinion of her really, truly mattered.

As if he had any right to judge Bailey Davis.

He reached out and tucked a lock of her hair behind her ear. "You mean, like a cat burglar?"

A giggle broke free, light and sudden. Cade's heart squeezed tight at the sound of her laughter.

"You're ridiculous," she said, but the smile still danced on her lips.

"Says the woman who's keeping a kitty cat captive," he teased.

The Ragdoll sat back on her haunches and watched their interaction with interest, blue eyes sparkling in the dim light of the closed coffee shop.

"You know what else is ridiculous?" Bailey tilted her head.

"Naming a cat 'Baby'?"

"Yes! Exactly!" She gave him a playful shove—something she'd done a million times before, but this time felt different. His chest tightened, a strange heat blooming in the place where her fingertips lingered.

Before he could stop himself, he reached down and covered her hand with his, anchoring it in place.

She glanced down at their fingers, which had some-how become intertwined, and to Cade's astonishment, she didn't look the least bit surprised. On the contrary, she looked—dare he think it—happy. Relieved, almost. As if touching like this had been a foregone conclusion.

"I approve of the choice to rename her," he said as he gave her hand a tender squeeze.

She blinked up at him, eyes full of secrets, and he wondered what else she'd been hiding from him and ev-eryone else in town. "Aren't you going to ask me how long I've had her? Or how she ended up here?"

"I'm pretty sure that would make me an accomplice—an accessory at the very least," he said as a smile tugged at the corners of his mouth.

"This entire conversation makes you an accessory, unless you plan on reporting me to the authorities." Her forehead puckered with worry. "Or taking the cat away."

Did she really think he would do something like that? Cade would never. He was Team Bailey, no matter what.

Besides, she wouldn't last a hot minute in a jail cell—not even the rinky-dink holding cell at the local law-enforcement office where the sheriff played old Johnny Cash records constantly and served "prisoners" biscuits and gravy from Hal's Diner for breakfast. Cade had be-come intimately familiar with this routine when he and Ethan had participated in an ill-fated, mascot-stealing prank during sophomore year. The rivalry between the Bishop Bulldogs and the Rustwood Roosters was legend-ary—then *and* now. Absconding with a live rooster had sounded like a walk in the park, but that thing turned out to be as mean as a snake. Cade still had a few physical scars from the incident. But, of course, there'd been no emotional scars from his short-term incarceration, because the boys had all been let go with a warning in plenty of time to suit up for Friday night's game.

"I'm not going to do either of those things, Bailey," he said quietly.

"Why not?" she asked, and her bottom lip began to quiver like she was trying not to cry.

If Cade wasn't careful, that quiver was going to be his undoing. *She's Ethan's widow*, he reminded himself, because forgetting was beginning to feel all too easy.

"Because," he said simply.

Because at last count, Mayor Pearl owns at least eight other cats. Because a poultry thief turning on a kitten thief seems highly hypocritical. Because if anyone deserves to feel happy and loved, it's you...

Bluebell rubbed against Cade's legs again and then tiptoed toward Bailey to rub against hers, moving between them in a serpentine pattern, almost like she was trying to force them closer together.

Bailey tilted her head and her voice dropped to a near whisper. "You're not even going to ask me why I did it?"

"I think I already know," he said, and without fully realizing how it happened, his forehead was suddenly pressed against hers and Bailey's hand was now splayed against his chest, directly over his racing heart.

Her bottom lip sank between her teeth as her gaze strayed to his mouth.

Cade cupped her face with his free hand and tilted her chin upward so their eyes met again. "Being lonely isn't a crime, Bailey Bear."

The endearment slipped out before he could stop it. He wasn't even sure where it came from. To his knowledge, no one had ever called her Bailey Bear before. As endearments went, it didn't even make sense.

But the sparkle in her eyes told him in no uncertain terms that she liked it—as did the way she rose up on tiptoe and wound her arms around his neck.

Cade wasn't sure who kissed whom first. All he knew was that, suddenly, his mouth was on hers, and the world seemed to tilt sideways under his feet and he had no desire whatsoever to right it. He'd done the forbidden thing. He'd kissed his dead best friend's wife, and he wasn't even sorry. Not yet, anyway. Come morning, when he returned to his senses, he'd probably feel like the biggest jerk in the world.

Not now, though. Now, even with Ethan's portrait looming behind him and a stolen cat at their feet, everything felt sweet and pure and warm. Like this moment was the culmination of months—maybe even years— of wanting and yearning and an ache that refused to go away, no matter how hard he tried to pretend it wasn't there. Like they'd finally managed to outrun yesterday's pain. Like, against all odds, this was the way it was meant to be… This was simply *right*.

Even though they, and everyone else in Bishop Falls, knew without a doubt it was wrong.

Chapter Three

The following morning, Bailey stood in her ordinary spot behind the counter at Huddle Up feeling anything but ordinary.

Cade had *kissed* her last night…or maybe she'd kissed him. The details were fuzzy. Every time she thought back on it, the logical part of her brain turned to mush. She felt all lush and delicious inside, like she had warm wildflower honey flowing through her veins all the way from the top of her head to the pointy toes of her cowboy boots.

She'd worn her favorite pair today—buttery, ballerina-pink leather with large inlaid ivory bows decorating the full length of the shafts. Bailey didn't always wear boots to work. Most of the time, she opted for sneakers.

Today felt special, though.

She felt special.

"What's going on? You keep staring at a spot just over my right shoulder," Calla said, swiveling on her barstool to glance at the exact place where Cade had turned Bailey's limbs to jelly last night. Her friend spun back around and frowned. "It's making me think someone is trying to sneak up behind me."

Bailey made a valiant effort at schooling her expression. She couldn't keep floating around the coffee shop with her head in the clouds. Someone was going to notice.

Someone already has, she told herself as she gave Calla what she hoped was a nonchalant flick of her hand. "It's nothing. I thought I saw a spider."

"A spider?" Calla's eyes went round. "Where?"

Ugh, Bailey had forgotten her friend had developed a touch of arachnophobia after she'd found a minuscule spider in her sleeping bag during a sleepover back in fourth grade. Never mind that the creature had been as dead as a doornail, smashed beyond recognition. To this day, Bailey thought it might've actually been a Texas-size mosquito. But that was beside the point. What were friends for, if not to support each other's harmless delusions?

"I promise there's no spider." Bailey crossed her heart and tried to steer the conversation back to safer territory. "Also, who on earth would be sneaking up on you?"

"Other than the Victory Club?" Calla said, invoking the name of the high-school football team's booster club. To say the Victory Club was intense would've been an understatement.

"I thought they weren't bothering you anymore now that you've been moved off the sports page?" Bailey said. Calla wrote big feature articles now, covering feel-good human-interest stories and motivational profiles. Her promotion had been a long time coming.

She scrunched her face. "They're mostly behaving themselves, but old habits die hard. You know how it is here."

Boy, did she ever. Once Bishop Falls slotted you neatly into a role, you were stuck there for life, which was precisely why Bailey would forever and always be known as the widow of the town's late, great football hero, Ethan Dunne.

Once upon a time she'd been perfectly fine with being put into that box. Lately, though, it had become suffocating. Clearly, the lack of oxygen was at least partly responsible for her recent unhinged behavior.

"You seem different today," Calla said, looking her up and down. "Why are you so jumpy?"

"I'm not jumpy," Bailey countered, feigning nonchalance as best as a cat burglar who'd recently kissed the stuffing out of her dead husband's best friend could. Which was not well at all, if the furrow in Calla's forehead was any indication. "How was the after-party's after-party last night?"

"Everyone mostly sat around the firepit at the town green and talked football until the wee hours of the morning. There was an overly competitive game of cornhole under the water tower." Calla shrugged. "You know, the usual."

Bailey didn't know, actually, since no one ever thought to include her in the town's late-night antics. She only ever heard about them the following morning—typically from the regulars at Huddle Up, desperate for an extra helping of caffeine. Not that Bailey minded...most of the time, anyway.

"That sounds fun," she said as she flipped a few levers on the espresso machine.

"Cade disappeared, though. It was the weirdest thing." Calla frowned into her coffee cup. "He walked over with us, and then poof. We didn't see him for the rest of the night."

Bailey cleared her throat. "Maybe he was just tired and needed an early night."

Or maybe I'm a big, fat liar, and I know exactly where Cade spent the rest of his evening.

She wasn't sure how long they'd stood kissing in the coffee shop, but when they'd finally pulled apart, the warm scents of roasted beans and cinnamon swirled between them.

Cade had rested his forehead against hers and fisted his hand in the back of her hair as a slow smile tugged at the corner of his lips. "Wow, that was…"

"Yeah, I know," Bailey had breathed and slipped her bottom lip between her teeth as she tried to catch up with the moment. She couldn't remember the last time she'd been kissed like that. She'd forgotten what it felt like.

Had it always been so all-consuming? Like the whole world had fallen away and narrowed to just…*him*?

Her pulse hammered in her ears as she'd searched his face. She'd half expected him to take a backward step and break the spell. He hadn't, though. He'd stayed close, hands lightly touching her waist, grounding her in a way she'd desperately needed.

Then he'd whispered her name again in a voice low and rough around the edges. *Bailey Bear.*

She'd swallowed hard, desperate for something cute or clever to say… Anything to make the moment feel less significant. But nothing came to her.

Because it *was* significant.

Even though Bailey still wasn't sure what any of it had meant.

Thinking about the kiss made her breath hitch. Her hands shook as she reached for the milk frother and pretended to focus. No one had even ordered anything requiring steamed milk. She was simply trying to buy herself some time to get a handle on her runaway thoughts while Calla kept talking about cornhole, team toasts and s'mores.

The bell on the front door chimed, and the sound barely registered in Bailey's consciousness. Then she spotted Cade's reflection in the polished silver surface of the espresso machine—broad shoulders, hair slightly mussed from the spring breeze and that unmistakable presence that sent a shiver up and down her spine.

Act natural. Bailey swallowed hard. *It's just Cade.*

He'd walked through that door every weekday morning for years and she'd managed not to go all fluttery inside. Today shouldn't be any different whatsoever.

Her hands faltered on the portafilter as she turned around, and ground espresso slipped through her fingertips, scattering across the floor in a rich, dark spill. She sucked in a sharp breath and stared down at the mess as if it could somehow save her from meeting Cade's gaze. She wasn't ready to face him…not after that kiss.

But he was already right there, on the other side of the counter, his tone low and sure. "Hey there, Bailey. Need some help?"

"No, I've got it," she chirped, her voice a notch higher than normal. She scooped the spilled grounds into her palm, willing her hands to stop shaking.

Pathetic much?

She'd lost her mind over a single kiss. This was precisely why she spent so much time at home reading or crocheting. Even the serial-killer documentaries she inexplicably loved so much seemed safer than dipping her toe into the dating pool.

She and Cade weren't dating, though. They were simply two friends who'd shared a moment—a moment that should never, ever be repeated.

Probably not, anyway.

Her resistance crumbled as she stood and finally met his gaze. There he was—the same Cade she'd known her entire life. Same generous smile, same crinkly gray eyes. The only thing different was the way those eyes now seemed capable of seeing straight through to her soul.

She cleared her throat. "Hey."

It took a second for her to notice the bulky cardboard box in his arms. She might've overlooked it entirely if Calla hadn't asked about it, which was a true testament to how rattled she was because the carton was at least a yard tall and a foot or so wide.

"What have you got there, Cade?" Calla's right eyebrow bounced upward. "That's not the Bulldogs's state-championship trophy in there, is it?"

Jackson—who always showed up with Cade to grab their regular morning coffee orders on their way to work at Bishop Falls High School—shook his head. "Nope. That shiny thing is already on prominent display in the school trophy case. Front and center, thank you very much."

Cade nodded. "As it should be."

"So what's that you're toting around?" Calla shot the box in his arms a curious glance.

"Something for Bailey, apparently," Jackson said with a shrug. Clearly, he'd already quizzed Cade during their walk down Bulldog Avenue.

Bailey's heart did a back handspring in her chest—the kind with a full layout like Bailey had done back when she'd been a cheerleader. She swallowed. "For me?"

"Yeah. It's the bulk order of supplies you asked me to pick up for you from the post office," Cade said smoothly, even though Bailey didn't have the first clue what he was talking about. "Remember?"

He gave her a look that seemed to carry a silent message. *Just go with it.*

"Right." Bailey nodded. What was happening? "I almost forgot. Thanks so much for grabbing that for me."

Who could possibly be buying this? Huddle Up's deliveries came right to her doorstep, like every other business in town. Or rather, the *world*. Barring some kind of serious mix-up, her branded to-go cups and coffee sleeves would never end up at the post office.

By some miracle, neither Calla nor Jackson seemed suspicious…probably because they were too busy making googly eyes at each other to notice the subterfuge going on right under their lovesick noses. For once, Bailey didn't even feel like a third wheel.

Cade readjusted his hold on the cardboard box. "I'm guessing you want me to take this to the back storage area?"

Well, obviously. The storage area was where she kept all her supplies…

And the occasional hostage.

"I'll come with you," Bailey blurted as she bustled her way around the counter before Jackson or Calla could offer to help. She shot them a parting smile as she tightened the sash of her apron. "Cade and I will be right back. Can y'all keep an eye on things for a quick sec?"

There. That should keep them up front for a few minutes. How was it so hard to hide a fluffy little kitten?

"Sure thing," Jackson said in his trademark lazy drawl. He was sounding more like a native Texan by the day.

Calla did a little dance on her barstool. "Oh! Does this mean I finally get to operate the espresso machine?"

Bailey snorted. "Not on your life. If anyone wants a latte, offer them a Bulldog Brew on the house while they wait."

Calla helped out at Huddle Up on occasion—only when Bailey was truly desperate for assistance—but she wasn't allowed to use the Bellisimo 9000. Nobody was. Bailey had spent her entire life savings on the machine when she'd opened the coffee shop, and it had been worth every penny. There was a reason why her coffee drinks were the best in town, and while her imported beans had a lot to do with her success, she knew the luxury espresso machine was a big part of it, too.

"Yes, ma'am," Calla called after her, but Bailey barely heard, because every last ounce of her attention was directed at Cade.

What could he possibly be hiding inside that box? Was it a gift? For *her*?

Her stomach did a giddy little somersault as the door to the supply room closed behind them, trapping them inside the small space. "Is that really for me?"

"Yes." Cade set down the cardboard box between them—probably a good thing, because it prevented her from throwing herself at him. "Well, you and Bluebell."

At the sound of her name, the kitten appeared from

behind a shelf, tiptoeing toward them with a flick of her fluffy tail. She let out a soft meow.

"Quiet now, little one." Cade scooped the cat into the crook of his elbow and let her nuzzle her sweet little face against his cheek. "You don't want to get your fur mom into trouble."

"'Fur mom?'" Bailey echoed, a ridiculous smile tugging at the corners of her mouth.

Cade shrugged, eyes sparkling with mischief. "It sounded better than 'captor.'"

It was official: Bailey's life had become a chaotic mess. And now, she'd dragged the Bulldogs's quarterbacks coach along for the ride.

She should be ashamed of herself.

She *was* ashamed of herself.

Mostly, anyway.

"When you decide to become an accomplice, you really go all in, don't you?" Bailey said, and the softness of her tone said all the things she couldn't bring herself to utter out loud.

She'd been on her own for so long now. And through it all, she'd done her best to put on a brave face. Ethan had been such a huge part of Bishop Falls. His passing had affected the whole town, not just her. The outpouring of grief had been overwhelming, and she'd known right away that she needed to stay strong. Not just for herself, but for all of Bishop Falls. At the funeral, people she'd never even met clasped her hands and tearfully told her how much her husband had meant to them. Their love story took on a legendary air, woven into whispered condolences and heartfelt memories.

Bailey felt she had no choice but to keep herself together. Staying strong and composed while everyone else fell apart seemed like the least she could do. No wonder she'd finally begun to crack.

It felt good to finally let someone in—to let someone see how messy she felt at times. *Too* good. If she wasn't careful, she just might get used to it.

"Open it," Cade said as he raised his brow.

Bailey peeled back the cardboard flaps and peered inside the box. The second her eyes landed on plush pink fabric, she knew exactly what she was looking at. A gasp escaped her, loud enough to stop Bluebell's rumbling purr in its tracks.

"Cade!" She grinned up at him. "Is this the flower-shaped cat tree from Howdy Pets?"

Bailey had been eyeing that cat tower for weeks. It sat directly in the front window of the local pet store, taunting her with its adorable kitty beds staggered at various heights. Two were shaped like pink-and-white daisies, and the third was a soft, cushy hammock. Pom-pom toys hung from the flowers, and the main stem doubled as a scratching post.

"It's not technically the same one. I didn't want to attract any unwanted attention by purchasing the one at Howdy Pets. I found a look-alike online last night and ordered it with express overnight delivery," he said.

Cade lifted the cat tree from the box and placed it in the corner of the supply room beside Bluebell's bowls and the pet bed that Bailey had purchased three days after the Ragdoll had shown up on her doorstep. She'd longed to buy the cat tree, but like Cade, she hadn't wanted to draw attention to herself. People without cats didn't normally go around buying cat condos.

Plus, investing in something that extravagant for Blue-bell meant she was intent on keeping her. Bailey knew she shouldn't—*couldn't*—do that. It was wrong.

Possibly even more wrong than kissing Cade Mont-gomery.

Last night hadn't felt wrong, though. And now that Cade was back at Huddle Up, snuggling with her cat and bearing gifts, she couldn't help thinking that it might be nice to kiss him again.

And again...

And again.

"I figured this might make things more fun for Blue-bell back here while you're working. If she's content, maybe she won't knock things off the shelf and get you into trouble," Cade said as he gently placed the Ragdoll kitten on one of the flower-shaped platforms.

"How did you know?" Bailey asked. Her heart felt like it was lodged in her throat all of a sudden. She could barely swallow. "About the cat condo, I mean. How did you know this is the exact one I wanted?"

"Because I know you, Bails." He looked at her with such tenderness that it hurt. "This thing has your name written all over it."

She beamed at him. Then, just as his warm smile went stiff around the edges, her mind snagged on something he'd just said. *This thing has your name written all over it.* Her name...

He'd just called her by the same old nickname he'd been using for years. Not Bailey Bear, like last night, but Bails.

She tried to tell herself it didn't mean anything. It was just a silly nickname, that's all. But when she blinked and then looked at Cade again—*really* looked—she realized his gaze held more than just tenderness. Deep in the smoky gray of his irises she spied a flicker of something else. Something all too familiar.

Pity.

Bailey's throat went as dry as sandpaper. She couldn't take that look—not from Cade. Anyone but him.

She crossed her arms and looked away so she wouldn't have to see it. She focused on Bluebell instead, curled into a ball and flicking the tip of her tail as she rested in the center of a plush pink flower. Her chest filled with warmth, but then an absurd thought struck her.

Is this a breakup gift?

Surely not. She and Cade weren't even a couple. They'd only kissed one time. Granted, it had been the single best kiss of Bailey's life—a fact that had filled her with elation until a smidge of guilt crept in. Poor Ethan.

It was hard to think about Ethan, though, when something so wonderful had finally happened to her. Clearly, Cade didn't see it that way, though.

"Bailey, about last night…" he began.

She glared at him. It was true, wasn't it? The cat tree was a breakup present. A sorry-I-kissed-you gift, at the very least.

Ugh. She wished the floor of the storage room would split wide open and swallow her whole. Bluebell, too, obviously. Bailey wasn't about to leave her kitten behind. She'd take the lovely cat condo as well, despite its humiliating origin story.

"Last night was a mistake," someone said, and it took a second for Bailey to realize it had been her.

Cade tilted his head, eyes narrowing ever so slightly.

"A mistake," he echoed.

Bailey smiled so hard that her cheeks hurt. No way was she going to let him see how much this stung. She'd been pitied enough for more than one lifetime, thank you very much. "Of course. We got caught up in the moment, that's all. It was a big night."

Cade gave her a blank stare like he had no idea what she was talking about.

"The ring ceremony," she prompted.

His forehead crinkled. "Right, the ring ceremony. How could I forget?"

"Winning State is huge. I know how much that means to you. It's all you've ever wanted." Bailey reached out to touch the hulking gold ring on his finger, but the instant her fingertips brushed against it, he caught her hand in his.

A knot formed in Bailey's throat as she took in the sight of their intertwined fingers.

"I'm sorry," Cade said quietly.

"It's okay. Really, Cade," she said, forcing herself to meet his gaze again. "It was just a silly little mistake. I'm fine."

He gave her hand a gentle squeeze. "Promise?"

"I promise," she lied and for once, she must've managed a passable poker face, because he gave her a quiet nod and took her at her word.

"We should probably get back out there." He hitched a thumb toward the door. "I don't want Jackson to burn the place down trying to make drip coffee."

Bailey nodded, still smiling even though her heart felt like it had been wrenched sideways in her chest. She bent to scratch Bluebell behind the ears, hiding her face for just a second longer. "You're probably right."

Cade moved toward the door but paused with his hand on the knob. "I meant what I said earlier. I'm sorry. About everything. I never meant to complicate things for you."

"You didn't." Bailey stood upright, brushing invisible lint from the front of her apron. "I mean, you did, but it's not your fault. We're adults. We kissed. It's no big deal."

What a whopper. It had, in fact, been A Very Big Deal. To her, anyway.

"Bailey…"

She shook her head. "It's okay. I get it. You and I can't go there because of Ethan."

And because the rest of the town would be well and truly horrified by their betrayal. She swallowed hard. Would it have really been such a betrayal?

"It just wouldn't feel right," she said quietly.

Cade didn't argue, and that was the worst part of the entire heartbreaking conversation.

Instead, he offered her one of his easy, lopsided smiles, the kind he always gave people when he was trying to make them feel better without saying too much.

That smile had been her lifeline these past few years. Now, it just felt like goodbye.

"Friends?" he asked gently.

Bailey hesitated for only a heartbeat before nodding. "Always."

Then she put down the cat, opened the door herself and walked out first, chin high and back straight. She didn't let herself glance over her shoulder. Didn't let herself look at him again. She couldn't, not without breaking.

Calla gave her a thumbs-up from behind the counter. "Everything okay back there?"

"Of course," Bailey replied, her voice as smooth as honey despite the way her insides trembled. "Just rearranging a few things."

Like all my recent hopes, dreams, and nonsensical expectations.

Cade followed her out a second later and gave Jackson a mock salute. "Let's get moving before someone asks me to mop floors."

"Too late," Bailey teased, keeping her tone light. "I've got a mop and bucket with your name on it."

He chuckled and tugged on the brim of his Bulldogs cap, and then they were gone. Just like that.

The bell above the door jingled behind them, the cheerful sound at odds with the sharp ache blooming in Bailey's chest.

She turned back to the espresso machine and went through the motions of pulling shots, steaming milk, forcing herself to focus.

But she couldn't quite forget the feel of Cade's hand around hers.

Or how it had felt, just for a moment, to be seen not as Ethan's widow, not as the girl everyone pitied...but as Bailey. Just Bailey.

And now, she had to find a way to forget.

Chapter Four

The late-afternoon sun slanted across the Bishop Falls High School football field, setting the freshly painted white lines aglow until Cade was forced to squint behind his aviator sunglasses.

Last fall, just a week after the Bulldogs won State, the school district had given the entire stadium a facelift. Months before they'd even received the engraved trophy for the glass case or slipped championship rings onto their fingers, the players had new turf under their cleats, a fresh coat of green and white pride on the stands and banners fixed to the chain-link fence that surrounded the field. It still smelled faintly of rubber and fresh paint—the scent of victory, Cade supposed.

It wasn't as if the field actually *needed* a makeover. Bishop Falls, Texas, always took the utmost pride in its football facilities. Whatever money the Victory Club had poured into the school after the championship game could've gone to better use. The school itself badly needed a new paint job and, judging by the way the windows in his classroom rattled and leaked every time it rained, a full set of replacements. Or fresh caulking, at the very least.

But Cade knew better than to expect new windows

when the town's pride and joy, the football field, could still be made shinier. Anyway, Cade wasn't in charge of spending decisions. His job was to make sure the product on the field lived up to all that polish.

Right now, as the offensive coordinator and quarterbacks coach, that meant watching his potential quarterbacks for next season like a hawk.

Down at the far end of the field, Noah Weaver was taking snaps. The sophomore had stepped into the starting role last fall, leading the Bulldogs through a surprise winning season after Jackson benched the entire starting lineup when a hazing incident left a younger player hospitalized. Cade had backed the decision without hesitation, even when the Victory Club and the assistant coach, Bob Simmons, had tried to run Jackson out of town for it. Even Principal Dean had taken the booster club's side for a time.

That had been months ago, though. Now, Jackson Knight and his championship team could do no wrong. But Cade knew the honeymoon wouldn't last. In Bishop Falls, the glow of a title faded with the first subsequent loss, and the unspoken rule was simple. Win again, or watch the same people who cheered for you start picking apart every decision you make.

Cade narrowed his gaze at Noah and flinched when the ball wobbled out of the teenager's grip. The kid's arm could still launch a pass halfway to Houston, but his mechanics were off—lazy feet, a half-second delay in his release and eyes that kept straying toward the sidelines, where the cheer squad was running through tryout routines. Noah's next throw sailed high, bouncing off his receiver's fingertips.

Jackson stepped up beside Cade, arms folded across his chest. "Your boy's out of sync."

Cade's gaze stayed on Noah. "Don't worry. We'll fix it."

A whistle blew on the other side of the field. The new eleventh-grade transfer student, Tyler Crenshaw, was jogging into position, helmet visor flashing in the sun as he took Noah's place. He barked out the cadence, dropped back and let the ball fly in a tight spiral. The pass cut through the air and smacked into his receiver's hands with laser precision. Tyler gave a little two-finger salute toward the sideline as if to say "you're welcome," then turned his back to the turf before the receiver had even jogged the ball back.

Bob Simmons gave a low whistle from the sidelines. "That kid's got quite an arm."

"A good arm isn't enough if he can't run the playbook and act like a team player," Cade said evenly, though he'd already clocked the kid's natural form.

Jackson's gaze followed Tyler as the teen brushed imaginary dust off his shoulder pads. "The boy's got swagger. And you know as well as I do that the only reason he's here is because we won State."

Coach Simmons shrugged. "It's not exactly a crime to switch schools after a big win. The kid's just looking to play for the best. Can you blame him?"

Cade bit back a comment. Simmons always had a way of framing ambition as an excuse for bad behavior.

But training the quarterbacks and getting them in shape for spring tryouts was Cade's job, not Bob Simmons's. He blew his whistle, sharp and long. "Weaver! Crenshaw! With me. Now."

Noah and Tyler jogged over, helmets tucked under their arms, the difference between them obvious. Noah closed the distance quickly, and was polite and attentive as he said crisply, "Yes, sir."

But Tyler trailed several paces behind, strolling at his own pace before he gave a lazy nod and casually said, "'Sup?"

Cade had been doing this a long time. He loved the kids. Every last one of them—even the ones who made him earn it. But days like this, with spring tryouts on the horizon and half the roster needing a tune-up, took it out of him. And once practice ended, he still needed to head over to the assisted-living facility to visit his grandmother. She'd been more forgetful lately, slipping further away, piece by piece, and he hated how little he could do to stop it.

He sent the boys back to the line, but instead of tracking the next few snaps, Cade's eyes wandered, almost against his will, to the thirty-yard line at the north end of the field. The patch of custom turf—Ethan Dunne's name and jersey number in white, framed by the Bulldogs's emerald green—stood out against the rest of the field.

Seeing his best friend's memorial turf logo hit Cade the same way it always did—with a strange mix of pride, grief and the uncomfortable reminder that he could never cross certain lines. Not with Bailey. *Never* with Bailey. Not when her late husband's memory was woven into the very fabric of this place.

He'd already crossed a line, though, hadn't he? And this morning, he'd tried to make it right with luxury pet supplies. As if a cat tree could somehow fix the ginormous mess he'd made.

What the heck was wrong with him?

She agreed the kiss had been a mistake, Cade reminded himself. *She even said it first.*

Bailey's words echoed in the back of his head like they'd been doing all day since he left Huddle Up. A song on constant repeat.

We're adults. We kissed. It's no big deal.

A sour weight settled in the pit of Cade's stomach. The kiss had been a big deal to him, no matter what Bailey said. He suspected it had been a big deal to her, too. He was almost certain she hadn't been with anyone since Ethan, and something in her eyes this morning told him she wasn't nearly as unaffected as she claimed.

But even if they were both lying, pretending it meant nothing had still been the right call. Bailey deserved more than a man who would always be compared to her late husband, and Cade owed Ethan enough to keep his distance.

His gaze flicked to the turf logo again, and the ache in his gut sharpened. Losing his best friend was a grief that simply refused to fade, no matter how much time passed.

Ethan's accident had happened during their senior year at Bishop Falls High. He'd been the star quarterback and Cade had been his trusted receiver. Together, they'd made magic on the very field where Cade still stood every single day. Like Brady and Gronk. Mahomes and Kelce. Joe Montana and Jerry Rice. They'd dreamed of attending the University of Texas together, rocking burnt orange jerseys and flashing the world-famous Longhorn sign. Scouts from UT had visited a couple of their games in Bishop Falls, so that fantasy had begun to feel like more than just a pipe dream during twelfth grade…

Until the Texas state championship game later that season.

With the championship that year being held at Longhorn Stadium, the very field Cade and Ethan had dreamed of since they were kids, they'd been on cloud nine. They'd never been so pumped up. Winning was a given. But late in the fourth quarter, Ethan suffered a catastrophic spinal-cord injury on the five-yard line. One bad tackle was all it had taken for a lifetime of dreams to fall apart.

After graduation, Ethan joined the Bulldogs's coaching staff and worked as an assistant for five years, coaching from his wheelchair. Through it all, Bailey never left his side. Her family urged her to move on, not to tie herself down so young to someone facing such a difficult road. But Bailey only ever wanted Ethan. She opened her coffee shop after graduation while Ethan coached, and a couple of years later, he proposed. In the middle of planning their wedding, he fell gravely ill. They married in his hospital room just before he was placed on a ventilator.

Two days later, he was gone.

In a lot of ways, Cade's memories of those years were just a painful, tragic blur. After Ethan's injury and their subsequent loss in the championship game, Cade's grades tanked. Practices felt hollow, football felt wrong and the hours he used to spend studying were eaten up by hospital visits and trying to help in whatever small ways he could. In May, he barely scraped across the graduation stage. The scholarship offers that had once felt so close slipped right through his fingers.

Instead of running out of the tunnel in Austin in a

Longhorns jersey, Cade ended up at a small Christian university in east Texas that no one had ever heard of. He still played ball, but it wasn't the same. Any shot he might've had at turning pro was gone before it started. By the time he earned his degree, he knew his playing days were numbered.

So he'd come home to Bishop Falls and taken a job in the athletic department at the high school. It had been a true full-circle moment, just not quite the circle he and Ethan had counted on.

The whistle blew again, dragging Cade back to the present as Jackson called practice to a close. Helmets were dropped into gear bags, cleats thudded across the turf. Cade turned his back to the turf logo and headed toward the sideline.

When his phone buzzed in his pocket of his khaki pants, he fished it out and glanced down at an unknown number. He almost let it go to voice mail, but he answered on the third ring, just in case it was news about his grandmother. Better to be safe than sorry.

"Coach Montgomery?" The voice on the other end was smooth, professional and just a little bit familiar. Cade's grip on the phone tightened. He knew that voice. He'd heard it barking orders across more than one sideline, always in the middle of a tense Friday night under stadium lights. "This is Mitch Callahan, the athletic director over at Rustwood High School."

Rustwood.

Cade fought back an eye roll. The Rustwood Roosters were the Bulldogs's oldest and most aggravating rivals. He was pretty sure he still had a scar on his left bicep from the ill-fated mascot-stealing prank. Roosters were surprisingly mean when cornered—both the feathered kind *and* the football kind. They fought dirty, plain and simple.

"Now really isn't a good time," Cade said, already scanning the sideline for Jackson, who was corralling the last of the players for his traditional end-of-practice pep talk.

"I understand," Callahan replied easily. "But I think you'll want to hear this. Why don't we grab a coffee tomorrow? I'll be in Bishop Falls. My treat."

Cade almost laughed. Coffee with Rustwood's athletic director? The Bulldogs and Rustwood had been trading barbs, cheap shots and stolen plays for decades. Accepting an invitation like that was practically asking to get roasted alive at the Victory Club's next meeting.

Still, there was something in Mitch Callahan's tone— he was calm, confident, a little too sure of himself—that made Cade hesitate. Just for a beat.

He probably just wanted to pick his brain, the same way a fox "just wants to chat" with the hens. Cade had better things to do with his time.

"I'll think about it," he said and then ended the call before the other man could press further.

Kissing Bailey Davis last night had nearly blown up his entire life. Tempting fate twice wasn't just reckless… it was asking for trouble. Everyone knew if you played with fire enough times, eventually you'd get burned.

Cade pushed open the heavy glass door of Maplewood Assisted Living an hour later and smiled at the receptionist.

"Good evening, Coach Montgomery. Congratulations

again on the state championship. I read all about the ring ceremony and trophy presentation in the *Gazette* this morning." The young woman—Shelby Parker, one of his former American history students from a few years back, now working the evening shift at the facility—let her eyes flit toward his right hand. "Are you wearing it? The ring?"

"Um, yeah." Of course, he was wearing it. Everywhere he went, it was the first thing people wanted to see. The town had waited fourteen long years to win the state title since the last time the Bulldogs had brought home the trophy. He couldn't so much as grab a cup of coffee without someone asking to catch a glimpse of it.

"Can I see it?" Shelby's eyes glittered under the lobby's fluorescent lights.

Cade hesitated, then gave a small nod. "Sure."

He held out his hand, and she caught it with both of hers, turning the ring this way and that as if it was some kind of crown jewel.

"So cool," Shelby breathed.

"Yes," Cade said, slipping his hand back with a faint smile. "Very cool."

He tipped his head in thanks and moved past the desk. A small group of residents sat gathered around the television, wheelchairs lined in a neat row, blankets tucked snug across their laps as they watched an old game-show rerun. Granny had always loved game shows, especially *Wheel of Fortune*. He wished she'd venture out more and join the group in the lobby, but lately she'd been spending most of her time in her room. Crowds confused her now that her dementia had begun to blur the edges of things.

Cade slowed as he passed the small group, who offered nods and quiet greetings. Everyone around here knew him by now. In truth, most of them had probably sat in the stadium bleachers years ago, cheering him on when he was just a boy with a football tucked under his arm.

At the end of the hall, he paused outside Granny's door, drew a deep breath and rapped softly before easing it open.

"Cade! There you are, sugar." Her eyes lit up the moment she saw him. As usual, she sat perched in her favorite recliner in the corner of the room. A lace doily she'd crocheted years ago was draped neatly across the headrest.

"Hey, Granny." Cade bent to give her a kiss on the cheek and handed her the white bag he'd picked up at End Zone Bakery on the way over from practice. "I stopped by the bakery and got you one of those peach hand pies you love so much."

"You spoil me so." She beamed up at him, her thin fingers brushing over the crinkled white bag as if it was a treasure. "I don't know what I'd do without my favorite grandson."

She winked at their running joke. He was her only grandson. Truth be told, he was the only family she had left nowadays. Cade had never known his mom. She'd left when he was still in diapers, and with his dad stationed overseas for most of his life, Granny had been the one to raise him. From scraped knees to his college send-off, she'd been there for it all, as steady as the sunrise. Now, the roles had flipped, and he was the one looking out for her.

Cade eased down on the ottoman at her feet, resting his forearms on his knees. "Good thing you'll never have to find out."

Her smile widened, though her gaze drifted toward the bag again. "Did I ever tell you my mama used to make peach pies in the summertime? Lord, the smell of them cooling on the windowsill…"

Her voice trailed off, eyes softening as her memories carried her someplace far away.

"You've told me," Cade said gently, his chest tightening. "Plenty of times. And I like hearing it every single time."

She nodded, satisfied, then leaned forward with a sudden spark. "How was the game tonight, son? Did you score any touchdowns?"

"We did alright," he said quietly, forcing a smile.

This happened sometimes. Her mind slipped backward, blurring years until he was seventeen again instead of thirty-two. It was easier to play along than to correct her, easier to let her live in the comfort of the past.

Granny's expression warmed, her face both proud and tender. "And your homework? You keeping up with it? Don't think I won't call your teachers if you start slipping."

Cade's throat tightened. He nodded, anyway. "Yes, ma'am. Staying on top of it."

"Good boy." She patted his hand, then her gaze drifted again, settling somewhere just over his shoulder. "Where's Ethan? You two are usually inseparable."

Cade froze. Ethan. His best friend. Bailey's husband.

Granny's face softened as she tugged the hand pie from the crinkled bag and broke off a small piece with her fingers. "Such a fine young man, always so polite.

And that girlfriend of his—Bailey? She's darling and just as sweet as this pie. I hope you boys are taking good care of her."

Cade bowed his head, her words cutting deeper than she could know. "We're doing our best, Granny."

She smiled at that, content, and nibbled at the edge of the pie, crumbs gathering on the quilt spread across her lap. Cade watched her with a lump in his throat, and the sweetness of the moment was soured by the guilt twisting in his chest. He thought of Bailey more than she, or anyone, could possibly know.

He forced himself to draw in a slow breath. Granny's memories had her stuck in a time when things were simpler, when he was just a high-school kid, Ethan was alive and Bailey was the head cheerleader who lit up the sidelines with her smile. Back then, everything was straightforward. Life hadn't split wide open with loss and responsibility and impossible choices.

Now, sitting here in the fading light of her room, Cade felt the weight of it pressing down on him—the ring on his finger, the strange call from Rustwood's athletic director, the ache of Ethan's absence and, most of all, the tender, unforgivable way his heart leaned toward Bailey.

He stood, bent and kissed Granny's temple. "Love you."

"Love you, too, sugar," she murmured, her voice already fading with drowsiness.

As he pulled the door shut behind him, Cade almost envied her...

How easy it seemed for her to live in yesterday, when he could never go back.

Chapter Five

Bailey wasn't sure when she'd started going over to Ethan and Calla's childhood home for family game night once a month. It had become such a regular part of her routine that she never really thought twice about the fact that she was no longer technically part of the Dunne family. After her parents tossed their hands up in the air and refused to attend her hospital wedding to Ethan, Dr. Dunne—Calla and Ethan's dad, and the beloved town veterinarian—had stepped quietly into the role of a surrogate father. They still attended all the Bishop Bulldogs games together every Friday night during football season. Bailey spent Thanksgiving Day and Christmas Eve at the Dunne house, and more often than not, she left with a container of leftovers tucked into her bag and the warmth of their laughter still lingering in her chest.

After she married Ethan, her relationship with her parents had unraveled completely. She'd been gutted when they refused to attend the wedding, and for months afterward she kept reaching out—calls, emails, quick visits whenever she found the courage—each time hoping for a crack in the wall they'd built between them. But every effort was met with silence, or worse, that polite, distant tone that told her she'd been shut out. Years passed without more than a strained holiday card, until after Ethan died, when her mother appeared on her porch with a tuna casserole and a smile like nothing had ever happened. They'd pieced together a fragile sort of relationship since then, careful and polite, but the damage had left a hollow place she wasn't sure would ever fully mend. The Dunne house, with its scuffed baseboards, mismatched mugs and the familiar scent of Dr. Dunne's aftershave, was the place where she felt like she belonged—where no one questioned whether she had a right to be there.

"Now, don't you worry," Bailey said as she placed a dish topped with Bluebell's favorite canned food on the floor. "Game night never lasts long. I'll be home before you know it."

Bluebell rubbed her face against one of Bailey's boots, purring her appreciation for the meal before diving in. The tip of her tail flicked as she ate, her ears twitching in time with each bite. Bailey lingered a moment, reveling in the cat's contentment before grabbing her coat from the peg by the door and making her way downstairs.

Her apartment was conveniently located directly above Huddle Up. She'd held out for three whole days after Bluebell slunk inside the coffee shop—okay, *technically* it might have only been two and a half—before she'd allowed the cat to set paw inside. Letting the kitty inside her home had felt dangerously close to admitting she was keeping her, and Bailey hadn't been ready to fully embrace her life of crime at that point. She still wasn't, even though the toy mice scattered across her living-room rug and the half-empty bag of salmon treats on the counter said otherwise.

Bluebell spent Bailey's work hours in the storage room

at Huddle Up because the kitten didn't like being left alone all day, and it allowed Bailey to pretend all of this was just temporary. Or maybe somewhere deep down, a small part of her wanted to get caught. She wasn't entirely sure why. Maybe being exposed as a petty thief of someone else's pet would finally shatter the image the town seemed to have of her as some fragile angel who needed protecting.

Of course, if anyone knew what she and Cade had been up to last night, that halo the town insisted on placing over her head would've slipped clean off.

Bailey's face flamed as she locked the front door of Huddle Up and stepped onto the sidewalk, the main drag of Bulldog Avenue, where all the town's mom-and-pop shops stood shoulder-to-shoulder. She wasn't supposed to be thinking about kissing Cade anymore, full stop.

It was a mistake, remember?

Right, a big, fat, Texas-size mistake. Which was why they'd agreed to pretend it had never happened.

She wondered how that was going for Cade, because so far, she was failing at the pretense in spectacular fashion.

She blamed her boots. After Cade's visit this morning and their subsequent awkward exchange in the storage room, she should've darted upstairs and changed into plain, boring sneakers. Every time she looked down and saw those whimsical bows inlaid in the pale pink leather, a knot formed in her throat. She'd been so hopeful when she'd slipped them on this morning—hopeful in a way she hadn't let herself feel in years. Those boots had made her believe, just for a moment, that romance might still be something meant for her.

And now, for some inexplicable reason, she was still wearing them, their fanciful heels clicking against the pavement as she made her way toward the town green.

The Dunne house sat in a cozy neighborhood just past the green, not far from where the old water tower kept watch over town. After Ethan's accident, Dr. Dunne had converted the garage apartment into an accessible living space for him, and that's where Ethan lived until he died. Mrs. Dunne had left shortly after the accident—she'd been too broken to stay, or maybe just unable to face what their lives had become—and the divorce had followed soon after. These days, Calla lived in the main house with her dad, while Jackson occupied Ethan's old apartment out back. Bailey had a feeling that arrangement wouldn't last much longer now that there was a wedding on the horizon.

Since pretty much everything in downtown Bishop Falls closed by six o'clock, most of the shops along Bulldog Avenue were dark, their window displays softly illuminated by the glow of the old-fashioned streetlamps. Somewhere down the block, the faint strains of an old George Strait song drifted into the cool spring air. People were probably hanging out under the water tower again. Bailey slowed her pace, letting the rhythm of her footsteps match the easy drawl of the music.

Then something in the corner window of the hardware store caught her eye. It was a single sheet of paper taped to the front of the glass. The edges fluttered faintly in the breeze.

Her gaze flitted over the word *Missing* printed in huge letters, followed by a grainy photo of a Ragdoll kitten. *Responds to the name Baby.*

Bailey's stomach gave a guilty twist. It truly wasn't her fault that the kitten had gotten out of the mayor's house. Maybe Bluebell, née Baby, had a good reason for running away from home. Mayor Pearl was known to be a tad unhinged at times. The memory of her throwing a pair of granny panties at Jackson during his welcome parade last fall sprang to mind…

Plus, she owned a lot of other cats. Bailey had recently read that a group of kittens was called a kindle, which, as a reader and ebook enthusiast, she found adorable. When exactly did a kindle of kittens become more of a hoarding situation than a sweet Hallmark movie scene?

Bailey wished she knew. More than that, though, she wished she could stop picturing Bluebell in Cade's arms last night… How easily the tiny kitten had nestled against his broad chest, and how ridiculously good he'd looked holding a cat, like some small-town calendar model for Hot Guys and House Pets.

Pretty sure that counts as thinking about him.

She cast an accusatory glare at the bows on her blush-pink cowgirl boots and kept walking.

The music grew louder as she neared the town green, a lush park that was home to the famed water tower, a historic Bishop Falls landmark since the early 1900s. The tower's silver steel gleamed in the fading light, its broad frame emblazoned with a painted bulldog, flanked on either side by bold sheriff-style stars. It had been a fixture in Bailey's life for as long as she could remember, so familiar she could sketch every curve and bolt from memory. She couldn't imagine Bishop Falls without it. Tonight, though, it looked different, almost magical, with strings of twinkle lights draped beneath the tank, casting a warm, starry glow over the park's lush green lawn.

For a moment, it felt like the whole town had been dusted in fairy sparkle. Small-town charm turned up to eleven. Bailey paused to take it all in, but then she froze when her gaze landed on the reason for the extra shimmer in the air.

There, just beneath the water tower, a man was down on one knee with a small velvet box open in his hand. The woman in front of him squealed.

"Yes!" she cried. "Of course, I'll marry you!"

Bailey's heart gave a sharp, traitorous kick. She told herself to look away with the same sense of urgency she used to change the channel when a sappy rom-com landed on her screen. Or worse, her ultimate kryptonite—*The Notebook,* starring Ryan Gosling. Nothing good ever came from seeing that kiss in the rain.

But it was too late. The damage was done. Ridiculous tears were already streaming down her face, even though Bailey recognized the couple as one of the tellers from Bulldog Savings & Loan and the hostess from Pigskin Pizza, and she had no vested interest whatsoever in their relationship.

She really wanted this, didn't she? Not just the romance, but someone to share her life with. Someone to make the ordinary days feel like occasions and the hard days feel a little less heavy.

To her utter horror, the first person who came to mind wasn't some safe, imaginary cardboard cutout of a romantic companion. It was *Cade*. Which meant she was going to have to take matters into her own hands.

She needed to take serious action and do something drastic.

Now.

Before her heart went and did something even dumber, like fall for him completely.

"I think I might be ready to start dating again."

The words tumbled out of Bailey's mouth before she could stop them. Granted, she'd been mulling them over all evening as she, Calla, Jackson and Dr. Dunne played Uno around the big oak table in the kitchen. There'd been a stretch during the game when Calla and Jackson kept slapping down "Draw Fours" and "Skips" on each other with laserlike precision, both of them far too competitive for their own good.

"Children," Dr. Dunne muttered at one point, though the faint smile tugging at his mouth gave him away.

Bailey's own turn kept getting delayed, leaving her with nothing to do but sit back, sip her sweet tea and let her mind wander. That's when the thought had first crept in. By the time the game ended in a surprise victory for Dr. Dunne after Calla and Jackson's mutual sabotage, it had crystallized into a concrete plan of action.

Now that Dr. Dunne had gone upstairs to bed, begging off on a rematch because he had an early morning surgery scheduled for tomorrow at the vet clinic, and Jackson had stepped outside to take Bishop for his nightly walk, she'd finally had a chance to say it out loud.

Calla's head snapped up, her eyes wide. "Excuse me? Did Bailey Davis just say she's ready to date?" Her grin spread slowly, like she'd just been handed the juiciest piece of gossip in Bishop Falls. "Should I grab my laptop and start you a dating profile right now?"

Bailey laughed, but it was a small, nervous sound.

Calla reached across the table and covered Bailey's hand with her own. "I mean it, Bails. I want you to be happy again."

Bailey blew out a breath. Even though Calla was Ethan's sister, she'd never given Bailey any reason to believe she'd mind if she started dating. In fact, she'd encouraged it from time to time, but Bailey had always shut down the suggestion immediately. A couple of years ago, she'd finally given up.

Still, it was good to hear Calla's support out loud, like permission Bailey hadn't realized she'd been waiting for.

"You deserve love, *real* love, and someone who makes you feel like the sun rises and sets just for you," Calla said as the diamond engagement ring on her finger twinkled beneath the kitchen lights.

Bailey shook her head, averting her gaze to focus intently on straightening the stack of discarded Uno cards and boxing up the game. "I didn't say anything about love. That's not what I meant."

The kitchen was quiet except for the steady ticking of the wall clock and the low hum of the fridge, each sound somehow making the moment feel more vulnerable than Bailey had anticipated. She and Calla were as close as sisters, but baring their souls to each other wasn't something they did with any sort of regularity. Mostly, things went unspoken between them. After Ethan's accident, they'd gone into survival mode and now they were stuck there.

Bailey was, anyway.

"Isn't that what dating is all about?" Calla countered. "Finding someone to love?"

"Not at all." Bailey opted not to remind her best friend how she herself had fought love kicking and screaming when she refused to admit she'd fallen for Jackson, even as everyone else could see the haze of lovesickness hanging over her like a neon sign. "I just want someone to spend time with. Someone predictable. Someone harmless. Someone content to sit quietly beside me on the sofa."

Someone I will never *actually fall for.*

The thought settled heavy in Bailey's chest, unspoken but absolute. She'd been hurt enough for one lifetime. Losing Ethan had been the hardest thing she'd ever endured. She couldn't go through that again. Ever.

Which meant whomever she ended up dating couldn't be Cade.

"Um, Bails?" Calla's eyebrows rose. "Why does it sound like you're describing an elderly dog instead of a real-life human man?"

"Because elderly dogs are sweet and predictable," Bailey said. *And an elderly dog would never break my heart. At least when it died, I would've seen the pain coming from a mile away.*

She cleared her throat. "I was hoping you might help me find someone. Not online, but the old-fashioned way."

"First of all, of course, I'll help. Nothing would make me happier." Calla scrunched her face. "But if you don't want to get on the apps, that means we might be limited to someone we already know."

Bailey nodded. "That's fine. I'm sure there are plenty of single men right here in Bishop Falls."

On the contrary, Bailey was sure of no such thing. The eligible-bachelor pool in Bishop Falls was more like a shallow puddle, but again, she wasn't looking for perfect. She was looking for safe. The human equivalent of a beige sofa—comfortable, dependable and unlikely to ever surprise her. If it disappeared overnight, she wouldn't miss it much at all.

"What about Dan Hobbs?" Bailey said, leaning back in her chair.

"Shop-teacher Dan?" Calla pulled a face. "Bails, he wears socks with sandals. To church."

"I don't mind," Bailey said with a shrug. "He's stable. And quiet."

Calla gave her a look. "Too quiet. The man could make reading a grocery list sound depressing."

She had a point. This whole exercise was supposed to help her forget Cade, but that didn't mean she needed to end up with someone who could put her straight to sleep. She just needed someone who wouldn't make her pulse do whatever crazy, fluttery thing it had been doing around Cade lately.

"Alright, forget shop-teacher Dan." Bailey sighed and moved on to the next name on the list she'd compiled in her head while she'd been losing at Uno. "What about Todd Beaumont?"

"Todd from the hardware store? With the collection of novelty farm-animal mugs that he keeps on display behind the counter?" Calla's voice climbed an octave, equal parts disbelief and amusement. "No. Absolutely not."

"He's a fixture in the community, and he owns his own business."

"He's a grown man who drinks coffee out of a ceramic cow," Calla said flatly.

"At least he's hydrated. And I'm not going to hold a man's choice of drinkware against him." Although, it was kind of gross when he brought his own mug into Huddle Up and expected her to fill it, even if it smelled faintly of whatever soup he'd eaten for lunch. Maybe she should scratch Todd off the list. "What about Carter McGraw?"

Calla blinked. "You mean Coach Carter? As in, the head coach of the high-school baseball team?"

Bailey shrugged. "Why not? I've never once seen him wear socks with sandals."

"The bar is literally on the ground, isn't it?" Calla snorted. "You do remember that I dated Carter a few times, right? I once saw him wear a baseball cap to a funeral."

"That was a million years ago, and you only dated him for like five minutes. I'm not sure a relationship that brief even counts. Besides, he's perfectly nice. He comes into the coffee shop every now and then and never makes a mess at the cream-and-sugar station or tracks mud on the floor," Bailey said.

Calla crossed her arms. "Again, maybe we should just set you up with the Labrador retriever my dad is neutering tomorrow morning."

"Calla, please?" Bailey gave her best friend her most ardent, pleading look. "I'm serious. Help me find someone who won't turn my life upside down."

Calla studied her for a long moment, then her expression softened. "Alright. I'll talk to Jackson. Between the two of us, we can come up with a better prospect than any of these guys."

Bailey nodded, though a flicker of unease curled in her stomach. She wondered if she should add one tiny disclaimer to make sure Cade Montgomery's name never even came up. But that felt unnecessary. No one in town would ever think to put them together.

"One more thing," Bailey added. "I don't want to date anyone in law enforcement."

That seemed crucial, given the circumstances. There was no sense romancing someone who might feel obligated to read her her rights once they discovered her dirty little secret.

Calla tilted her head, brow furrowing in mild confusion. "That's oddly specific, but okay, I guess."

"Just trust me on this one." Bailey kept her expression neutral as she stood to collect the dessert plates and carry them to the sink. She was either going to end up in a relationship or a jail cell by the time this was over.

Either way, it was better than the status quo.

Chapter Six

Cade strode through the door of Huddle Up the following morning, solo this time. He usually walked to work with Jackson and they grabbed coffee on the way, but today Jackson had an early department-head meeting, so Cade was on his own.

The familiar chime of the bell above the door mingled with the comforting scent of roasted coffee beans and warm cinnamon. Bailey stood in her usual spot behind the counter, chatting with a customer as she flipped levers and turned knobs on the espresso machine. Cade's heart turned over in his chest at the sight of her, and he told himself he had no reason whatsoever to feel apprehensive about seeing her again. They'd agreed to act like nothing had happened. He could do that.

Right?

He cleared his throat and reminded himself that she was the same Bailey he'd known since they were kids. His *good friend* Bailey. Period.

The tables in the coffee shop were filled with the usual early morning crowd. A couple of ranchers nursed their mugs at a table by the window, and a half dozen or so members of the Victory Club were gathered around the big farm table by the front, decked out in full, head-to-toe

Bulldog gear. Earl Whitaker, the booster-club president, was bellowing something about the upcoming spring scrimmage, and Cade pulled the bill of his Bulldogs cap low over his eyes, hoping to avoid being pulled into their line of fire. He angled toward the counter instead, weaving between chairs like a running back avoiding a tackle.

Todd from the hardware store sat at his usual spot drinking his coffee from a ceramic cup shaped like a pig. He had one thick finger looped through the handle, which, naturally, was the pig's curly tail.

"Hey, Cade," Todd said, lifting his mug in greeting.

Cade responded with a quick nod. "Morning, Todd."

"Congrats again on the ring ceremony." Todd tipped his head toward the table where the Victory Club was gathered. "Earl Whitaker is about to bust a button bragging on y'all over there."

Out of the corner of his eye, Cade caught Bailey watching the exchange, her gaze flicking between him and Todd before she quickly looked away. Not before she'd lingered an extra second on that ridiculous pig mug, though. A faint flush had crept into her cheeks, though Cade couldn't begin to guess why. He only knew that seeing her blush did something to his chest he wasn't prepared to examine this early in the day.

With a word of thanks to Todd, he slipped into place behind the customers. Just as he noticed someone sitting alone in the back corner—shoulders squared, the brim of a Stetson shadowing most of his face—Bailey called him forward. By the time Cade reached the counter, the stranger had already angled slightly away, as if deliberately trying to avoid being seen.

"Good morning," Bailey said, her voice a touch too

bright. She slid a steaming Bulldog Brew across the counter without even asking what he wanted. Of course, she hadn't needed to. She always knew his order.

"Morning," he returned, his throat tightening more than he cared to admit. Their fingers nearly brushed as he wrapped his hand around the cup.

Bailey leaned in a fraction, nodding subtly toward the back corner. "That guy over there got here almost an hour ago. He came in and asked if you'd shown up yet. He made it sound like you had an appointment?"

Cade followed her gaze toward the stranger in the Stetson he'd noticed earlier. The man's posture was stiff, purposeful, the kind of guarded body language that made him seem more like an outsider than a local.

"No appointment," Cade said slowly, the words tasting wrong in his mouth.

Then, like a light flicking on, he remembered the call he'd ignored yesterday from the Rustwood athletic director wanting to "chat."

His gut churned.

"Is everything okay?" Bailey gnawed on her bottom lip, and her voice dipped low enough that only he could hear. "Should I ask him to leave?"

"No, it's fine. Nothing for you to worry about." He offered her the kind of wink he'd tossed her way a dozen times before. Funny how even that felt different now. "I'll take care of it."

"Great." Bailey nodded, then immediately busied herself with rearranging a stack of napkins that didn't need straightening.

Cade felt like he should say something, but he wasn't sure what. He'd have to deal with fixing things between him and Bailey later. Right now, he needed to deal with the Rustwood situation.

Cade took a long pull from his coffee, buying himself a second before he headed over. He could practically feel Earl Whitaker's gaze boring into the back of his head, but when he risked a glance toward the Victory Club table, no one seemed to be paying him any mind. Earl was still mid-story, waving his arms around like he was coaching a two-minute drill.

The man in the corner looked up as Cade approached. He rose partway out of his chair, tugged off his cap and extended a hand. "Coach Montgomery? I'm Mitch Callahan, the athletic director over at Rustwood."

"Yeah, we've met before." Cade shook his hand and slid into the chair opposite. "I'm a little curious what you're doing here, though. This is pretty intense for the offseason. You're not planning on forking our field again while you're in town, are you?"

Two years ago, a bunch of Rustwood players broke into Bulldog Stadium the night before the teams were set to square off and stuck thousands of plastic forks into the turf, tines up, like a plastic porcupine had exploded across the fifty-yard line. It had taken the janitorial staff, the entire varsity team and the Bulldogs coaches hours to defork the field.

Classic Rustwood.

"It's nothing like that, I promise." Mitch held up his hands. "I told you I'd be in town today. Besides, I don't know anything about that forking business. Boys will be boys, though."

Cade's jaw tightened. *Boys will be boys.* That was Rustwood in a nutshell—never holding anyone accountable, chalking everything up to mischief. No wonder they'd happily scooped up the star players Jackson had suspended last season for hazing, like discipline didn't matter as long as the roster stayed stacked. Cade had been involved in plenty of pranks when he'd been a kid, but at least his coaches had made sure there were consequences.

"I'll get right to it, Coach Montgomery," Mitch said with a practiced smile. "You and I both know the Bulldogs had an impressive season. On paper, Rustwood had all the advantages, and your team still managed to pull off a state championship. I was surprised, and frankly, more than a little impressed. Your team's got heart."

He was being too complimentary. Cade didn't trust it for a hot second.

"And?" he prompted. He didn't have time for this. He needed Mitch to get to the point so he could get on with his life. Noah Weaver wasn't going to get his mojo back on the field as long as Cade was sitting here drinking coffee with the AD of their biggest rival.

"And that's something we're obviously lacking over at Rustwood." Mitch cleared his throat and let the startling admission sink in. "Which is why we'd like to bring you on board."

For a second, Cade wondered if Mitch had spiked his coffee, because there was no way he'd just heard that right.

"I beg your pardon?" he said after a beat of stunned silence.

"Head coaching position. You'd start immediately, and the salary is a significant step up from what you're getting here in Bishop Falls," Mitch said with the air of a man who thought he'd just laid down the winning hand.

Cade leaned back in his chair, his jaw tight. "I appreciate the offer, but no."

"Maybe I should repeat myself," Callahan said lightly, as though Cade hadn't heard him. "This is Rustwood. Bigger program. Bigger budget. You'd be set up for years."

"I heard you the first time." Cade's voice stayed even, but steel threaded through it. "I'm not interested."

The other man steepled his fingers on the table, the easy smile never leaving his face. "Look, Coach, I get the loyalty thing. Bishop Falls is a nice little program, but you and I both know how this goes. With Jackson Knight at the helm, you're never moving up. Rumor had it he just inked a five-year contract to stay put. We both know Bob Simmons isn't going anywhere, either. That man's practically a fixture, which means you'll be stuck teaching history and coaching part-time until you're old enough to retire."

Cade felt the jab land, but not the way Callahan intended. Truth be told, he was glad Jackson was staying. The town needed a steady leader, and Jackson was good for Bishop Falls in ways no other outsider ever could be. More than that, over the past season he'd become Cade's closest friend—aside from Bailey, of course. His friendship with Jackson was different, though. They shared the kind of brotherhood Cade hadn't thought possible since losing Ethan. The idea of resenting him for signing on to coach the Bulldogs long-term was laughable.

Callahan leaned in and lowered his voice. "Rustwood is offering you a chance you'll never get here. Head coach. Full control. A salary that'll make whatever you're making in Bishop Falls look like pocket change. You could set yourself up for life, Montgomery."

Cade set down his Bulldog Brew on the table with a deliberate thud. "Let me make this real clear. I'm not leaving Bishop Falls. I'm not leaving Jackson, the boys, or this program. And I'm not selling out to Rustwood, no matter how much money you dangle in front of me."

For the first time, Callahan's smile faltered, but then he quickly recovered. He slid a business card onto the table with two fingers, the glossy Rustwood Roosters logo catching the light. "No need to get worked up, Coach. I'm not asking for an answer this minute. Just don't make any rash decisions, okay? Think it over. The offer stands—" his smile thinned as he rose and adjusted his Stetson "—but not forever."

Mitch tucked in his chair, then added, almost casually, "The Bulldogs and the Roosters might be squaring off again sooner than you expect. Stranger things have happened." He tipped the edge of his cowboy hat and walked out, the bell over the door chiming once before the morning noise swallowed it.

Cade let out the breath he'd been holding and stared at the card. Earl Whitaker would no doubt have his hide for even having the thing in his possession. When he glanced across the coffee shop, though, the Victory Club was still loud and oblivious. Earl was in mid-rant with his arms windmilling like he was drawing up a two-point conversion on the fly.

He picked up the card and thought about crumpling it, then slid it into his wallet away from prying eyes. His

Bulldog Brew had cooled a shade, but he took a steady-ing drink and headed for the counter.

Bailey was wiping down a metal pitcher that didn't need wiping. Her eyes flicked to the door, where Calla-han had exited, then back to Cade's face.

"Everything okay?" she asked. "That guy looked fa-miliar."

"It's fine," he said, and the words came out rougher than he meant. He softened his expression with a half smile. "Just a nobody from out of town."

Her gaze narrowed. Cade could never hide anything from Bailey. She knew him too well. "He seemed…de-termined."

Cade shifted his coffee to his other hand. "That's one word for it. I doubt he'll be back, though."

He couldn't have been any clearer. He wasn't leaving Bishop Falls, end of story.

Something eased in Bailey's shoulders. "I'm glad you got it sorted. You want a kolache?" She ducked her head, tucking a loose wave of chocolate-brown hair behind her ear. "On the house."

He should've said no, but he nodded, anyway. "Jala-peño if you've got it."

She slipped one into a warm bag with a pair of tongs and slid it across to him, their fingers skimming the same inch of countertop. "Here you go, Coach."

"Thanks." Cade was about to step away from the counter when the bell over the door jingled again.

"Good morning, Bishop Falls!" Mayor Pearl Atkin-son swept in, floral scarf trailing behind her like a pa-rade banner.

"Morning, Mayor," Bailey called, straightening automatically.

Cade turned to nod at the mayor…then stopped short. Just above the strap of Bailey's apron, clinging to the dark knit of her puff-sleeved sweater, was a single tuft of cream-colored fur.

Cat hair.

His pulse kicked. Before he could think better of it, Cade darted behind the counter and slipped an arm around Bailey's shoulders as if leaning in with some intimate, private word. With the motion, his thumb brushed swiftly over the incriminating cat hair, flicking it away.

Bailey went perfectly still, eyes wide as saucers. From her vantage point, it surely seemed like he'd just pulled her close right there in front of God, Mayor Pearl and half the town.

"Um…lint," Cade said quickly, dropping his arm and lifting his coffee in his other hand to gesture at her sweater. "You had a little something on your sweater."

Her cheeks went scarlet, her lips parting like she couldn't quite find words.

"Bailey, dear, I'll have my usual," Mayor Pearl chimed, none the wiser. She prattled on about the upcoming town-council meeting, but Cade barely heard her. His focus lingered on the flush in Bailey's cheeks, the way her hands trembled ever so slightly as she prepared the mayor's order.

When Mayor Pearl finally bustled off toward a table, Bailey dared a glance at him, her eyes bright with nervous energy.

"What was that?" she whispered fiercely.

Cade kept his expression carefully neutral, though one

corner of his mouth twitched. "I just saved you from a heap of trouble."

Her eyebrows knitted. "Trouble?"

He glanced meaningfully at the spot by her apron strap where the fur had been. "If Mayor Pearl had caught you with cat hair on your sweater, she might've sent it out for DNA testing. We couldn't have that, could we?"

Bailey's flush deepened until she looked ready to dive headfirst into the pastry case just to escape. She muttered something unintelligible under her breath—something that might have been "thank you," but Cade couldn't be sure. Then she grabbed the dish towel she always kept folded by the register. The counter was already gleaming, but she wiped it down with brisk little strokes, her movements betraying more fluster than purpose.

Cade took a slow sip of his coffee, watching her from the corner of his eye. He fought the grin tugging at his mouth, the one that threatened to break past his carefully neutral expression. He had no business enjoying this— her pink cheeks, the way she couldn't quite meet his gaze, the quick efficiency of her hands trying to look busy.

None of it was his business. And yet, for reasons he refused to name, it felt a little too much like it was.

Cade had barely settled into one of the chairs opposite Jackson's desk when the thud of boots in the hall made him glance up. Bob Simmons slowed in the doorway, his brow furrowing the second he spotted Cade's feet propped comfortably on Jackson's desk. The older man muttered something under his breath and kept walking, his disapproval clear from the expression on his face.

"Sometimes I think you do that just to rile him up,"

Jackson said, shutting the door behind Bob's retreating figure. Bishop the bulldog lifted his head from his custom-made dog bed—stitched in the school colors of green and white, naturally—and regarded Jackson with sleepy interest.

"That's because I do," Cade drawled, not bothering to move his feet. "The man is a grump. Always has been, always will be."

Jackson chuckled and dropped into the chair across from him. Bishop waddled over and flopped heavily at Jackson's feet with a groan. Jackson reached down absently to scratch behind his ears. "True, although I'll give him this—he's come a long way. Simmons has been playing awfully nice lately."

Cade snorted. "Funny how a championship ring will do that."

Bob Simmons hadn't always been so agreeable. In the beginning of Jackson's tenure as head coach, he'd made it his personal mission to stand in Jackson's way at every turn. Simmons had lobbied hard for the head-coaching job when it opened up and made his displeasure clear when the school hired an NFL player with no coaching experience under his belt instead. Winning State hadn't erased all that history, but it had quieted Simmons down, at least for now.

He was in the same boat as Cade, anyway. With Jackson's new five-year contract, Simmons had likely peaked as second-in-command for the Bulldogs. He might as well settle back and enjoy the ride. There were far worse fates than being the assistant coach of a state championship team, especially in Texas.

Cade folded his arms behind his head, studying his

friend. "So how was your big department-head meeting this morning? Anything earth-shattering?"

Jackson leaned back in his chair and twirled a pencil between his fingers. Bishop rolled onto his side with a grunt, snoring almost immediately. "Not really. We've got a whole slate of spring fundraisers coming up, and Principal Dean wanted reassurance that the football staff and boys would show up to support. I told him we'd be there, starting with the chili cook-off tomorrow afternoon."

Cade nodded. He'd never once skipped the annual chili cook-off—after all, he was the one who made the Bulldogs's entry every year. Granny's recipe was a guaranteed crowd favorite. Free food and bragging rights came with the territory, but he doubted chili was what had Jackson twirling his pencil like a majorette during halftime. "And?"

"And," Jackson continued, "the athletic director called a little bit ago. That's where the bigger news comes in. The spring scrimmage is going to be a little different this year."

"Different how?"

Normally, two weeks after tryouts, the Bulldogs split into two squads and went head-to-head in a spring scrimmage. It was rough-and-tumble fun, a chance for the boys to show off, and the crowd always ate it up. Like everything else remotely related to football, the annual showdown had become as much a community tradition as it was a team workout.

Jackson flicked the pencil onto his desk. "This year, the AD wants to treat it more like a preseason game. Instead of scrimmaging ourselves, we're lining up against another school."

Cade straightened, his sneakers thunking down from the desk. Bishop startled at the sound, blinked, then settled back down with a sigh. "That's not nothing. It won't really count, sure, but this is Bishop Falls. Folks around here don't care about stats. They'll expect us to win."

Jackson gave a half smile. "Exactly."

"Let me guess," Cade said as the realization settled in like a stone in his gut. "The other team is Rustwood, isn't it?"

The look on Jackson's face confirmed it before he even answered.

Cade let out a humorless laugh. "So that's what Callahan was hinting at this morning."

"Callahan, as in *Mitch* Callahan?" Jackson's brow furrowed. "What are you talking about?"

Cade hesitated, then blew out a breath. "Listen, there's something I need to tell you."

He told Jackson about the coffee-shop meeting, about the Rustwood AD's slick pitch and the not-so-subtle lure of a fatter paycheck if he'd agree to take over their program. The whole thing had reeked of desperation disguised as charm—a sales job more than a serious conversation.

"I said no, obviously," he said, finishing, his voice clipped. The memory still left a sour taste in his mouth. Bishop Falls was home. He wasn't about to jump ship for a rival school with shady ethics, no matter how much money they waved under his nose.

Could he have used a salary increase? Sure. Things had been a little tight since Granny moved into the assisted-living facility a few years ago. It had been her choice, one she made even before her dementia diagnosis, though Cade sometimes wondered now if she'd already been noticing lapses and didn't want to admit it. There'd been no sudden emergency, just Granny's determination to simplify her life while she still had the clarity to make the call.

He'd offered to move into her house with her if she felt like it was too much to manage, but she'd waved him off with that stubborn spark in her eyes and told him it was time for her to let go. Instead, Cade had packed up his little apartment and settled into the home where she'd raised him. Without a monthly rent or mortgage payment hanging over his head, he could afford to supplement Granny's retirement income and cover the cost of a comfortable apartment at Maplewood on his teacher's and part-time coaching salary.

They were doing just fine.

He'd meant every word of his refusal, and he was certain Jackson understood where he was coming from. And Cade knew that Jackson wouldn't want to lose him as quarterbacks coach.

Sure enough, relief flickered across Jackson's face, but not quite as much as Cade might have expected.

"As your head coach," Jackson said finally, "I'm certainly glad to hear that you turned him down. But as your friend, I have to ask…are you sure? It sounds like a good offer. A big career move, for certain."

Cade shook his head firmly. "No way. I'm not going anywhere—not to Rustwood, not anywhere. Bishop Falls is home, these boys are my team, and you…" He gave

Jackson a pointed look. "You're my head coach. That's all I need."

Jackson studied him another moment, then nodded slowly, a smile tugging at one corner of his mouth. "Alright, then."

"Besides," Cade added with a smirk, "if I left, who would keep Simmons in check?"

That earned him a full laugh from Jackson, the kind that eased the tension humming between them. Even Bishop cracked open one eye at the sound before resuming his nap. Cade leaned back again, more anchored this time. The offer from Rustwood was already behind him. He'd made his choice the second Mitch Callahan opened his mouth.

And there wasn't a chance in the world he'd regret it.

Chapter Seven

Bailey snuggled Bluebell in the crook of her neck, inhaling her sweet kitten smell as she flipped the sign on the front door of the coffee shop to Closed and shut the blinds. The high school's annual chili cook-off was scheduled for this afternoon, and as usual, Huddle Up was one of the event's main sponsors.

Bailey always did what she could to support the school, particularly the football team, not just because it was good for business, but because the Bulldogs were stitched into the very fabric of Bishop Falls. Their Friday night lights drew the whole town together during football season, and Bailey knew from experience how much those boys counted on community support.

Once a cheerleader, always a cheerleader.

She set Bluebell gently on the ground and let the kitty weave around her feet as she glanced around the shop, making sure everything was ready for the big event. The air still smelled faintly of espresso and the warm chocolate croissants she'd served as a special treat for her morning customers since she was closing up shop early today, a cozy contrast to the chili that would be simmering across town in just a few hours.

Her booth always offered free cups of iced coffee,

which required large silver dispensers for the brew, coolers packed with ice and stacks of clear plastic cups that sweated in the spring sun almost as fast as she could hand them out. She stacked sleeves of clear plastic cups into a box, tucked in napkins and straws and added a few bottles of flavored syrup, along with a large pitcher of cream. By the time Calla was almost due to arrive to help her carry things over, the neat pile on the counter looked less like clutter and more like a mobile version of Huddle Up, complete with a folded green-and-white tablecloth and the chalkboard sign that proudly proclaimed, Compliments of Huddle Up. Go Bulldogs!

She carried Bluebell upstairs to the apartment at the last minute, fantasizing about being able to take the cat with her. That was impossible, of course, and not just because she didn't possess a cute backpack-style cat carrier…yet. Someday, maybe. It would be fun to take her places, the way Jackson carted Bishop around town. For now, though, Bluebell had to remain her little secret. By the time Bailey darted back downstairs to the shop, Calla was already knocking on the front door and trying to peer through a crack in the blinds.

"Hey! Sorry, I was just upstairs," Bailey said as she swung the door open and waved her friend inside.

Calla stepped in, shaking off the wind and eyeing the neat stacks of boxes by the counter. "All good. I figured you were finishing up."

A faint thud echoed from above, followed by the jingle of something rolling across the floor. Bailey's stomach dropped. No doubt, Bluebell was playing with one of her little stuffed mice.

Calla's head tilted. "What was that?"

Bailey pasted on a smile that felt two sizes too tight. "The pipes are rattling again. You know how this old building is. Sometimes they sound like a herd of elephants."

Another noise followed—a tiny *scrape-scrape* that could only be kitten claws skidding over hardwood.

Calla's eyebrows arched higher. "Elephants, huh?"

"Look, the iced coffee is all ready to roll. I even packed the caramel syrup this year. Big improvement over last time, right?" Bailey said a little too brightly, swooping toward the counter before Calla could ask more questions.

She pointed at the silver dispensers waiting to be carried out. Calla gave her a funny look but let it go, reaching for one of the boxes. "If you say so. Let's get this stuff loaded before the field gets too crowded."

Bailey exhaled through her nose, relief washing over her until a faint mew drifted down the stairs.

She coughed loudly, clattering a stack of cups into her arms. "Right! Off we go!"

Bailey managed to herd Calla out the door before any more suspicious noises could escape from upstairs. Between the two of them, they juggled the dispensers, coolers and boxes to Calla's car, the clinking of glass syrup bottles mingling with the chatter of townsfolk already making their way down Bulldog Avenue toward the high school.

By the time they pulled up to the practice field, the place was already alive with energy. Booths lined the edges of the grass, each one decked out in colorful banners and Bulldog spirit. Kids in Bulldog T-shirts darted between the yard lines with paper sample cups in hand, eager for the official start of the event. Bailey could already overhear the competitors ribbing each other, and die-hard locals arguing the eternal question of beans versus no beans. In Texas, the definitive answer was always no beans, but there were always a few outliers. Bless their hearts.

Bailey spread the tablecloth across her table while Calla set out cups, straws and napkins. She propped up the chalkboard sign, arranged the bottles of flavored syrup and creamer and adjusted the silver dispensers so they gleamed in the light. When everything was ready to go, she glanced up and her stomach gave a little hitch.

Directly across from her, the football team's booth was already bustling with players ladling chili into Styrofoam bowls and slapping high fives. And right in the middle of it all—tall, broad-shouldered and very much at ease—stood Cade, front and center with a ladle in hand and his Granny's famous recipe simmering in a massive pot.

Bailey handed someone an iced coffee and averted her gaze to Bishop. The bulldog was sprawled directly in front of the football booth like he owned the place. The big dog had a green-and-white bandana tied around his neck and his usual droopy expression that made him look unimpressed by all the excitement. Every so often, one of the players bent to scratch his ears, and Bishop's stubby tail thumped lazily against the grass. Kids kneeled to hug him, and adults paused to take pictures. It was all very wholesome and adorable, but not nearly enough to keep her eyes from drifting back to Cade.

He looked maddeningly at ease in the role of chili king, joking with the line of people at his booth as if he had all the time in the world. His laugh carried easily across the field, and Bailey kept catching herself glancing his way. Worse, she kept catching him doing the same. Their eyes would lock for a beat, too long to be accidental, before she turned back to her coffee urn with cheeks warmer than the spring sunshine.

She busied herself filling a stack of plastic cups and lining them up for easy pickup. Anything to stop thinking about Cade in the coffee shop yesterday, particularly the sight of Cade and Todd from the hardware store, side by side. Todd with his ridiculous pig mug, Cade with that easy smile. Put together, there'd been no comparison. And really, what business did she have even considering Todd as a significant other when Cade Montgomery existed?

That's the whole point, she reminded herself. *To find someone you won't get overly attached to.*

Bailey straightened the chalkboard sign for the third time. "So," she said, lowering her voice so only Calla could hear. "Any luck on our little matchmaking project?"

She tried to keep the wobble out of her voice. Honestly, she was a grown woman. The prospect of going on a date shouldn't make her this nervous. Still, it had been years since Ethan, and the thought of stepping into something new carried a quiet ache she doubted would ever fully fade.

Calla offered her a smile that felt a little too familiar...and a little too sympathetic. There it was again— pity. "Not quite yet, hon. I'm working on it, don't worry. These things take time."

"That doesn't sound promising," Bailey murmured as

she stacked sleeves of cardboard cup holders to give her hands something to do.

"Relax." Calla topped off a cup of coffee with exaggerated cheer. "I promise I'm on it, and Jackson is, too."

Bailey forced a smile, but her attention drifted across the field again. She wasn't the only one watching Cade. A steady stream of women came by his booth—teachers, booster moms, women she vaguely recognized from the coffee shop. They all seemed to laugh a little too hard at his jokes. And was she imagining things, or were they also leaning just a little too close across that massive pot of chili?

Even Bishop seemed to notice. When one woman leaned in far enough to brush Cade's arm, the bulldog gave a loud grunt, lifting his head and fixing her with a baleful bulldog stare until she stepped back.

It wasn't anything new. Back in high school, girls had practically tripped over themselves to catch Cade's attention. Bailey remembered girls crowded around his locker every afternoon with offers to "help" him with his homework—offers he'd always brushed aside, to her knowledge at least. She used to tease him about it, laughing at the way he'd duck his head and mutter something gruff to send them scattering. At the time, she'd thought it was funny.

But now, when one of the single moms sidled up to his booth, twirling her hair and practically purring over her chili sample, something hot and sharp curled in Bailey's chest… Something that felt way too much like jealousy.

She tried to swallow it, but it sat heavy in her chest, impossible to ignore.

Calla noticed instantly. "What's with you? You look like you're about to bite the head off that poor spoon."

Bailey snapped her gaze away, realizing she'd been gripping one like a weapon, despite her sample bowl of chili remaining untouched. "Nothing. It just looks like Cade might need rescuing over there."

Calla snorted. "Please. He's fine. Look at that smile on his face. He doesn't look like he's suffering to me."

That only made it worse. Bailey's stomach twisted as she watched the woman linger, hand brushing Cade's forearm as she laughed. He didn't seem to be encouraging her, exactly, but he wasn't exactly shaking her off, either.

And Bailey hated it.

The crowd bustled between them, oblivious. A gaggle of middle schoolers sporting bulldog face paint waved sample cups at the booth next door. Somewhere behind her, the marching band warmed up for a short set, and the first few off-key notes of the fight song carried on the breeze. Bailey tried to keep her focus on the familiar rhythm of pouring coffee, but her pulse beat too loud in her ears.

Before she could second-guess herself, she pressed her dish towel into Calla's hands. "Wait here. I'll be right back."

"Bailey—" Calla began, but Bailey was already marching across the field, her white cowboy boots leaving faint impressions in the grass.

The football booth buzzed as she approached. Two linemen were mock-arguing over whether Granny's chili was better with cornbread or saltines. A group of cheerleaders squealed when Cade ladled generous helpings into their bowls. Someone shouted his name from the twenty-yard line, and Cade lifted a hand in easy acknowledgment, as if he'd been born in the center of all this noise. Bishop perked up, too, his tiny tail wiggling as if he sensed something more interesting coming his way.

Bailey stopped directly beside the flirty mom and thrust a fresh iced coffee toward Cade.

"I thought you could use this," she said, voice sharper than she intended. "It's so hot out."

What on *earth* was wrong with her? She'd thought kitten stealing had been her rock bottom, but this was a new low. Here she was, practically throwing herself at a man who wanted nothing to do with her...

Again.

Except he wasn't exactly looking at her like he regretted their kiss. Quite the contrary, actually.

Cade's eyes flicked from the cup to her face, and the corners of his mouth curved, his smile slow and knowing. "Thanks. Just what I needed."

The single mom hesitated, then mumbled something about checking out another booth and drifted away.

Finally.

Bailey handed him the cup, pulse thudding in her ears. Cade's fingers brushed hers deliberately as he took it, his gaze never wavering. The crowd around them kept laughing, the hum of conversation blending with the distant pulse of the marching band, but in that moment it felt like the whole field had gone still.

And Cade knew. Bailey could see it in his eyes. He knew exactly why she'd come over.

Her stomach gave a little lurch. The problem wasn't

that he knew. It was that he was right—she had a serious case of the green-eyed monster.

She pasted on a smile and forced her attention to the pot bubbling between them. Steam rose in curls, carrying Granny Montgomery's secret blend of spices. The smell made her chest ache with a peculiar mixture of hunger and memory. Cade had always made this chili for team fundraisers, ever since high school. Bailey could still picture him in his Bulldogs jersey alongside Ethan on this very practice field, stirring the pot while his grandmother barked instructions from a folding chair.

Now, he was grown, confident, utterly at ease with himself...and apparently completely capable of tying her heart into knots. The tug in her chest startled her, laced with a whisper of guilt she couldn't quite shake. As if noticing Cade this way somehow erased the years she'd spent loving Ethan.

"Busy afternoon," she said, trying for casual as she gestured at the crowd pressing toward the booth.

"Best turnout yet," he agreed, lifting his chin toward the judges making their way down the row. His grin widened. "Granny's recipe is about to sweep again."

Of course, it was. Cade Montgomery didn't lose—not on the field, not in the kitchen. And not, Bailey realized with a pang, when it came to the steady line of women waiting for his attention.

She should turn around, march back to her booth and pretend she hadn't felt this spark of irrational jealousy. Pretend she wasn't standing here like a schoolgirl with a crush, bristling because Cade Montgomery hadn't swatted away a woman's flirtation fast enough.

But her feet refused to move.

A football arced high over the grass where a handful of kids had started an impromptu game. Jackson stood off to the side, arms crossed, calling out something that made the boys hoot with laughter. The loudspeaker crackled to life with an announcement about the bake-sale table, followed by a choreographed chant from the cheerleaders near the fifty-yard line.

None of it mattered. All Bailey could hear was her own heartbeat. All she could see was Cade, smiling at her over the rim of the cup she'd just handed him, as if the entire cook-off had been staged for this moment alone.

And for one dizzying second, she let herself imagine it... What it might feel like if she stopped fighting this pull between them. If she admitted what the heat curling in her chest really was.

But then Calla's voice rang across the lane, breaking the spell. "Bailey! We're out of lids!"

Bailey blinked, her grip on reality snapping back into place. She stepped away from the booth with a quick nod, retreat already burning in her veins.

The floodlights above the practice field flickered on against the dimming sky, their glow catching on empty Crock-Pots and crumpled napkins as the chili cook-off wound to a close. Most of the booths had already begun packing up, tables scraped clean and folding chairs stacked in messy rows.

At the football team's table, Cade stood with his players as they wiped down the long trestle and collapsed the legs beneath it. As expected, Granny's chili recipe reigned triumphant again. The plaque on their shiny gold trophy read Best Bowl, but Cade suspected the real prize was the way his boys puffed their chests and ribbed each other as though they'd just won State all over again.

Noah cradled the trophy like a football. "We did it, Coach. Granny Montgomery's secret recipe lives on."

"Granny's going to be proud. I can't wait to tell her," Cade said.

She'd known the chili cook-off was today and had smiled when he offered to bring her along, but she'd insisted she was happier staying home. Large gatherings weren't her thing anymore, and Cade respected that. The last thing he wanted was for her to feel uneasy.

At the moment, though, his mind wasn't on the chili. Or Granny...not really.

He was still back in the moment from earlier, when Bailey had stood before him with pink cheeks and her chin tipped a little too high. She'd been defensive in that way only she could be, pretending she wasn't jealous while practically daring him to say otherwise. Her voice and her flustered expression had been humming in the back of his mind ever since, louder than the crowd, louder than the music.

He helped one of the linemen tip a cooler to drain melted ice, then clapped him on the shoulder. "Good work today. Get the rest of this loaded in the truck, then you guys head on home. Or wherever."

"Under the water tower," one of the juniors said with a grin. "Where else?"

The after-parties under the water tower had been a Bishop Falls tradition for as long as Cade could remember—lawn chairs, cheap sodas, somebody with a Bluetooth speaker, the comfort of familiarity under the old steel landmark.

Everyone went.

Well, almost everyone.

His gaze drifted across the field to the Huddle Up booth. Bailey was bending over her table, sliding the silver dispensers back into their crates. Calla carried stacks of cups toward a trash bag and was chatting animatedly with a couple of choir moms. Bailey, though, was alone in the corner of the booth, her movements quick and efficient, her smile polite but distracted.

Cade knew that look. It was the look of someone wrapping up early, getting ready to head home because no one expected them to do anything else. Just like the last time, when no one had bothered to invite her to the water tower after the ring-ceremony party.

Something tugged hard in his chest. Before he could second-guess himself, he called across the field, "Bailey!"

Her head snapped up, eyes searching until they landed on him. He lifted a hand in greeting and started over, closing the distance with easy strides.

By the time he reached her booth, she'd straightened, and was brushing a strand of hair from her face. "Congratulations," she said, nodding at the trophy Noah still paraded around behind him. "The football boys are never going to let anyone forget this, are they?"

"Probably not," he said, unable to hold back a grin as he stopped at the corner of her table. "We appreciate you coming out."

I *appreciate you*, he wanted to say. Why did everything between them feel so loaded with meaning now? They'd known each other their entire lives. He really needed to get a grip.

"You know I never miss it," she said.

There was that flicker again—the guarded smile, the distance she carried like armor. Cade shoved his hands into his pockets and tried for casual, though his pulse had kicked into something sharper. "Listen, a bunch of us are heading over to the water tower. Just the usual...hanging out, cornhole, that kind of thing. You should come."

Her eyebrows rose, and for a second, she didn't answer. He could almost see the gears turning in her head, calculating whether he was serious or just being polite.

"Me?" she asked at last, the word slow and careful.

"Yeah, you." He forced a shrug, aiming for nonchalance. "I'm sure Calla and Jackson are going. Half the team will probably be there, too. It's not a big deal."

But it was, and he knew it. No one had ever invited Bailey to those gatherings, not since Ethan. Maybe not ever.

It wasn't intentional, at least not on Cade's part. In the beginning, maybe folks had felt awkward inviting a widow to party under the water tower so soon after losing her husband. And as time passed, the invitations simply stopped coming, until no one thought to include her at all.

Cade hated the way that realization burned in his gut.

Bailey blinked, then nodded. "Okay."

"Okay," he repeated, the simple word charged in ways he hadn't intended. "See you there."

The water tower loomed tall against the dusky sky, its tall metal legs anchored in a patch of worn grass that held more town secrets than Cade cared to count. Tonight, string lights were looped between the beams, casting soft pools of light over the crowd that gathered below.

Still, it shouldn't have felt romantic. Half the town was here, including a good portion of Cade's students. But while he waited for Bailey, he felt like a nervous teenager on a first date, jittery in a way he hadn't been since his own high-school days.

It's not *a date*, he reminded himself. *Asking her here was just a friendly invitation...*

Emphasis on *friendly*, though his heart clearly hadn't gotten the memo.

He spotted her the moment she arrived, and a wave of inappropriate heat rushed through him before he could stop it. Bailey walked slowly into the glow, her eyes scanning the crowd as though half-expecting someone to tell her she didn't belong. Calla was by her side, but even Calla looked surprised when heads turned, voices dipping for just a beat too long.

Cade didn't give the whispers a chance to settle. He stepped forward, waving her over like it was the most normal thing in the world. "There you are. Thought you might've bailed."

Bailey's gaze found his, and she smiled faintly. "Thanks for inviting me."

He shrugged, shoving his hands in his pockets. "Sure thing."

For a second, neither of them spoke. Then someone hollered his name and tossed a beanbag at him. "Coach Montgomery! You're up!"

Cade caught the bag and jerked his chin toward Bailey. "Come on. You're on my team."

Her eyes widened, but she followed him to the handmade cornhole boards. The wooden planks were painted a bright Bulldog green with a snarling mascot's mouth cut out as the target. The paint had chipped years ago, but tradition was tradition. Cade doubted the cornhole game would be replaced until this one rotted into pieces.

"Do you know how to play?" he asked, handing her a beanbag. Cornhole was pretty straightforward, but he didn't want to make assumptions.

Bailey laughed. It was good to see her having fun like this. "I'm pretty sure I just throw it in the dog's mouth."

Cade winked. "Bingo."

They took turns, beanbags falling against wood and sliding just shy of the hole. When Bailey sank one clean through the opening, Cade raised a fist in triumph. "That's my teammate."

That's my girl, he'd nearly said. At least he hadn't made that mistake.

Her laugh carried in the night, lighter than he'd heard it in years. When the game ended—with Cade and Bailey victorious, thank you very much—Jackson shoved cups of soda into their hands, and the crowd drifted back to the firepits. Cade and Bailey lingered by the cornhole boards.

"Congratulations again on the cook-off win," she said, sipping from her cup. "Granny Montgomery's recipe does it again."

He tipped his head, studying her. "Thanks. It was an… interesting afternoon."

Her eyebrows drew together. "Interesting?"

"Yeah," he said, letting his eyes meet hers. "Especially when certain people showed up acting a little jealous."

Her cheeks pinked immediately. "Jealous?"

"You heard me," he said quietly, and the words seemed to hang between them, heavy with implication.

"Don't be ridiculous. You're free to date whoever you want." Bailey tilted her chin just a little too casually. "Whatever happened with Lauren Jennings, anyway? Weren't you two seeing each other before the Christmas holidays?"

Lauren Jennings, the local librarian with her sleek blond ponytail and cropped cardigans, hadn't been the right fit for Cade. Not even close.

He shrugged, casual on the outside, even as something heavier pressed inside his chest. "Didn't work out."

Bailey fiddled with her cup, avoiding his gaze. "Why not?"

"I guess I wasn't as interested in her as I thought I was," he said. "The library's big black-tie gala was during our district playoffs, and I had to make a choice."

Her eyes flicked up to search his. Cade met her stare, unflinching. Should he tell her the whole truth about how things had ended with Lauren, or was it too soon?

"That's a shame." Bailey's face tipped toward the firepit. The warm light brushed over her skin, highlighting the delicate curve of her jaw, and Cade couldn't look away.

"Not really," he murmured.

"What about Rachel?" she asked with an adorable little furrow in her brow. Bailey couldn't bluff to save her life. Her interest in his dating history was about as subtle as the Bulldog marching band. "You two were quite the item last year."

Cade huffed out something between a laugh and a sigh. "Rachel? That wasn't anything serious, Bails. I thought you knew that."

Bailey's brows knitted tighter. "Everyone was sure it was."

"Everyone was wrong." His tone came out firmer than he intended, so he softened it with a shrug. "Rachel and I wanted different things. That's all."

Bailey tilted her cup, staring down into her root beer like it might give her answers he wouldn't. "Different how?"

Different, as in Rachel had guessed where his heart really leaned, and it wasn't toward her.

He swallowed hard. "Just different."

For a beat, neither of them moved. Bailey's eyes lifted slowly, meeting his across the narrow space between them. Her expression was guarded, but her gaze lingered, as if she was trying to read the truth he wasn't saying. Cade held her gaze, although something inside of him twisted tight.

Bailey looked away first, back toward the firelight, where Calla was laughing with Jackson.

"Well," she said lightly, "maybe the third time's the charm."

"Maybe," he said in a voice low enough for only her to hear. "But only if it's the right person."

Her breath caught in her throat. It was the smallest, quickest sound, but Cade noticed. He always noticed.

The music shifted to an old country ballad that seemed to hush the chatter around the firepits. He leaned down slightly, and whispered, "You know, for someone who claims she's not jealous, you sure have a lot of questions about my love life."

Bailey's lips parted, and he fully expected some clever retort. But she sighed instead, and her shoulders sank, like she'd given up pretending this was just a casual conversation between two friends.

"You're not making this easy," she whispered, her dark eyes flicking up to his. She tried to smile, but it wavered, the truth written too plainly in her expression for either of them to ignore.

His heart kicked hard, steady as a drumline. "Easy's overrated, Bailey Bear."

The space between them seemed to shrink, and the laughter and music blurred into background noise, replaced by the thud of his own pulse. He wanted to close the gap, to prove to her that what had passed between them before hadn't been a mistake.

But just as his fingers brushed the edge of her sleeve, Bailey startled. She stepped back fast, and root beer sloshed over the rim of her cup as her eyes widened with a flash of something vulnerable.

Fear? Guilt? Possibly both. Cade knew those feelings well, after all.

"I should probably get going. I've got an early day tomorrow," she said, grasping at an escape.

"Bailey—"

"Thanks for inviting me," she interrupted quickly, the words rushed. Her smile was back, fixed in place like armor. "Really. It was fun."

And then she was gone, weaving through the crowd toward Huddle Up before he could say another word.

Cade leaned back against one of the steel legs of the water tower, staring up into the darkness. Stars swirled overhead, big and bright, just like the song. Deep in the heart...

His gut churned. Deep in Cade's heart, things were

a mess. Were he and Bailey really going to keep doing this? Circle closer and closer until neither of them could pretend anymore?

He didn't blame her for walking away. Because another, more pressing question stuck sharp in his chest— a question he didn't dare utter out loud.

What would Ethan think?

Ethan, who'd been his teammate, his best friend and Bailey's whole world. Cade had been there the night Ethan first asked her out, he'd stood beside his hospital bed at their last-minute wedding and had carried his casket when the unthinkable happened. Their lives had been intertwined from the start. No wonder it felt like a betrayal to want what was right in front of him...

No matter how many years had passed.

Chapter Eight

Bailey didn't get a wink of sleep after the party under the water tower, and the next morning, it showed.

She was a wreck, plain and simple. Less than an hour after opening, the counter was stacked with half-empty coffee cups and the muffins in the pastry case were going faster than she could bake them. Every time she started a task, she abandoned it to jump to another. The espresso machine hissed behind her, the cash-register drawer kept popping open all on its own, and there was still a smear of cinnamon sugar on one of the tables she hadn't wiped down.

She couldn't even blame the party. Not really. She'd gotten home in plenty of time to get a full night's sleep, but after taking a bubble bath and slipping into her pajamas, she'd stared at the ceiling for half the night with Bluebell curled against her side. She couldn't stop replaying every second with Cade—the way he'd looked at her under the string lights, the low rasp in his voice, the almost touch that had sent her pulse skittering.

Another sharp hiss from the espresso machine jolted her back to the present. Bailey spun, fumbling with the portafilter before the steam could scorch the milk. Behind her, someone dropped a spoon into the tip jar, and the sharp clang made her wince. The line at the counter had doubled while she'd been off in la-la land again, and the register drawer had popped open again like it was purposefully mocking her.

She was already stretched as thin as she could possibly get when she heard the faintest creak from the storage room.

Bailey froze. The storage-room door! Panic prickled down her spine as her stomach dropped. Had she been so distracted this morning that she'd forgotten to latch it after getting Bluebell settled inside on her cat tree?

Before she could move, a blur of chocolate-and-cream-colored fluff shot through the narrow crack in the door. Bluebell's little paws skittered against the wood, and then the kitten launched herself straight into the middle of Huddle Up as though she owned the place.

"Whoa!" a customer yelped, stumbling back with his latte as Bluebell streaked past his shoes. He windmilled his arms, barely keeping his balance.

Bailey lunged, her heart jackhammering. "I'm sorry! So sorry. Just, um, don't mind her!"

If Mayor Pearl or anyone from city council caught sight of that cat in her shop, she was toast.

She scooped up Bluebell before anyone else could get a good look, tucking the squirming kitten against her chest. The cat let out a defiant little meow, loud enough to draw a curious glance from the two high-school girls at the corner table. Bailey pasted on a bright smile, babbling something about the delivery truck making a noise out back, and bolted for the storage room.

Once she was safely out of sight, she set Bluebell on the middle petal of the cat tree and pressed a hand to her chest to slow her breathing. The kitten tilted her head and blinked up at her, all innocence and wide blue eyes, as if she hadn't just blown Bailey's cover wide open.

"What am I doing?" Bailey whispered, leaning against the wall.

Her whole life, she'd prided herself on being the good girl. She always did the right thing. Huddle Up ran like clockwork, her routines kept her sane, and she never, ever invited trouble. But lately, everything was unraveling.

First, the kitten—an impulse she'd hidden from everyone but Cade. Then Cade himself—just looking at him across the practice field at the chili cook-off yesterday had made her heart race like she was a teenager again. And then she'd accepted his invitation to go to the water tower, of all places, and let herself feel like maybe she belonged there with him.

It was all too much. Too messy and way, *way* too dangerous.

By the time Calla pushed through the front door fifteen minutes later, Bailey was nothing but a raw bundle of nerves. She'd managed to get Bluebell secured again, but her heart was still thudding from the scare. The cracks in her carefully ordered life were widening by the second.

Calla grinned as she slid onto her favorite barstool at the coffee counter. "Good morning. As per usual, I'm in desperate need of sugar masquerading as coffee. What's today's special latte flavor?"

Bailey barely heard her. She twisted the lid on a whipped-cream canister until a puff of cream sprayed the front of her apron. "You need to set me up with someone. Soon."

Calla's eyebrows lifted. She eyed the mess Bailey had just made and then pressed her lips together like she was fighting laughter. "Excuse me?"

"I'm serious." Bailey grabbed her dish towel and dabbed at her apron. It was official: she wasn't meant for a life of secrecy. She needed to get control of herself and her emotions again, starting with forgetting about the one man in Bishop Falls who had the unique ability to completely unravel her.

"I mean it, Calla. I need you to find me someone safe. Someone predictable. Someone who won't…" Her throat closed up, and she shook her head. "Someone who won't turn my life upside down."

Calla's eyes narrowed with concern. She flattened her hands on the counter and took a deep breath. "Bails, I'm going to ask you something, and I want you to know that however you answer it, everything is okay. I promise." The quiet compassion in her gaze nearly broke Bailey in two. "Do you think maybe you're developing feelings for Cade?"

The question pressed against something tender inside her. She straightened, defenses rising, despite Calla's gentle expression. "Why are you asking me that?"

Calla tilted her head. "Just a hunch."

Of course, she'd noticed. She was a journalist, for goodness' sake.

"I don't have feelings for Cade," Bailey said quickly. *Too* quickly. She tried to keep her voice steady, but the lie throbbed inside her like a bruise. *I can't*, she thought. *Cade is just… Cade. He's just a friend.*

Calla didn't look convinced. "Ethan's been gone a long time, Bails. It's okay if you want something more."

Bailey's chest clenched so tightly she almost couldn't breathe.

That's just it, though. It's not *okay.*

She'd been just a girl when she'd fallen in love with Ethan. After his injury, she'd grown up overnight. She remembered the hospital, the silence that had followed and the hollow ache that had settled in her bones when he was gone. She'd gambled everything on a forever with him, and it had all crumbled to dust. Even the strongest, most sacred vows hadn't been enough to save them from the fragility of life.

Bailey had once told Calla that even though losing Ethan had hurt more than anything she'd ever experienced, she wouldn't have traded their years together for anything. She had no regrets. She'd do it all over again in a heartbeat…

But she'd never confessed the rest. What Bailey hadn't admitted was that as much as she cherished every memory, every kiss, every dream they'd shared, she could never risk that kind of love again.

Because what if she lost Cade? The thought alone was unbearable. He was rooted too deeply into her life, into Bishop Falls itself, into the spaces Ethan had once filled. Losing him would rip her apart all over again. Maybe worse, because with Cade she wouldn't just be risking her fragile heart. She'd also be risking their entire friendship, the one anchor she still had in a world that had already taken so much.

Bailey's throat ached with unsaid words, but she forced a bright, practiced smile and looked at Calla. "Just please find someone nice and boring for me, okay?"

Calla studied her for a long moment, a wistful smile

tugging at her mouth. "If that's really what you want, of course, I'll do it."

"It is," Bailey said firmly.

But the lie echoed inside her, settling deep in a place she didn't dare touch.

Cade thought that winning the chili cook-off might light a fire under Noah and remind the sophomore quarterback what it felt like to come out on top again, even if it was just over a bowl of chili instead of a football game.

Unfortunately, he'd thought wrong.

The Bulldogs were in shells at Monday afternoon's practice, not full pads, which meant agility and timing were the whole ballgame. Cade planted himself near the hash marks and gripped his whistle a little too hard as he watched Noah stumble through his reads like his cleats were made of concrete.

"Noah, reset your feet," Cade called, cupping his hands around his mouth to project across the field. "Don't marry the back foot—drive off it. Let's try that again."

Noah nodded, jaw set. He took the snap, his first steps crisp and on time, but then he paused as he searched for an opening. That tiny delay threw everything off. When he finally let the ball go, it sailed high and behind the receiver.

"Dang it," Noah muttered with an apologetic wince for the receiver.

"You're fine," Cade said automatically, even as his gut churned.

Tryouts were this Friday. They were running out of time, and Cade didn't want to be forced to name the new transfer student as starting quarterback. Tyler's attitude was going to be a problem down the road. Cade could feel it.

He nodded at Noah. "Go ahead and run it back. Same concept. Keep your eyes on the safety, and trust the first window."

Three yards away, Tyler rolled his eyes. Instead of stretching, calling out encouragement to his teammates, or running after loose balls, he'd been spending his time on the sidelines smirking at Noah's mistakes, making no effort to hide his impatience for his turn. Now, he flipped a spare ball into the air with a lazy spin, then snatched it behind his back and launched it in a tight spiral to a receiver who wasn't even looking. The kid caught it out of pure instinct, blinking in surprise as Tyler lifted his chin like he'd just scored the winning touchdown.

Cade felt his molars grind.

"Save the circus throws for TikTok," he said.

"But bro, he caught it." Tyler spread his hands wide, like the evidence spoke for itself. A couple of the receivers chuckled under their breath, and Cade's blood pressure ticked up another notch.

"That's not the point." Cade stepped forward, planting himself squarely between Tyler and the rest of the group. "Being a quarterback isn't about showing off. It's about running the play, keeping your guys steady and making the right read. It's about being a team leader. If you can't figure that out, you'll be warming the bench no matter how pretty your spiral is. And unless you want to be running bleachers for the rest of practice, you may address me as Coach Montgomery."

Tyler smirked.

"Yes, sir," he drawled, the picture of polite disrespect.

Across the field, Jackson found Cade's gaze. Bishop sat at his feet, jowls sagging in a bulldog scowl that mirrored his owner's. The head coach lifted an eyebrow, a silent question in his eyes. *Everything okay over there?*

Cade gave a small nod. *I'm on it.*

He *was* on it, but the clock was not his friend. Tryouts for spring placement were bearing down on him, and the victorious glow from the chili cook-off hadn't changed the fact that his sophomore quarterback looked like a kid still learning to trust his feet. Meanwhile a showboat with a cannon arm had landed in their backyard.

Noah lined up again, shoulders squared, determination etched deeper this time. He took the snap and moved through his drop with more purpose, his weight shifting cleanly as he scanned the field. This time he didn't hesitate—he let the ball go early, and though it wasn't perfect, the pass hit his receiver in stride. The kid tucked it and kept running, and Cade felt a flicker of relief stir beneath the tension in his chest.

A chorus of cheers rang out from the cheer team hopefuls practicing their routines at the edge of the field. One of them waved her pom-poms and yelled Noah's name, and Cade was pretty sure he could see the kid's ears turn pink even under his helmet.

He caught Noah's sleeve as he jogged past.

"That was better," he said in a low voice, so only Noah could hear. "I don't need fireworks. I need first downs. Don't force it and remember to breathe."

Noah nodded, Adam's apple bobbing. "Yes, Coach."

"Your feet are the foundation," Cade said, tapping the toe of his own sneaker to the grass. "If they're late, your eyes are late. We'll fix it. Are you free before first period tomorrow morning?"

Noah blinked. "Yeah. I mean, if you are."

"I'll be here. Bring your cleats. We're going to get you nice and bored of the right footwork. Then your brain won't have to think. It'll all be muscle memory."

A shy smile ghosted over Noah's mouth. "Okay."

"And Noah?" Cade added as the kid started to jog off. "Don't worry about him." He jerked his chin toward Tyler, who was lounging on the grass under the guise of stretching. "The job isn't about flash. It's about trust. Win the trust of your teammates and everything else will follow."

"Okay," Noah said again, this time with a steadier spine.

The rest of practice moved along, the boys running drills and hitting their marks, but Cade's mind kept circling back to the quarterback situation. After the final whistle, Jackson ambled over as the players headed to the locker room. Bishop waddled alongside him, true to form.

"He's coming along," Jackson said, eyes on Noah.

"Not fast enough." Cade blew out an exhale. "But he's coming."

Jackson's mouth tugged into a grin. "That transfer kid is going to force him to grow up."

"Or make him implode," Cade said under his breath.

"Only if we let it, and I know you won't, Coach." Jackson clapped Cade's shoulder and peeled off toward the field house with Bishop lumbering faithfully after him.

By the time the last cones were stowed, twilight had settled across the field and the water tower beyond the bleachers cut a dark angle against the sky. Cade's eyes went to it before he could help himself. He pictured the string lights from that night with Bailey, heard the echo of her laughter and remembered the way she'd stepped close to him before pulling away.

You should be relieved, he reminded himself for the fiftieth time since the night of the water-tower party. *It's good that nothing happened.*

They didn't need to let momentum and music push them someplace they weren't ready to go. Cade had enough on his plate without tangling himself up in feelings he wasn't sure he could handle. Bailey had thanked him for the invitation with that brave, careful smile, and then she'd bolted. Maybe that was just the Good Lord saving them both from a mistake.

He gathered his duffel bag and headed for Maplewood, the ache of unfinished business trailing after him like a shadow.

"There's my boy," Granny said as Cade strode into her room at Maplewood. Thankfully, there was no hint of fog in her eyes this time. Not even the slightest hesitation as she said his name. "You didn't bring me any chili, did you? I was hoping you might sneak me a bowl. Although if you did, that would mean there were leftovers, and we can't have that."

"No, we can't. And don't you worry. We scraped that pot clean." Cade laughed, the knot in his chest loosening a bit. "Besides, if I'd brought you chili, every nurse on this floor would have tackled me at the door."

"I suppose that's true." Granny patted the arm of her recliner. "Come and sit. Tell me everything."

Cade took a seat and scanned the area around her chair. The television was turned on, but the volume was muted. Granny's Bible was lying open on the side table beneath a pair of reading glasses smudged with fingerprints. The crossword puzzle from the Sunday edition of the *Lone Star Gazette* sat beside it, every square filled in with bold strokes of blue ink. Cade felt himself smile. Granny only attempted the crossword in pen when her mind was sharp and her spirits steady. Today must've been a good day.

He told her about the cook-off and all about how his players hovered around the booth like a pack of wolves and swaggered like champions before the judging was even finished. He saved the big win for last.

"And we took home the trophy," he said, grinning broadly. "Best Bowl, for the fifth year in a row."

She preened. Actually preened. "Well, of course, you did. It's my special recipe, after all."

He grinned. "I guess we'd better start engraving your name on it."

Granny's laugh softened into a smile as she folded her hands on the blanket spread over her lap. "Now, tell me more about your boys. Are they behaving themselves, or running you ragged all over that field?"

She leaned forward, eyes shining the way they always did when football came up. Granny loved Bishop Falls football as fiercely as anyone else in town. It was always a topic of conversation on his visits, whether she remembered he was a coach now or thought he still suited up in Bulldog green and white. Cade never corrected her. Either way, it meant she was proud.

"They're doing okay," he said, and the statement

covered a multitude. "We've got a transfer student who thinks he invented the forward pass."

"That arrogance is going to get knocked off him quick," she said primly. "Pride goeth before a fall."

"Amen," he said, because yes, indeed it did.

They chatted a while longer and watched a few silent rounds of *Wheel of Fortune* on the muted television. When the conversation began to wander and the loops in Granny's stories started to curl back on themselves, he kissed the top of her head, straightened her throw blanket and stood.

"I'll be back soon," he promised.

"You better. Tell that Jackson I expect another state championship trophy next season," she said with a grin.

"Yes, ma'am. No worries. We've got it on the schedule," he said, absently twisting the championship ring on his finger.

He stepped into the hallway, and his good mood lasted all the way to the front desk before Shelby gave him an apologetic look and held out an envelope.

"Hey, Coach. I hate to bother you, but these went out today." She slid the envelope across the counter. Maplewood's logo was in the top left corner, his last name stark in the little window. The kind of envelope that never contained anything good. "It's the new rate schedule. Administration wanted families to get them sooner rather than later."

Worry coursed through him. This didn't sound good.

"How bad is it?" he asked as he tore the flap and scanned the letter's opening paragraph. His attention snagged on the words *adjustment* and *operating costs* and *effective June 1*.

The figure at the bottom made his mouth go dry.

Shelby's expression flickered. "I know this isn't what anyone wanted."

"It's not your fault," he said immediately, because none of this was Shelby's doing. She was just the messenger. "I appreciate the heads-up."

"Of course. Granny Montgomery had a really good day today, just so you know." Shelby offered a small smile, like she wanted to leave him with something good.

"Thanks for letting me know." Cade's throat went thick.

He needed to get out of here, pronto. He managed to make it all the way to his truck before he closed his eyes and let his forehead rest against the steering wheel. For a long moment he just sat there. Numbers tumbled through his mind, but none of them added up.

What was he going to do?

A head coach's salary would solve everything. Rustwood had practically dangled it in front of him—the promise of stability, of not lying awake at night wondering how to keep Granny where she belonged. And if he was honest, maybe putting a little distance between himself and Bailey wouldn't be the worst idea in the world. It would mean less temptation…less risk of ruining the fragile balance between them.

Cade exhaled hard through his nose and stared at the water tower looming in his rearview mirror.

He couldn't go to Rustwood. Rustwood wasn't home, and it never would be. The Roosters stood for everything he despised. They cut corners and played dirty instead of teaching boys how to be men. Cade couldn't stomach it, no matter how big the paycheck.

He told himself he was staying for Granny, because she needed him. For Jackson, because loyalty ran deeper than money. For Noah and the rest of those kids, because they deserved someone in their corner.

And all of that was true…technically.

But none of those things was the reason that pressed hard against his chest as he let his eyes drift closed again. It was Bailey—her laugh, her stubborn chin, the way she'd looked at him under the water tower before she'd bolted like they'd just stepped onto unsteady ground.

"There's got to be another way," Cade muttered out loud to the empty truck.

He scrubbed his face. Walking away had never been his style, even when the odds were stacked against him. Some might even say he was loyal to a fault.

If staying in Bishop Falls and keeping Granny at Maplewood meant finding a miracle, then he'd just have to do his best to dig one up.

Chapter Nine

Cade's first stop after his early morning practice with Noah the next day was Jackson's office in the field house.

Do not pass go. Do not collect 200 dollars. Do not even stop at Huddle Up for a Bulldog Brew.

Too bad this wasn't *Monopoly*, because Cade would've given anything for a do-over card. This was his life, though, not a board game, and he had people depending on him. If he wasn't going to defect and go to Rustwood, he needed to ask Jackson for a raise.

Cade was well aware that the odds weren't good. The school budget was already set, and everyone knew how tight the district kept the purse strings. Still, if they'd managed to scrape together enough for football-field renovations after the state championship, maybe they could find a way to tack on a few extra dollars for the quarterbacks coach and offensive coordinator. Technically, his role on the coaching staff counted as a part-time position, but in reality, he spent far more time on football than he did teaching history and grading papers. If he ever sat down and divided his stipend by the hours he actually put in, the rate would shake out to pennies. Possibly less.

His stomach knotted as he strode down the hall, and he reminded himself that this wasn't greed. It was survival. Granny's care was climbing faster than his paycheck, and something had to give before he ended up in a Rustwood red-and-gold polo shirt come football season.

Cade rapped his knuckles against the open door to Jackson's office and leaned against the doorframe like he did at least three times a day. The familiar creak of the hinges and the faint scent of coffee and worn leather footballs were comfortingly normal. He could do this. Asking was the hard part, but like he told the boys, you can't win if you don't run the play.

He was surprised to find Jackson on the phone with his pen tapping absently against a notepad covered in half-finished play diagrams. Jackson caught sight of him and waved him inside, mouthing a quick *one minute*. From the relaxed grin tugging at his mouth, it seemed like a personal call. Calla, most likely.

Cade sank into the chair across from Jackson's desk, the knot in his stomach pulling tighter as he waited.

"Okay, okay. I'll ask him again," Jackson said into the receiver. He had the distinct tone a man used when he was trying to placate his fiancée. "But I'm telling you, Calla, I got nowhere the first time. Coach Carter shut me down cold. Isn't there someone else we could ask?"

He listened for a beat and then chuckled, shaking his head like he couldn't believe he was even humoring the conversation. "Well, maybe Carter doesn't wear socks with sandals, but that's a pretty minimal standard for a date, don't you think? Also, oddly specific."

From his spot on his dog bed, Bishop lifted his head with a snort, as if unimpressed by Jackson's matchmaking commentary. The big dog's jowls quivered as he yawned wide enough to show every tooth in his mouth, then he flopped back down with the dramatic sigh of someone who had heard it all before.

Jackson's voice softened. "Calla, you know how things are around here. Carter said no before I could even get the words out. Nobody wants to risk hurting her. Not after everything with Ethan."

Cade froze as Jackson's words hit him square in the chest.

Bailey.

Who else could they possibly be talking about?

Jackson set down his phone with a sigh and leaned forward in his chair. Bishop's ears perked at the sound, his big brown eyes following Jackson's every move with comical intensity.

"Sorry about that," Jackson said. "That was Calla again."

Cade narrowed his eyes. "Were you two talking about Bailey just now?"

Jackson blinked, clearly caught off guard by the seriousness in Cade's tone. "Yeah. Who else? Calla's been on a mission to set her up since Bailey told her she wanted to start dating again. I thought you'd be in the loop since you and Bails are so close."

The words landed like a sucker punch. Cade's pulse quickened, and for a moment, he couldn't draw in a full breath.

Calla was trying to set Bailey up? At *Bailey's request*?

He dragged a hand across his jaw, incredulous. "And she wants to date *Carter McGraw*?"

"Apparently," Jackson said with a wry lift of his brow. He tapped his pencil against the desk for emphasis. "Bailey mentioned Carter specifically, but he's not too keen on the idea."

"You're kidding me." Cade sat back hard, as if the air had been knocked clean out of him. "Carter McGraw? Bailey's too good for that guy. Way too good."

Not to mention, he was the varsity baseball coach. Bailey didn't even *like* baseball. She'd once called it the world's slowest sport when he and Ethan had dragged her to a Bulldogs game. He could still hear the way she'd sighed through extra innings, bored out of her mind, counting the minutes until it was over.

Bishop punctuated Cade's sentiment with a loud grunt, as if agreeing wholeheartedly.

Cade shot Jackson a look. "See? Even the dog thinks it's ridiculous."

Jackson chuckled and held up his hands. "You'll get no argument from me, but this seems to be a recurring problem. No one wants to date Bailey because the whole town is too protective of her. Or maybe no one wants to replace Ethan, the hometown hero. Either way, Calla keeps striking out on Bailey's behalf." He pulled a face. "Apologies for the baseball metaphor."

Cade's jaw worked, muscles tightening as if he'd just been asked to hold a plank indefinitely.

"Are you absolutely sure she specifically mentioned Coach Carter?" he finally asked.

Jackson nodded. "More than once, according to Calla."

"Fine. I'll handle it," Cade said flatly.

If Carter McGraw was whom Bailey wanted, then Cade would make it happen…even if it killed him. No one deserved happiness as much as Bailey did.

Jackson arched an eyebrow. "Handle it? Meaning what, exactly?"

Cade waved him off, already rising from the chair. "I'll talk to Carter."

Jackson studied him for a long beat, clearly trying to decide how serious he was, then shook his head with a smirk. "Alright. But before you go storming the dugout, what did you actually come in here for?"

The question stopped Cade cold. He sat back down slowly, heat prickling the back of his neck. What *had* he come in here for?

The real reason felt suddenly too heavy, too vulnerable.

He'd rehearsed the conversation in his head all morning, all the way down to the calm, reasonable tone he'd use. But now, with Bailey's name still hanging in the air, the words stuck in his throat like dry bread.

Admitting he needed help, right after finding out Bailey wanted someone else? It felt impossible. Like showing too much of what was really under his skin.

He shifted in his seat. "Doesn't matter. It can wait."

Jackson gave him a long look. Before he could press, Bishop heaved a long, rattling sigh and stared at Cade as if to say *get it together, man*.

The sound broke the tension enough for Cade to stand.

"I'll catch you later," Cade muttered, pushing to his feet.

Jackson let him go, but his gaze followed him to the door.

Before Cade even reached the hallway, Bishop lumbered after him, nails clicking on the smooth tile floor.

The dog stationed himself in the doorway, staring up at Cade with mournful eyes and droopy jowls.

It felt uncomfortably like judgment.

What am I doing here?

Bailey smoothed her napkin over her lap, her fingers trembling just enough to make her press harder than necessary against the stiff white linen.

She had asked for this. Correction: she'd *begged* for it, practically ordering Calla to find her someone safe, predictable, and normal. She'd even mentioned Carter by name. Now, here he was, sitting across from her at the best table in the Copper Lantern, the fanciest restaurant in Bishop Falls.

And he was perfectly nice.

Carter McGraw—Coach Carter to the baseball team—was exactly the kind of man she should have wanted. Tall, broad-shouldered, with neatly combed sandy-blond hair and a polite smile. When he'd called this afternoon to ask her out, Bailey had actually been excited. Her heart had even skipped a beat from sheer relief. Calla had come through! Or maybe Jackson had nudged him in her direction. Granted, it was a Monday evening, not exactly a date night. But what did either of those things matter? At long last, she had a date. She could finally stop thinking about Cade and get on with her life.

Carter had even shown up at the restaurant tonight sans baseball cap, which seemed like a step in the right direction. He'd also brought Bailey flowers, a cheerful bundle of bright yellow daffodils tied with a pale pink satin ribbon. That had been unexpected. And a little strange. How had he known that daffodils were her favorite flower?

Still, she'd smiled and accepted them, because that's what she was supposed to do. When a man brought you flowers, you smiled, you said thank you and pretended they brightened your whole evening…even when they didn't stir so much as a flicker inside of you.

Which was precisely what you wanted, remember?

She pasted a smile on her face as she sat perched across the table from Carter, doing her absolute best to conjure a spark. Not butterflies, not anything as dangerous as that. But a twinge of *something* would have been nice. Instead, there was only the low hum of conversation from the other diners and the clinking of silverware against china as she felt nothing at all, unless she counted the creeping sense that this entire date had been a huge mistake.

Be careful what you wish for.

Carter cleared his throat and leaned back in his chair with his menu already folded neatly on the table. "So, um, how's the coffee-shop business?"

Bailey gave a polite nod. "Busy, especially in the mornings. You know how it is. Half the town needs caffeine to function."

"Yeah." He chuckled stiffly, then reached for his water glass. "I guess I'm more of an herbal-tea kind of guy."

Of course, he was. Bailey nodded and took a sip of her own water to cover the awkward silence stretching between them.

She tried again. "How's the baseball season looking? I heard you've got a good group of seniors this year."

Carter's face brightened. Finally, something he cared

about. "Oh, yeah. We've got a real strong lineup. If we can just get the pitching consistent, I think we've got a shot at District."

Bailey nodded again and waited for him to elaborate, but he seemed content to let the subject drop after that one enthusiastic burst.

The server came by and jotted down their orders—steak for Carter, grilled salmon for Bailey—and Bailey found herself wishing for Bluebell curled in her lap, or the warm comfort of her coffee shop. At least there, she knew who she was and what she was doing.

Here, she felt like she was trying on someone else's skin.

"So, Carter, would you say that you're more of a cat or a dog person?" she asked, trying valiantly to make conversation.

"Ah." He rubbed the back of his neck. "Truthfully, I'm neither."

"Neither?" She tipped her head, amused. "That's a bold stance to take in Bishop Falls."

He looked at her like he had no idea what she meant.

She pumped a fist half-heartedly in the air. "Go, Bull-dogs!"

"Oh, right." He cracked a millimeter of a smile and then winced. "I'm allergic to pretty much everything with fur. A lot of other things, too, but pet dander is the worst. I like the idea of having a pet, though. Lately, I've been thinking about getting a lizard."

"A lizard," she repeated, trying very hard not to picture a gecko running amok in Huddle Up. Weren't cats and lizards on the opposite ends of the food chain? "Like, what kind?"

"A bearded dragon, maybe? They look chill." He brightened. "And they don't shed."

"Hard to argue with that," she said, although she was one-thousand-percent certain she'd never before heard the words *chill* and *bearded dragon* in the same sentence.

Their salads arrived, mercifully giving Bailey something to do with her hands. She speared a cherry tomato with her fork and tried to imagine future versions of this—Carter telling her about lineups and pitching rotations… Her bringing him late-night cinnamon rolls after a win…so long as he wasn't allergic. The two of them sitting in these same chairs on some future date night, maybe even an anniversary.

The lizard.

It should have made her feel safe. Well, except for the bearded dragon and a lifetime of allergy meds for Carter if she somehow managed to keep Bluebell. Instead, something restless prowled behind her ribs, looking for a way out.

She tried another smile. "The daffodils were such a surprise. Thank you again for bringing them. They're my favorite flower in the whole world."

"Yeah, that's what Cade said." Carter cleared his throat, eyes darting away as though he hadn't meant to say it out loud. "Sorry, forget I said that."

Bailey blinked. Cade? Why on earth would Carter be talking to Cade about her favorite flowers? The two of them weren't exactly friends, and she couldn't picture Carter going out of his way to chat about her with anyone, least of all Cade Montgomery.

A prickle of unease slid through her, sharp enough

to make her grip her napkin tighter. Something about it didn't add up.

"Too late. Why would you want me to forget it, anyway?" she asked.

Carter sighed and set down his fork on the edge of his plate. "Because Cade specifically said not to let on that he was the one who told me to ask you out."

For a moment, Bailey couldn't breathe. The words slammed into her, knocking the air from her lungs.

Cade.

Of course. Of course, it had been him.

Heat rose in her cheeks, not the pleasant warmth of flattery but the scalding burn of humiliation. This wasn't her date. It was Cade's idea. Cade's arrangement. Cade's…game.

Carter must have seen something in her face, because he leaned forward, his hands lifted as if in surrender. "Hey, don't be mad at him. He meant well. He said he just wanted to help out a friend."

"A friend," Bailey repeated, her voice sharper than she intended. She gripped her napkin with white-knuckled fingers, her pulse thudding so hard she felt it in her temples.

Carter breathed out, a slow exhale that said he'd been dreading this part. "I should probably tell you that I said no at first."

"No to what?"

"To…this." He gestured between them. "To our date."

A hot prickle crawled up her skin, mortifying and fierce all at once. "Carter."

He winced. "Look, Bailey, you're great. Everyone thinks so. But, well…everyone also knows you're kind of off-limits. Not because you aren't attractive. I mean, obviously you are. You're amazing and nice and smart. It's only because of Ethan."

He looked like he wanted the ground beneath the Copper Lantern to open up and swallow him whole. "It's just…you're kind of untouchable because of him, you know. You and Ethan were epic. Nobody wants to be the one who messes that up."

Her throat tightened. "And Cade? What does he think?"

Carter blinked, clearly caught off guard. He shifted in his chair, fingers drumming against the edge of the tablecloth before he finally shook his head. "I don't know what Cade thinks. He doesn't talk about it much. About you, I mean."

He hesitated, then added with a grimace, "But if you ask me? He's probably the most protective of all. I can read in between the lines. The guy isn't exactly subtle."

Protective.

The word made her feel like a fragile glass figurine, something kept on a high shelf where no one dared touch it. She swallowed hard and forced her expression into something neutral as Carter reached for his water glass, clearly wishing he'd never said anything at all.

"Like I said, he meant well. He said I'd be doing him a solid if I took you out tonight and that you deserved to be wined and dined." Carter's eyes flicked up. "I'm not saying that he threatened me or anything, but he was awfully convincing."

The room wavered, just for a second. The restaurant's cozy brick walls and mason-jar candles blurred at the edges, like she was underwater looking up through ripples. Cade had arranged this entire evening. He'd cho-reographed the whole date, all the way down to forcing Carter to participate.

"Bailey?" Carter's voice was tentative now. "Are you okay?"

"I'm fine," she said, and the lie scraped her throat raw. "I just— Excuse me."

She pushed back her chair before he could finish. The legs dragged hard against the polished floor, drawing the attention of a few nearby diners. Bailey didn't care. She couldn't sit there one second longer, not when her insides were unraveling.

"Thank you for a lovely evening, Carter." She grabbed the bouquet of daffodils and clutched it to her chest. "But I'm afraid this was a mistake."

"Bailey—"

But she was already on her feet, grabbing her purse and storming toward the door. Outside, the night air hit her like a slap, cool and sharp against her heated cheeks. She sucked in a breath, but it didn't help. Nothing would at this point.

Cade Montgomery.

He was the last person she wanted tied to this mess. He had no right to meddle in her life, no right to orches-trate her dates like some well-meaning puppet master, and no right to shove her toward someone else when he was the one making her heart race… The one making her feel alive in ways she'd sworn she never would again.

Yes, she'd wanted the comfort of a safe, boring date, but not one arranged by Cade, of all people.

She hugged her arms around herself as she walked down the sidewalk, daffodils still clutched in one hand.

Their petals trembled in the spring breeze. She should toss them in the nearest trash can, but her fingers wouldn't let go.

What did Cade think he was doing? Protecting her? Pushing her away? Did he really want to see her with another man after the way he'd kissed the breath right out of her?

Her throat tightened, but she forced herself to keep moving, her steps quick, her jaw set. She had one destination in mind, and she wasn't going to stop until she got there.

"Convincing," she muttered under her breath as fury crackled like ice in her veins. That's how Carter had described Cade's behavior when he'd strong-armed him into asking her on a date.

Convincing.

Ugh.

She hastened her steps. "I'll show *him* convincing."

Chapter Ten

The knock came just as Cade was drying the last supper plate his grandmother had owned—the one with the hairline crack spidering out from the rim. He set it gently on the dish towel like it might break in his hands if he breathed wrong.

Another knock. Quicker. Impatient.

He wiped his palms on his jeans and crossed the narrow kitchen, the old linoleum soft under his sock feet. The house creaked like it always did when the wind nudged at the eaves, familiar as his own heartbeat. He wondered who would be knocking on his door on a random Monday evening, but anything was possible in Bishop Falls. He just hoped it wasn't anyone from the Victory Club. The boosters had a tendency to overstep, to put things mildly. Although, he couldn't figure out what they'd have to complain about during the offseason. Knowing Earl Whitaker, he'd find something.

Whoever was at the door knocked a third time before he could get there. Antsy, much?

Cade pulled open the door, and a bouquet of daffodils hit him square in the chest.

He caught them out of reflex. A single yellow petal

tore loose and stuck to his T-shirt. Another drifted down to the porch like a surrendered flag.

Bailey stood on the top step, eyes bright and furious. She was in a red polka-dot dress he'd never seen before, nipped in at the waist and flaring into a full skirt that skimmed the tops of her knees. Her hair was curled into loose waves, a soft frame around her flushed face, and for one irrational second, he had the urge to reach out, to thread his fingers through the silky strands just to feel them slide against his skin.

"Hi," Cade said, because his brain had apparently short-circuited.

"Don't 'hi' me." Her voice was low and shaking, and somehow more dangerous than if she'd shouted. "I can't believe you, Cade Montgomery."

He took a step back, then remembered the manners that Granny had drilled into his head and held the screen door open wide. "Do you want to—"

She barreled past him before he could finish.

"—come in?"

"No, I don't," she said, despite the fact that she was already standing in his living room.

Cade needed to tread lightly here. Clearly, she was upset, and he had a feeling it might have something to do with her date with Carter McGraw. The daffodils had been a pretty good hint, plus the new dress, which he was trying very hard not to think about.

He couldn't remember the last time he'd seen Bailey in anything other than her usual casual Western wear—denim and either boots or sneakers softened by some whimsical feminine touch, like a lace-trimmed blouse or a bow in her hair. Something about those polka dots was getting under his skin.

He clenched the flowers so hard a stem snapped.

"You forced Coach Carter to ask me out," she spluttered.

Cade squirmed. He should have expected this. In truth, some part of him had. Carter McGraw couldn't keep a secret to save his life. Once, during a baseball game, he'd gotten so excited about a surprise bunt that he hollered it across the field before the batter even stepped up.

"Bailey Bear…" He sighed.

He'd told himself she wouldn't find out. He'd also told himself that if she did, she'd laugh it off and he'd absorb whatever heat came his way because he could handle it.

All lies, it turned out. She didn't look a bit like laughing. In fact, she looked like she might cry. Her eyes were shining, tears pooling at the edges like she was trying her hardest to hold them back. If even one of those tears fell, Cade was going to lose it.

"Do *not* call me that," she said. Her bottom lip quivered, and it made his gaze go straight to her mouth.

He had absolutely zero business thinking about kissing her right then, but suddenly his mind was filled with only one thing—how very badly he wanted to just kiss her and make all of this better somehow.

He was a terrible person, wasn't he? A terrible friend, that's for sure. He'd been trying to do the right thing setting her up with Carter, though. According to Jackson, it's what she'd wanted. Plus, if Bailey was with someone else, Cade could go back to pretending his own feelings didn't exist. He could shove them back where they belonged. Buried deep and locked up tight.

"Sorry, I didn't realize you don't like it when I call you that," he said quietly. The house was so silent, you could hear a pin drop. The only thing louder than the tick of Granny's old mantel clock was the sound of Bailey's breathing, shaky and uneven.

Yep, she was definitely going to cry, and every single one of those tears was apparently going to be all his fault.

"I love it, and that's precisely the problem," she said, the words catching like they hurt on the way out. A tear slipped free, and she swiped it away quickly, as if she hated to let him see it. "Why did you do it, Cade? Why would you possibly think that forcing a man to ask me out on a date was a good idea?"

Cade held her gaze. "Because Jackson told me you wanted to go out with Carter."

"So you thought it was a good idea to strong-arm him into doing it behind my back?" she countered.

When she phrased it like that, his behavior did sound a tad unhinged.

"I didn't force him," Cade said, and then he winced because that sounded weaker out loud than it had in his head. Maybe there'd been a tiny mention of shoving Carter's precious baseball-card collection into the school paper shredder, but that had been a joke. Mostly. "I encouraged him. I tried to make it easy."

"So you told him I like daffodils." Her gaze flitted to the flowers, and this time it lingered, her expression wavering. Just a little. "The pink ribbon was a nice touch. I should've known you had something to do with it as soon as I saw it. You didn't just 'arrange' my date, but you also micromanaged it, didn't you? I bet you even chose the restaurant. And told Carter not to wear his baseball cap."

Cade snorted. "Someone had to tell him to ditch the hat."

A flicker of a smile tipped her lips before she could stop it. Once she'd carefully rearranged her expression into a scowl, she crossed her arms, the movement deliberate, like she was building a wall between them, flimsy as it might be against the pull they felt toward each other.

"If it makes you feel any better, I didn't choose the restaurant. That was all Carter. Scout's honor." Cade held up three fingers in a mock salute, though he'd never been a Boy Scout a day in his life. He truly hadn't picked that snoozefest of a place, though. "I would never take you there on a first date."

That appeared to pique her curiosity, although she seemed to be putting a lot of effort in feigning disinterest. She squared her slender shoulders, arms still folded across her chest, and muttered, "Not that I care, but what exactly would you have done differently?"

Cade's mouth curved, not quite a smile. "You don't want to know, Bails."

Was he imagining things, or did she seem disappointed that he hadn't used the Bailey Bear nickname this time?

Watch it, he warned himself. One wrong move and he'd give away more than he meant to…more than either of them was ready for.

Her soft, doe-brown eyes narrowed. "You're right. I don't."

A beat of silence passed.

"Not even a little," she added.

Another pause stretched, heavy enough to make his chest tight. Then, with a huff, she unfolded her arms. "Fine. Where would you have taken me?"

He hadn't meant to picture it…hadn't meant to let the thought fully form in his head. But once she asked, the answer tumbled right out. "Not the Copper Lantern, that's for sure. I'd have taken you out to Miller's Bluff. You remember it? That field where the fireflies come out so thick in the springtime it looks like the stars dropped down to earth."

Her eyes flickered, softening, and Cade's throat worked.

He swallowed and kept going. "I'd bring a quilt and cherry pie. We'd sit under the dogwoods with the river below us and the sky wide open overhead. Just us, and nobody else—no nosy servers, no other diners craning their necks to eavesdrop on every word, no Carter Mc-Graw *or* his baseball cap."

"And?" Bailey whispered.

He looked at her long and hard until he could see the word *more* shining in her eyes…until he was sure that she wanted him to go on, to know what else he'd dreamed up, as if she needed to hear every last piece of it before she could let herself believe.

"And you'd wear that dress." He reached out and brushed a fingertip along a polka-dot circle near her waist, barely skimming the fabric. "I'd lie back on the quilt, and you'd rest your head on my chest while the fireflies flickered around us like candlelight."

He hadn't noticed how close he'd gotten until he took in the uneven rise and fall of her chest. Then her gaze slipped, slowly and surely, all the way down to his mouth.

She lifted a hand until her fingers brushed against his knuckles, feather-light, but the touch nearly undid him. Somewhere in the periphery, he was vaguely aware of the daffodils slipping from his hand and falling to the floor.

Cade bent toward her without thinking, drawn like a magnet, until there was only the smallest breath between them. His heart slammed against his ribs, and he could practically taste her lips already.

"Why did you really do it, Cade?" Her whisper cut through the rush in his ears.

He paused, their mouths separated by the barest sliver of space. She wasn't asking about Carter anymore, not really.

"And don't tell me it was because Jackson said I wanted to go out with Carter. I need the real reason." Her eyes searched his, raw and pleading, and he knew— *knew*—he couldn't hide behind jokes or excuses this time.

"Because I'd do anything to see you happy," he said, and it was the God's honest truth. The words felt torn straight from his chest, too naked and dangerous to take back.

"Bailey," he said, gentler. "Is Carter what makes you happy?"

The question lodged in his throat, rough-edged, because she was so close he could feel the warmth of her body and see the way her eyes dilated when she looked at him.

"No," she said.

There it was. A single word that might as well have been a door swinging open inside his chest.

"Who is it, then?" Cade asked, even though every

cell in his body already knew the answer, even though the asking felt like stepping to the edge of a cliff and looking down.

Her eyes went glassy, luminous in the dim light of the living room. Behind her, the kitchen was lit up like a Christmas tree, the dishes long forgotten.

"It's you," she whispered.

Cade didn't move. He wanted to kiss her, and he wanted to drop to his knees, and he wanted to run, all at the same time.

"Bailey," he said, rougher than he intended. "Are you sure?"

She nodded once. Then again, harder. "I'm so tired of pretending...of being careful."

He lowered his face toward hers, just a fraction, and then took a ragged inhale.

"Tell me to stop," he said, mustering up his last morsel of restraint.

She smiled into his eyes. *That's my girl*, Cade told himself. The thought should've been edged with guilt, but in this moment, Ethan was the furthest thing from his mind. All he could see was Bailey...

Choosing *him*.

"Don't you dare stop," she whispered, and then she closed her eyes and rose up on her tiptoes to close the distance between them.

The first brush of Cade's mouth against hers was lightning. Not the terrifying kind that split the sky wide open, but the kind that made every nerve hum, that told Bailey in no uncertain terms that she was alive all the way down to her soul. A soft sound escaped her before she could stop it, and suddenly there was no living room, no Bishop Falls, no weight of the past pressing in…

Just Cade.

He threaded his fingers into the hair at the nape of her neck, and she wrapped her arms around him like she'd been waiting to meet him halfway for years. Because she had, and it was finally happening…again. Only this time it wasn't born of impulse or circumstance. This time, every brush of his lips was deliberate, every breath between them a choice. This was a kiss steeped in intention.

His mouth moved over hers with aching reverence, slow at first, then deeper, hungrier, until she couldn't tell where her heartbeat ended and his began. The warmth of him, the strength of his arms, the way he held her like she was the only thing in the world—it all unraveled every careful wall she'd built.

Bailey clung tighter, afraid to let go, afraid the moment might shatter like a dream she'd wake from too soon. His lips tasted faintly of honey and determination, a mix that was uniquely Cade. He kissed like a man who had waited too long, who had fought himself every step of the way, and she couldn't help the flood of emotion that welled up in her chest.

Memories spun through her—the ache of losing Ethan, the long months of pretending she was fine, the way the whole town seemed to have wrapped her in bubble wrap. But Cade wasn't treating her like glass. He was kissing her like she was fire, like she might burn him, but he'd risk it, anyway. For the first time in forever, she felt wanted, not because she was safe or fragile or someone else's memory, but because she was Bailey.

Her fingers tightened against his back. She didn't want

to think about tomorrow, about explanations, or small-town gossip. Right here, right now, she only wanted this.

And then a knock rattled the front door.

They broke apart, both of them breathless, staring at each other in disbelief.

Another sharp rap sounded on the wood, and Cade's jaw clenched. "Who could it possibly be this time?"

He scrubbed a hand over his face, clearly torn between ignoring it and yanking the door open just to yell "go away" at the top of his lungs. Bailey was fine with either choice, so long as he kept kissing her.

"Maybe they'll leave," she whispered.

Cade's mouth curved, a glimmer of mischief breaking through the frustration. "This is Bishop Falls, or have you forgotten? Folks around here don't leave. Not when they've got a chance to get up in somebody else's business."

He made a valid point, and then, as if to emphasize its accuracy, the knocking came again. Only it was louder this time, followed by a familiar voice booming through the door.

"Cade? You home? It's me."

Bailey's stomach plummeted. Jackson...of all people.

Cade muttered something under his breath that sounded suspiciously like "oh, boy," his jaw tightening as he looked at her. The weight of what they'd just done, what they'd just started, hung thick in the room.

She swallowed hard, heat rushing to her cheeks. "Maybe I should just—" She hitched a thumb toward the kitchen, her voice trembling.

Cade frowned. "Seriously?"

"Only until we have a chance to tell everyone about…"

She waved a hand helplessly between them. "Whatever this is?"

What *was* it, anyway? It felt like more than a kiss. Her lips still tingled, and her heart still raced, but underneath the rush was something that felt dangerously real, like the beginning of something they couldn't take back. It scared her and thrilled her in equal measure.

Cade's gaze softened, but his voice was rough with conviction. "This is me wanting you all to myself for a while, before the whole town starts chiming in on it."

Relief slipped through her chest like air after a held breath. She hadn't realized how badly she needed to hear that until this moment.

Carter's words from earlier flickered in her mind. He'd called her off-limits and untouchable, like she was a prize no one would ever dare try and win. She'd hated the word then, and yet some part of her had believed it. Carter's offhand comment had sliced deeper than she'd let on, because hadn't she wondered the same thing herself? Only worse, because deep down she knew that the town hadn't been the one to stick her on a shelf. She'd climbed up there all on her own, telling herself it was safer that way. Safer not to be touched, not to be chosen, not to risk breaking all over again.

But Cade's kiss had stripped away that lie in an instant, leaving her shaken and achingly alive.

Bailey's breath stuttered. She looked at Cade and whispered, "Maybe I should go."

His hand caught hers before she could slip away. "Don't," he said quietly. "Not like this. Just…give me a minute. Stay."

Her throat tightened. "Then I'm going to hide."

She gave a shaky, almost embarrassed laugh, hitching her thumb toward the kitchen again.

Cade's eyes locked on hers, all heat and stubborn resolve. "Alright. But just for now."

The words sank into her like a promise. For now...

This was a secret. *Their* secret.

What's one more? she asked herself, thinking of Bluebell as she darted into the kitchen and closed the swinging door behind her.

From the other side of the door came another knock, followed by Jackson's voice calling Cade's name. Something seemed off. Jackson was never this impatient.

Or maybe Bailey was just a hot mess, overall, and everything was fine. Probably that.

"Yeah, I'm here," Cade called back, his voice clipped but calm. "Hold your horses. I'm coming."

She held her breath, every nerve still buzzing from the kiss, her palm pressed flat against the cool counter to steady herself.

The kitchen smelled faintly of daffodils and the lemon soap Cade's grandmother used to favor, grounding her in the smallest way. But her heart still pounded wildly out of control, because somewhere beyond the fog of longing and the gnawing fear of what might happen once the town weighed in on things, Bailey knew the truth.

Secrets in Bishop Falls never stayed hidden for long.

Chapter Eleven

Cade took a deep breath as he strode toward the door, more than mildly aware that Bailey had seemed to take all the oxygen with her when she'd left the room.

How and why, exactly, had this evening spun so completely off the rails? He wasn't altogether sure, but he hadn't minded a single bit...until Jackson had started pounding on his door.

Bailey had just disappeared into the kitchen, but the weight of her presence lingered—her perfume soft in the air, her warmth still bottled up in his chest. He hadn't wanted to let her go, but she'd been right. Now wasn't the time for a hard launch as a couple. Not with Jackson knocking like a battering ram at his front door, and not when their brand-new more-than-friends status had barely lasted two minutes.

"Hey," Cade said as he swung the door open to let in Jackson. "Sorry, I was tied up with something."

He forced himself to focus when all he really wanted to do was drag Bailey out of hiding and pretend the rest of the world didn't exist. But no amount of distraction could mask the tension radiating off Jackson. His friend's shoulders were tight, and his jaw was set in a way Cade recognized all too well.

Something was eating at him.

"Hey," Jackson said as he walked in, the lines of fatigue carved deep around his eyes. His gaze flicked to the daffodils scattered on the floor. "What happened here?"

Beside him, Bishop waddled in with his usual entitlement, nails ticking against the floorboards, snuffling like he was casing the joint. The bulldog immediately shoved his nose toward the flowers, tail wagging.

Cade moved fast, scooping the bouquet off the ground before Bishop could do any damage. "I broke a vase earlier. No big deal."

The excuse slipped out smoother than he expected, and Jackson, distracted, let it pass.

Cade let the flowers drop onto the table in a clumsy heap and turned back to his friend, steeling himself. "Why do I get the feeling this isn't just a social call?"

Jackson didn't even try to soften the blow. "You might want to sit down."

Cade stayed on his feet, folding his arms across his chest. "I'll take my chances."

Jackson rubbed the back of his neck, a habit Cade had learned to recognize months ago. Something was wrong. Bad wrong.

"Bob Simmons quit," Jackson said flatly.

Cade stared, waiting for the punchline that didn't come. "Quit what?"

"The Bulldogs." Jackson's gaze didn't waver. "He walked this afternoon right after practice. He dropped his keys on my desk just after the locker room cleared out and said he was finished. An hour later, Rustwood announced him as their new head coach. They have a big splashy post on social media. My phone started blow-ing up the instant it dropped. Earl Whitaker is about to come unglued."

Cade could scarcely make sense of what he was hearing. Bob Simmons had taken the Rustwood job? Just yesterday morning, the Roosters AD had texted him with a last-ditch offer, upping the ante to a yearly salary that made Cade's eyes water. Still, his response had been a curt No, thank you.

Mitch Callahan hadn't wasted any time finding someone else to defect, had he?

"You're kidding," Cade said. Of all the plays Simmons could've run, this was the dirtiest.

"I wish. Unfortunately, I'm dead serious." Jackson slung his hands on his hips like he was on the sidelines of a big game.

Maybe they needed to slow down and think this through. Simmons wasn't exactly the easiest man to get along with. Half the time he barked louder than the refs, but he'd been loyal to the bone. And with him gone, Jackson finally had a clear field to direct the team without someone second-guessing every call.

"Have you considered that maybe this isn't such a bad thing? You and Simmons haven't always seen eye-to-eye," Cade said. Did *anyone* see eye-to-eye with that grump?

Jackson gave a short, humorless laugh. Bishop shoved his snout against Jackson's knee, demanding attention, but Jackson barely noticed. "He knows our entire playbook. And after that meeting we had this morning where we sat there and laid out our picks for the new team, he's walking away with all of that information in his back pocket, as well."

Tryouts weren't until Friday, but they'd already drafted a rough depth chart, penciling in who looked ready to step up and who needed more time on the bench. It wasn't just notes on a clipboard. It was the future of the Bulldogs, sketched out in black and white. And now, the new head coach of the Roosters had every bit of it.

"The spring scrimmage is probably going to be a disaster, but it still won't count toward our stats," Cade said. The Victory Club wouldn't be happy if they lost, but they'd get over it once the real season started. This still wasn't an end-of-the-world scenario. At least he didn't think so…yet. "We'll have all summer to come up with a new playbook."

Jackson dropped onto the sofa and gave Cade a look that said he *really* wasn't going to like what came next. "There's more."

More? *How?* Had Simmons planted covert listening devices in their locker room before walking out the door?

"He took Crenshaw with him," Jackson said.

"What?" Cade felt all the blood drain from his face as he tried to process this latest development.

He'd been debating what to do about the transfer player for weeks. In the meeting this morning, he'd gone ahead and placed Noah as his pick for QB one. Preliminarily, anyway. He'd been doing better at their private morning sessions. At afternoon practices, he was still shaky, but they had time to fix that. At least that's what Cade had been telling himself since State.

Still, even with Crenshaw's abominable attitude, Cade needed him. *Noah* needed him. Without Crenshaw, they'd have to tap their third-string players for a backup quarterback. To say that was less than ideal was putting things mildly.

"I'm guessing that Simmons told him all about your thoughts for QB one," Jackson said.

"And he convinced the kid to jump ship to Rustwood, where Simmons will use him as a starter," Cade said grimly. He let out a low curse. "Forget ethics. That's not even legal."

Jackson snorted. "Not that legalities have ever stopped Rustwood."

True. They'd poached the Bulldogs's top three seniors last year after they'd been suspended for hazing.

And we went on to win State, anyway, Cade reminded himself.

This situation was no different. They'd adapt. They always did.

Still, Cade's jaw ached from the effort of holding it tight. Without a decent backup quarterback, the whole upcoming season suddenly felt a lot more fragile, never mind the ridiculous spring scrimmage that everyone was suddenly treating like a playoff game.

Cade was getting a monster of a headache. He massaged his temples and tried to focus on everything Jackson was telling him. From the other side of the wall came the faintest sound—a creak, maybe, or the shuffle of a foot against linoleum. Bailey. Listening.

He coughed into his fist to cover it, praying Jackson hadn't noticed.

Jackson went on. "Look, I know you've been worried about compensation. You didn't say it, but I could see it on your face."

Cade's eyes dropped to the floor. He hated that Jackson had read him so easily. "Was it that obvious?"

"We make a good team." He shrugged. "Teammates know how to read each other."

Cade huffed out a breath, not quite a laugh. "I guess my game face needs work."

This wasn't exactly a conversation he wanted to have with Bailey in the next room, but he didn't have much of a choice. It was already happening, even if Cade's personal life was hanging by a thread on the other side of that kitchen door.

Jackson smiled but it didn't quite reach his eyes. "Your game face is fine. What matters most right now is figuring out how to keep the team steady while the grown-ups make a mess of things. I figured I could kill two birds with one stone and promote you to assistant coach. Simmons is gone, which means his spot is open. I don't have to think twice about who I want filling it. It's you. The job would mean a large pay increase, a full-time coaching position and a solid step up in your career."

Cade blinked, sure he'd misheard. Jackson had to be joking, except Jackson never joked about football.

"I already talked to the athletic director and Principal Dean," Jackson added. "I told them both I wanted you on board as assistant head coach. Full-time. Salary. Benefits. The whole package. They agreed you were the right pick."

Relief hit like a wave. Cade swore he could feel his knees weaken. For the first time since he'd opened the Maplewood letter, he felt like he could see daylight. Even if his promotion and pay raise didn't go through until the end of the school year, he'd be fine.

But then Jackson hesitated, and Cade knew the other shoe was about to drop.

"There's a catch, isn't there?" he asked.

Jackson blew out a long breath. "The athletic director wants results. He's got Earl Whitaker in his ear, and the entire Victory Club breathing down his neck. They never saw Simmons's betrayal coming. He bled green and white as far as they were concerned. The bottom line is that the job is yours—on paper, officially—with one condition."

Cade was almost afraid to ask. He lifted one eyebrow instead.

Jackson met his gaze squarely. "We have to beat Rustwood in the spring scrimmage. That's the condition."

Cade let out a short, bitter laugh. "My entire livelihood hangs on a glorified practice game?"

"That's how he wants it. Simmons walking makes us look weak, and the athletic director—along with the rest of the town, once word spreads tomorrow—wants to prove we're not. Nothing will quiet the noise faster than a win over Rustwood."

Cade dragged a hand down his face, trying to breathe past the pressure closing in around his chest. He saw Crenshaw in Rustwood red and gold, slinging passes for Bob Simmons. He saw Noah, eager but still green, carrying more than he was ready for. He saw Granny with her Bible open on the side table, at peace in the one place that still felt familiar. Uprooting her now, with the dementia closing in, would be like pulling the ground out from under her.

And behind it all, he felt Bailey's presence in the kitchen.

"Then we beat Rustwood," Cade said, his voice low.

Jackson's eyes narrowed. "It's that simple for you, huh?"

"Hardly," Cade admitted. There wasn't anything simple about this mess. "But it's clear, at least. They took Crenshaw? Fine. We put Noah in until his arm gives out. We run plays Simmons never heard of. And we remind Rustwood that Bishop Falls doesn't roll over for anyone."

For the first time, Jackson's mouth twitched into a grin. "Somehow I knew that's what you'd say."

They talked strategy for a few minutes, and all the while, Cade's mind whirled. He was already cataloging drills, making adjustments, shaping an offense Simmons wouldn't recognize until it was too late. But beneath the tactics, anger hummed. This wasn't just about football. It was about teaching the boys how to be honorable men. About proving Simmons wrong. About protecting Granny.

About not letting everything he'd built fall apart.

By the time Jackson finally rose, Bishop was already waiting impatiently at the door.

"Let's meet up tomorrow night after practice," Jackson said, and Cade had a feeling those evening meetings were about to become a regular thing. "We've got our work cut out for us."

"Yeah." Cade's jaw tightened. "We do."

He watched Jackson and Bishop disappear into the night as the screen door whispered shut behind them.

Cade stood for a beat, his fists clenched at his sides. Then he turned toward the kitchen. The swinging door creaked, and Bailey stepped through. Her eyes—wary, unreadable—searched his face. She'd heard everything, of course.

Her gaze darted to the coffee table, where the rescued daffodils sat in a haphazard bundle, petals bruised but hanging on, not unlike the way he felt.

"So," she said softly. "You're the new assistant coach."

Cade swallowed hard. "If we beat Rustwood."

Her chin lifted, steady as a rock. "Then you'd better beat them."

Something inside Cade's heart twisted. Not hope... not yet.

Something fiercer.

Something that felt like fight.

By the end of the week, Huddle Up had turned into a makeshift war room.

Bailey didn't hate it. Quite the opposite, actually. With the Bulldogs in panic mode, Cade didn't seem to have a spare second of free time. At least she got to see him every evening since he and Jackson had taken to meeting at one of the corner tables after practice.

Bailey wiped down the counter late Friday afternoon after the results of the Bulldogs's team tryouts had been announced, acutely aware of Cade's presence. A huge bouquet of daffodils brightened the end of the counter, their yellow petals spilling like sunlight over the edge of a vase from Field Goal Flowers. These weren't Carter McGraw's daffodils—the ones she'd hurled at Cade after her disastrous date with the baseball coach. These were from Cade himself, a fresh, new bouquet he'd given to her in a stolen moment Tuesday morning. He'd brought

them by Huddle Up on his way to early morning practice with Noah Weaver.

It wasn't until after he'd gone that she'd discovered
a tiny surprise tucked among the blooms—a little cat-
nip mouse for Bluebell. The tiny felt toy, hidden among
all that beauty, had undone her more than the daffodils
themselves. Flowers were romantic. The cat toy was personal. It was Cade telling her without words that he saw
her whole messy life, cat fur and all, and he wanted to
be part of it.

Her gaze darted to him now, and she caught him
watching her as she looked at the flowers. They shared
a secret smile while Jackson scribbled a rough field dia-
gram on a napkin, arrows and *Xs* overlapping in a tangle
of felt tip ink.

"Why here, again?" Calla asked from one of the other
tables, her laptop open in front of her. She'd been working on a big feature article for the *Lone Star Gazette* all
week, with a Friday midnight deadline. Aside from the
hours she'd spent at Huddle Up banging away at her key-
board, Bailey had hardly seen her. "Don't you guys have,
I don't know, an office?"

Bailey knew she was only teasing…mostly. On the
very day Bailey opened her coffee shop, Calla had declared dibs on the corner table as her writing spot, because it was the biggest table in the place, perfect for
spreading out her notebooks and research binders. But
lately, that prime real estate had been hijacked. Cade
and Jackson had swiped it right out from under her, their
mountain of football binders and formation charts spilling across the surface like an invading army. Calla's sleek
laptop looked downright dainty compared to the chaos.

Calla sighed dramatically, but Bailey wasn't fooled. For all her mock complaints, Calla loved and supported her fiancé with everything she had. She cared about the Bulldogs, too. More than she ever let on.

"Sure, we do," Jackson said, without looking up. "We also have a fluorescent light that flickers every two seconds and a thermostat that only knows how to crank itself to eighty. We need caffeine. And air that doesn't smell like Icy Hot and gym socks."

"Ah, the glamour of football," Calla said, deadpan.

Jackson blew her a kiss, and Calla practically melted, her sharp edges giving way to the kind of warmth that left no doubt how deeply she loved him. She closed her laptop, pushed back her chair and headed for the counter.

"Did you get your article finished?" Bailey asked as Calla set her empty mug down on the bar.

"I just pressed Send," Calla said with a satisfied sigh. Then she winced. "I'm sorry I've been so buried this week. Between my deadline and the Bob Simmons disaster, I haven't even had a chance to check in with you since Monday."

She leaned closer, conspiratorially. "So how did it go? Did you have a good time?"

Bailey blinked. "How did what go?"

"Your date with Carter, silly." Calla grinned, waggling her eyebrows.

"Oh. That." Bailey's mind scrambled for something to say. Her evening listening to Carter wax poetic about lizards felt like a lifetime ago.

Calla's eyes flicked to the daffodils at the end of the bar. "Are those flowers from him? They are, aren't they?"

Bailey's throat went dry. "No. They're from Field Goal Flowers."

Not a lie, technically.

She tucked a loose strand of hair behind her ear and forced a smile. "I just felt like brightening the place up."

Across the room, Cade's pen stilled. At the sound of Carter's name, his jaw flexed hard.

"So," Calla went on. "Tell me about the big night. Was it everything you wanted it to be?"

You have no idea. Out loud, Bailey said, "I don't think Carter and I will be seeing each other again."

"Why not?"

"We just…aren't compatible."

Calla pursed her lips, then shrugged. "Fair enough. Should we move down to the next name on your list? How about Todd from the hardware store? You know how I feel about that idea, but if you insist, I'll make it happen."

Cade practically choked on his coffee. Jackson shot him a look over the rim of his mug, his expression a mix of confusion and amusement.

Bailey let out a shaky laugh and shook her head. "No, thank you. Let's just shelve the whole dating thing for now."

Calla narrowed her eyes, her reporter's instincts kicking in. "Why? Don't tell me you're going to hibernate forever. You've been hiding out behind that counter since—" She stopped short, her expression softening before she said Ethan's name. Instead, she reached across the counter and squeezed Bailey's hand. "You deserve happiness, too, you know."

Bailey swallowed hard. She wished she could tell her

best friend the truth and that maybe happiness had already found her, quietly and unexpectedly, sitting at the corner table with a football binder.

But she settled on a different reply. "I've just got enough on my plate right now. Between the coffee shop and helping with the pep rally before the spring scrimmage, I don't exactly have time to swipe through Bishop Falls's eligible bachelors."

"You're volunteering at the pep rally?" Calla wrinkled her nose. "I suppose this means I'm also 'volunteering.'"

"It sure does. I signed both of us up to help out selling raffle tickets. Huddle Up is donating a pair of branded mugs and a bag of Bulldog brew coffee beans. The basket also includes two Dogs Hunt Roosters T-shirts and a pair of boots from Giddyup Western Wear," Bailey said. She shot Calla a warning glance. "Don't laugh, but Todd offered to donate a pair of ceramic salt-and-pepper shakers. The salt is a bulldog, and the pepper shaker is shaped like a rooster."

Calla's mouth twitched. "I'm not laughing."

Bailey threw a dish towel at her, but Calla caught it before it made contact.

"Back to the topic at hand, if you can make time for the Bulldogs, I think you can make time to date someone." Calla reached across the table, her fingers brushing Bailey's hand. "No one wants you to feel alone, you know. My brother wouldn't want that, either."

She was really going there. She was bringing up Ethan, even if she wasn't exactly saying his name out loud.

"I hear you, and thanks. But also, no." Bailey forced a breezy tone. "Not if it's Todd from the hardware store."

Cade's pen skittered across the napkin, leaving a dark streak. He muttered something under his breath that sounded suspiciously like "over my dead body," and Jackson had to cough to cover his laugh.

"What was that?" Calla asked, narrowing her gaze.

"Nothing," Cade said smoothly, without glancing up.

Bailey felt a bubble of laughter rise in her throat. She bit it back, shaking her head as if she couldn't believe her life had come to this—dodging her best friend's match-making while watching her secret boyfriend choke on his coffee.

If that's even what Cade was now. Bailey honestly wasn't sure.

Before Calla could push further, the bell over the door jingled and in strode Mayor Pearl, dressed in her signature florals with her gray hair teased into a formidable helmet.

"Hello, Bishop Falls," Pearl boomed to the half-empty coffee shop. It was almost closing time, after all. She marched right up to the register, seemingly unbothered by the lack of fanfare. "How are you, Bailey?"

Beneath her larger-than-life persona, coupled with her flair for the dramatic, Bailey had always thought Mayor Pearl was a nice person. A *good* person. She truly wanted what was best for the town, even if her methods sometimes made people raise their eyebrows.

Which was exactly why Bailey's guilt gnawed at her, because good people didn't deserve to be lied to. Especially not by their neighbors.

"I'm great, Mayor Pearl." *Other than harboring your missing cat in my apartment right now like a criminal.*

"Would you mind if I tacked one of these up by the

door?" She held up one of her missing-cat posters. Blue-bell's wide-eyed face stared back at Bailey, practically daring her to confess. "The more eyes looking out for Baby, the better."

"Of course," Bailey said, her voice steady even as her heart thudded against her ribs.

As Pearl bustled away to find a thumbtack, Bailey bit the inside of her cheek. If only the mayor knew. She couldn't keep doing this. She was going to have to fess up and tell the truth...*soon*.

One secret at a time, though.

Cade caught her gaze from across the room, and Bailey's breath bottled up tight in her throat. Then he looked back down and scribbled something on yet another napkin. Was she going to have to start charging them for paper goods?

Jackson leaned over to study the napkin, and Cade shifted, folding one corner under his palm. His pen moved again, slower this time, the line of his shoulders taut with concentration. When Jackson turned back to his coffee, Cade slid the napkin across the table, keeping his expression blank.

Bailey frowned, confused, until she realized he was nudging it in her direction, like some secret grade-school note. If she wanted to know what it said, she was going to have to walk over there and claim it.

She straightened her apron and passed with the cof-feepot a few seconds later, careful to make it look routine. Cade's mug tilted toward her, a silent request for a refill. She topped him off, fingers brushing his for the briefest second, and with her other hand, she palmed the folded napkin from the table.

Back behind the counter, she smoothed it open while Calla made chitchat with Mayor Pearl. In Cade's unmistakable scrawl were only five words:

Tomorrow night. Our first date?

Her pulse skittered. She glanced up, and his eyes were already on her, daring her to say yes.

Chapter Twelve

The gravel path out to Miller's Bluff felt the same under the tires as it had when they were kids. More rattle than road, it wound a slow climb that made conversation lapse into companionable quiet. Cade drove with one hand on the wheel, the other resting lightly on the basket between them, while Bailey watched his profile in the glittering light of the sunset.

She studied the clean line of his jaw, the little notch in his eyebrow from a childhood rookie tackle football game gone wrong, and the way his mouth softened into a smile when the truck crested the hill and the trees opened up to a tall, grassy field. The view up here took her breath away, just like it always had. A river rippled at the bottom of the hill, and the outlook was dotted with dogwood trees, their pale pink blooms catching the last honeyed rays of sunshine.

Cade parked beneath one of the trees and turned off the engine. A gentle quiet settled over them at once. No football stadium, no clinking of coffee cups, not even a hint of the small-town foot traffic on Bulldog Avenue. Out here, the only sounds were the crickets starting up for night, the river far below and Bailey's heart doing its level best to escape her chest.

Cade glanced at her, a crooked grin tugging at one corner of his mouth. "You wore the dress."

She smoothed a hand over the polka dots and felt shy all of a sudden. *It's only Cade. You've known him your entire life.* "You gave it such a glowing review. I figured it deserved a second chance."

His smile deepened, and he climbed out of the truck and came around to open her door like it was second nature, like he'd been practicing for exactly this moment for years. When she stepped down, he wrapped his hands around her waist to steady her. His fingertips lingered, even after her feet were on solid ground.

"Come on," he said with a wink. "We don't want to miss the firefly show."

Cade grabbed the picnic basket and a folded quilt from behind the seats. It was the faded patchwork one she recognized from his grandmother's house, a jumble of calicos and ginghams, each square a little story in itself.

He placed a hand on the small of her back as they crossed the field together. The grass brushed Bailey's calves, and the spring air smelled green and new. A few stubborn lightning bugs flickered ahead of schedule, testing the edges of twilight.

Cade spread the quilt under the dogwoods where the ground sloped toward the water. He shook it once and let it fall, then set the basket on the corner so the breeze couldn't get carried away.

"Your table, ma'am," he said, mock formal, but his voice was a shade deeper than a joke.

Bailey sat, tucking her legs to one side. The quilt was cool through the cotton of her dress. When Cade lowered himself beside her, their shoulders brushed, and goose bumps rose instantly on her arms.

"What's on the menu?" she asked, because talking felt safer than the rush of everything else.

Cade lifted the lid. "Cherry pie from End Zone Bakery. Did you know that place is for sale?"

Bailey felt her eyes widen. "No. Are you sure? The same folks have been running the bakery since we were kids. It's hard to picture Bishop Falls without Mrs. Miller behind the counter."

"There's a For Sale sign propped right in the front window. The Millers are finally retiring. From what I hear, they're ready to trade their bakery for a big RV." Cade handed her a slice of cherry pie on a paper plate.

Bailey shook her head, still trying to take in the surprise news. She got all the baked goods for Huddle Up from the Millers, and now, she'd likely have to change her routine. Unless someone actually bought the place. "Wow. End Zone Bakery changing hands? It's hard to imagine."

Cade slid his fork through the flaky piecrust, his tone a little gentler than before. "Some things do change in Bishop Falls. People get used to it, eventually."

He was still talking about the bakery, or at least he wanted her to think he was. But the way his eyes lingered on hers made it clear they'd both heard the unspoken part, the shift that had nothing to do with pie or pastries.

Bailey laughed a little too quickly, tucking her hair behind her ear. "Well, let's hope the new owners know how to make a decent blueberry scone, or I'll never forgive them."

Cade's mouth curved, but his eyes stayed serious. "I

don't think blueberry scones are the only thing people adjust to."

For a dizzy second, Bailey wondered if he was trying to push them out of the shadows, trying to say he didn't want their secret to stay one forever. She dropped her eyes to the quilt, tracing one of the faded seams with her fingertip. She wasn't ready for anyone to know. She couldn't imagine ever being ready, honestly, even though she knew that wasn't fair to Cade.

It was only their first date, though. They still had time to find their footing before the whole town started watching.

The light slid toward deep violet as they ate their pie and drank homemade root beer from Hal's Diner. More fireflies drifted up from the grass until they were everywhere, soft points of light blinking on and off. Cade set aside the empty basket and stretched his legs out, boots crossed at the ankles and an arm behind his head like he intended to stay there as long as she'd let him.

"Is this okay?" he asked quietly.

"Yes," she said. He'd been right. This was infinitely better than the Copper Lantern. "More than okay."

He patted the quilt beside him, and Bailey eased down, stretching out along his side. Their shoulders brushed again, a warm line of contact that sent another ripple of awareness through her. For a moment it felt like the whole world had gone still, holding its breath all around them. Then the edge of the quilt lifted and fell with the evening breeze.

The first time she'd come to Miller's Bluff with him and Jackson, they'd been twelve and sticky with soda, legs pumping as they chased one another in the tall grass.

Later, when Ethan came into the picture, she'd come here with a crowd, with bonfires, with laughter echoing down the hill. The field had filtered through a dozen versions of her life, and somehow it was both exactly the same and nothing like it had ever been.

She thought of Ethan. The ache that used to bite down hard surfaced and then softened. He'd been the boy next door, her best friend and first everything. Then his injury had shoved them into adulthood before they were ready. They'd loved each other the only way kids know how—completely and all at once. Looking back, Bailey could see how naive she'd been. As much as she hated to admit it, her parents had been right about some things. She hadn't realized how much of her heart she'd staked on the idea of forever at the tender age of seventeen.

Ethan had been her whole world, and when that world shattered, she hadn't known who she was without him. For the longest time, she'd thought she wasn't allowed to be anyone else. Sometimes she still believed it.

Cade's thumb traced an absent circle on her upper arm. His touch was tender, carrying more patience than she thought she deserved.

Bailey had never had this before. Not like this. Ethan had been a chapter. Cade felt like a door—a door to a life with room enough for grief and laughter, for patience and heat, for what they'd been and who they were now.

"Penny for your thoughts," Cade murmured.

"They're worth at least two pennies," she said, because she needed a second to collect them. Then she breathed out the truth. "I was thinking about how different this is."

He didn't pretend not to know what she meant. "Different good?"

She nodded against his shoulder. "Different real."

He was quiet for a beat. "I want real with you, Bails."

She didn't pull away to look at him, because sometimes the most honest things were easier to say to the dark. "I do, too."

The river tumbled below them, and somewhere in the tree branches, an owl hooted. Fireflies flickered all around them, just like Cade said they would. Like falling stars.

Make a wish, Bailey thought.

Cade shifted just enough to face her, his knee bumping against hers. "Tell me something," he said. "Something you want. It doesn't have to be anything big. Just some small dream you have."

She scrunched her face as she thought. So many answers rose to her tongue, but the one that surprised her with its simplicity came out first. "I want to not have to be careful all the time."

Her laugh was small and a little sad. "I didn't realize how exhausted I've been from tiptoeing around other people's expectations. From trying to be the version of me that made everyone the most comfortable."

His hand closed gently around hers. "You don't have to be careful around me. I like you just the way you are."

Her eyes prickled, and she squeezed his fingertips. "Now, you tell me something."

"I want to win the scrimmage," he said without missing a beat.

Laughter bubbled up her throat. "I walked right into that, didn't I?"

"Practically begged for it."

She swatted his shoulder lightly, and the teasing settled the moment back on its feet.

Cade sobered a notch. "And I want time. With you... without everybody else chiming in. I know we'll have to tell them. I'm not trying to hide you. I just want the part that's ours to feel like ours before we share it with a hundred opinions."

She let that sink in, warmth blooming behind her ribs. "I like that plan."

"Good." He tipped his head. "Another thing I want? For you to lay your head right here." He patted his chest, and his eyes still held a teasing glint, but she knew the ask was real.

She pretended to deliberate, then eased down until her cheek met the cotton of his T-shirt and the steady beat beneath it. He smelled like cherry pie and fresh-cut grass.

His breath tickled her hair when he spoke again. "Comfy?"

"Annoyingly so," she murmured. "I think I could get used to this."

His hand found the curve of her shoulder again and stayed there. Their words spun between them, and Bailey could hear a smile in his silence.

They talked about simple things for a while. Bailey told him about the plans for the raffle basket, and Cade talked about a "promposal" that had brought his class to a standstill the day before. And all the while, Cade's thumb kept moving in that small, steady circle on her arm. A breeze slid down from the trees, and the sky did its quiet work of turning day into night.

"Do you ever feel guilty?" she asked suddenly, braver

than she'd felt earlier in the evening. "For liking this? For even wanting it."

He didn't flinch from the question.

"Sometimes," he said, and she could feel him swallow hard against her temple. "But then I remember that caring about someone and wanting them doesn't take anything from what came before. It doesn't erase it. It just makes room for more."

He pressed a kiss to the top of her hair and whispered, "I know Ethan is part of you. I'm not trying to take his place."

"I know you're not," she said. "And I don't think of you as a replacement. I promise."

He exhaled. "Okay."

"And Cade?"

"Yeah?"

"You're part of me, too. You have been for a long time. Even when I was trying very hard not to admit it."

His laugh was a little unsteady. "I can work with that."

She turned her face toward him because it felt impossible not to. He was already watching her. The look on his face wasn't hungry exactly. It was reverent.

And certain.

He didn't move right away. He just waited. Then she nodded, and he kissed her with a tenderness that stole her breath and gave it back, all in the same heartbeat.

If the kiss in the living room had been a spark catching tinder, this one was a warmth she wanted to lean into. When he coaxed her closer, she went without thinking, one hand braced on his shoulder, the other sliding up to the back of his neck. He tasted faintly of warm cherries and the kind of devotion she'd never seen coming.

The night settled around them, alive with fireflies, and Bailey let herself rest in the quiet of Cade's arms. His kiss stayed gentle, unhurried, never asking for more than she was ready to give. And as his lips lingered on hers, the ache of the past loosened its hold, leaving space for this new thing between them to take root.

Maybe it was still a secret, maybe it was still uncertain, but in this moment beneath the dogwoods, it felt like the truest thing Bailey had ever known.

Chapter Thirteen

Cade leaned back in his chair and rubbed at the crease between his eyebrows. A half-graded stack of essays glared up at him from the desk in his classroom, every one of them on the same topic: the causes of the American Revolution. He'd chosen it because he figured it was broad enough to give his juniors room to breathe, but now, midway through a dozen nearly identical paragraphs about taxation without representation, he was rethinking that decision.

The classroom was mostly quiet, save for the scratching of pens and the occasional squeak of a sneaker against the tile floor. His sixth-period students bent over their own drafts, some with heads propped in their hands, others chewing on their pens like the answers might materialize if they gnawed long enough.

Cade forced his eyes back to the essay in front of him. Between the extra hours he'd been putting in with the Bulldogs and his full teaching load, exhaustion was beginning to press down on him in a major way. Snagging the assistant-coach position would fix so many things. He could fully commit to the team without thinking about money, he wouldn't have to worry about Granny and he could pour his whole heart into the Bulldogs, where it belonged.

Most of his heart, anyway. The rest had been stolen last Saturday night, out on the bluff with Bailey. It didn't matter how pressed he was for time. He'd never trade the memory of her lying on the quilt beside him with her head on his shoulder.

His pen stilled on the margin as he remembered the hitch in her voice when she'd asked if he ever felt guilty. Of course, he did. He probably always would, but he hated the thought of her carrying that weight. If being with him was ever going to hurt her, he'd step aside in a heartbeat. He just prayed it would never come to that.

A throat cleared at the front of the room. "Coach Montgomery?"

Cade blinked and looked up, pulled from his thoughts. One of the boys in the back row of class was pointing toward the door.

That was when the music started.

The door banged open, and in marched a senior he recognized from his third-period class, trailed by two friends lugging an enormous Bluetooth speaker. It sputtered to life with the tinny beat of a Taylor Swift classic, the song where she turned Romeo and Juliet into a say-yes moment.

The classroom erupted into instant chatter, the writing assignment completely forgotten. A collective gasp went up as the boy in the lead whipped a poster board out from behind his back that was practically drowning in glitter glue. A cascade of sparkles shook loose, scattering across the floor, and Cade's sympathy immediately shifted to the janitorial staff, who would be cursing this display long after the romance faded. Glitter would still be sparkling in the grout after graduation.

Across the front of the poster, in letters big enough to clock from the back bleachers of Bulldog Stadium, it read: Prom With Me, Kaylee?

The class went wild.

Kaylee, a quiet honor student who usually kept her head down, froze. Her pen clattered to the desk. Her eyes widened, and both hands flew to her mouth.

The boy grinned, then took a dramatic bow before striding straight to her desk. His friends fumbled with the music volume, one of them clearly suppressing laughter as the song skipped awkwardly between verses.

"Oh, my gosh," someone whispered. "He's really doing it."

The boy dropped to one knee right beside Kaylee's desk and pulled a bouquet of daisies from behind his back. Even the flowers were covered in glitter, each white petal sparkling under the fluorescent lights like they'd been dusted by a rogue fairy. Or, more likely, Marigold Knox from Field Goal Flowers. Cade had the sudden, sinking thought that Kaylee would be finding sparkles in her backpack until graduation.

A few petals rained down in the commotion, but Kaylee's suitor didn't seem to care. "Kaylee," he declared, loud enough for the whole hallway to hear, "will you go to prom with me?"

Half the class broke into applause, while the other half *awwed* in unison. A few even pounded on their desks like they were at a football game. Cade had seen touchdowns celebrated with less enthusiasm.

Kaylee's cheeks blazed scarlet. She looked from the

daisies to the glitter poster to the boy kneeling in front of her. For a heartbeat, Cade thought she might faint, and he braced himself for a sprint down the hall to fetch the school nurse. The woman already kept a cot warm for kids trying to skip algebra. No doubt, she'd make room for swooning over a glitter-soaked promposal, too.

Then Kaylee nodded furiously, laughter spilling out around the hands still covering her mouth.

"Yes! Yes, of course," she said, falling into perfect timing with the chorus, right as Taylor hit the part about saying yes.

The windows rattled as a fresh round of cheers, whistles and shouts went up from Cade's students. Kaylee's friends swarmed her desk, squealing and fanning her with looseleaf paper. The boy stood, triumphant, and delivered a fist pump so dramatic that it sent his friends into hysterics.

Cade folded his arms over his chest. Another promposal in the middle of class? He couldn't allow this to become a thing. He fought for a stern expression, but a smile tugged at his mouth anyway.

"Alright, alright," he finally said, raising his voice over the din. "You got your answer. Now, get this circus out of my classroom before Principal Dean shows up and I'm the one sweeping up glitter for detention."

The seniors retreated with their boom box and bedazzled poster to another round of cheers. Cade shook his head as the door closed behind them. Their whoops echoed down the hall, chased by the fading strains of Taylor Swift from the Bluetooth speaker. For a moment, the silence that followed felt deafening. Then a stray note crackled back from the boom box before finally dying out.

"Kaylee, that was so cute," one girl gushed. "You're like, promposal famous now."

Kaylee blushed furiously, though the dazed little smile on her face made it clear she didn't really mind the attention. "I can't believe that just happened."

Gradually, the noise died down to a dull roar. Cade tapped his pen against the desk and gave the class his best coach's look. "Let's get back to your essays, guys. The Boston Tea Party is not going to analyze itself."

Pens hit paper again, though the buzz of leftover excitement lingered.

"Coach Montgomery?" A girl in the front row raised her hand. "What about you? Did you ever do a promposal for your date?"

The class perked right back up as Cade arched an eyebrow. "Promposals weren't even a thing back in the Dark Ages when I graduated."

A wave of laughter broke out.

"The Dark Ages?" Someone snorted.

"Well, if you didn't do a promposal, then how'd you ask your date?" another girl persisted.

Cade shifted in his chair. He could feel twenty pairs of eyes waiting for him to spin some story, but he wasn't about to lie.

He cleared his throat. "I didn't ask anyone. I didn't go to my senior prom."

The room fell quiet. A couple of students blinked, surprised.

Someone muttered, "Seriously?"

Another whispered, "But you were a football star."

He gave a shrug that he hoped looked casual. "Sometimes life doesn't line up the way you think it will."

That seemed to satisfy them. The chatter shifted back to Kaylee's daisies, then to complaints about word counts, and soon everyone got back to work on the assignment.

Cade bent low over his desk, pen poised, pretending to be absorbed in a messy paragraph about Paul Revere. At least the kid had remembered the lanterns—one if by land, two if by sea—even if he'd spelled it "lantrin."

The question about his prom date nagged at him, though.

Cade hadn't gone to prom. Neither had Bailey. Prom had taken place just a few months after Ethan's injury, when everything they'd known had been shattered. The thought of tuxedos and corsages had just felt wrong, so he'd skipped it. Bailey had, too, but for different reasons. She should've been on Ethan's arm, and instead she'd been sitting in his hospital room helping him learn to deal with his new reality. Cade had never regretted not going, exactly. But in the end, it was one more thing they'd both lost to the accident, one more piece of normal that had slipped through their fingers.

His jaw tightened, and he shoved down the memory, refusing to let it show on his face. Prom had passed them by. But maybe, just maybe, their moment was finally catching up with them.

Bailey slipped the lock on the front door to Huddle Up, wiped one last coffee ring on the espresso machine and stood still just long enough to feel the quiet settle in around her. She'd barely had time to take a single exhale when a gentle knock sounded at the back entrance.

Two quick taps and a beat of silence, followed by one more knock—Bailey and Cade's not-so-secret code for their very much secret relationship. She felt a smile tip her lips as she unlatched the back door. The lock on it was always tricky, but once she jimmied it free, she went a little swoony at the sight of Cade filling the frame with his easy confidence and the grin that did dangerous things to her resolve.

"Hey, Bailey Bear," he murmured.

"Hey, Coach," she replied, lifting one eyebrow. "You know we closed at least six whole minutes ago."

"Then I'm right on time." He leaned to give her a tender kiss on her cheek, like it was habit now.

It *was* habit now. That tiny, secret kiss had become the sweetest sort of habit imaginable, and it had wrapped itself around Bailey's heart and refused to be shaken loose.

The first time Cade turned up at the back door of Huddle Up had been the night he'd slipped her the note asking her out for their first date. He'd left the shop with Jackson and Calla, walking with them just far enough down the sidewalk to make it look like he was headed home. But a few minutes later, there he was again, double-backing to the alley and knocking softly at the back entrance. Now, it had become their pattern whenever he could steal the time. He'd stop by after practice with his hair still damp from the shower and a tired grin on his face like she was the part of the day he'd been saving himself for.

It made her feel safe in a way she hadn't realized she'd been missing. Every time his knock sounded, it was like a promise that he'd always come back, that she wasn't alone in this. Cade didn't just bring her excitement or butterflies. He brought her something solid to hold on to. He always had. She just hadn't realized quite how much until now.

"Come in before Marigold from the florist catches us and activates the Bulldog phone tree," Bailey said, tugging him inside. She slid the bolt, then reached for the light switch, dimming the overhead chandelier to a soft, golden hush.

Bluebell scampered straight toward him, and Cade picked her up, letting her rub her face against his cheek. Then he took in the surroundings with an expression that he only seemed to get here in Bailey's cozy coffee shop. She'd started to think that maybe Huddle Up was the only place where he could let himself exhale. He carried so much responsibility. For the boys, for the school, for Granny…

Even for me, she thought with a pang. She didn't want to add to the weight he already shouldered, but the look on his face told her otherwise. Like being with her wasn't a burden at all, but a relief. Like maybe she could be his safe place, the way he had so easily become hers.

"It smells like cinnamon and victory in here," he said with a grin.

She laughed. "Practice was that good, huh?"

"Actually, no. Noah looked great this morning, but this afternoon…" Cade sighed and dropped down on one of the barstools. Bluebell leaped gracefully to the floor to lick one of her paws. "Not so much."

Bailey winced. "I'm sorry. I wish there was something I could do to help."

Cade's mouth curved again. "You could come watch practice tomorrow. The guys always show off when there's an audience. Maybe a little extra motivation is just what Noah needs to stop tripping over his own feet."

Her chest gave a little squeeze at the thought that he wanted her there. "You really think that would help?"

"I know it would for a certain member of the coaching staff," he said, his grin turning boyish.

Bailey bit her lip. She was touched in a way she hadn't expected by the simple invitation. "Then I'll be there. Front row, cheering section of one."

"Actually, Calla's been a regular fixture in the bleachers lately. I'm pretty sure it's not the drills she's watching as much as the way Jackson fills out his Bulldogs polo. That girl has really gotten over her aversion to professional athletes."

"Cheering section of two, then," Bailey said. She sat beside him and gave him a shoulder bump, although it was more like nudging against a brick wall. Jackson Knight wasn't the only guy around Bishop Falls who could fill out a Bulldogs polo.

His eyes warmed, and for a beat the whole shop seemed to hum with something unspoken, sweet and impossible to ignore.

Bailey cleared her throat. "Can I get you something to drink? You've been outside all afternoon. Do you want a glass of water?"

Or perhaps she'd just pour it over her head to cool the ridiculous surge of attraction buzzing through her. He'd invited her to watch football practice, not run away together.

"Water?" Cade put a hand to his heart, mock wounded. "I set a new personal best for stacking tackling dummies so I could get here as fast as I could. I need something with a little more kick than water."

She ducked behind the counter and grabbed a mug, fighting the urge to smile at the thought of him hurrying straight here just to see her. "What are you in the mood for?"

"You're the boss," he said, drumming his fingers on the polished wood of the bar.

"Seriously? You always get a Bulldog Brew. Are you really telling me I can whip up anything I want for you?" she asked, already reaching for syrups.

"Why does that sound so ominous? Coffee is coffee, right?"

Bailey gave a mock gasp. "Cade Montgomery, did you just say 'coffee is coffee' in my shop?"

He spread his arms out wide. "Fine, then. Let's do this. Give me something so good that I'll never look at a Bulldog Brew the same way again."

"You jest, but I'm about to change your entire world." She pulled a double shot, the coffee pooling in the cup with a swirl of golden froth on top. "Espresso, cinnamon, a whisper of honey—don't look at me like that, it's manly—and a dash of my special house-made vanilla."

Cade's eyebrows rose. "That whisper of honey looks more like a shout."

"Trust the artist. You gave me full rein, remember?" She swirled and then tasted her creation with a spoon. After a few small adjustments, she topped it with a thin layer of frothy milk and, because she couldn't quite resist, a generous dollop of whipped cream.

Cade eyed it like it might bite. "That looks like something Calla would order. Do I need to sign a waiver before I consume all that sugar?"

"What you need is gratitude. Welcome to the dark side. It's about time, my friend. You've been drinking plain black coffee for *years*. You deserve to have a little fun." She slid the mug toward him. "Presenting the Hail Mary, created especially for my favorite football coach."

A smile teased the edges of his mouth. "You named my drink after the most desperate move in all of football?"

She nudged the drink closer to him. "It might have a low probability of success, but when it works, it's spectacular. The kind of play people never forget."

"That almost sounded like a metaphor, Bailey Bear."

Maybe it was. Whatever they were doing together wasn't in the playbook, but then again, the best wins rarely were.

"Just drink," she said with a roll of her eyes.

He took a careful sip, then another, and the teasing dropped out of his face.

"Wow," he said, sounding more than a little bit surprised. "That's actually really good. I think I might like it over here on the dark side."

She leaned one elbow on the counter, savoring his reaction. "Shall I add it to the chalkboard menu? It could be a special limited run."

He gave her a look that warmed something low in her belly. "Put it up there. I kind of like the idea of our secret hiding in plain sight."

She reached for a piece of chalk and lifted it to the chalkboard that hung over the pastry case. In a corner of the board, under Staff Favorites, she drew a tiny football and wrote Hail Mary. Then she added a heart the size of a pea before immediately erasing it with the side of her hand.

The heart was too much, wasn't it?

Cade rounded the counter to her side, close enough that she could feel the heat of him. He set down his mug and tapped a finger over the smudge where the chalk heart had just been. "I saw that."

"I doodle sometimes," she said without looking at him.

"You also rescue tired men with cinnamon and honey."

"It's part of the Huddle Up mission statement." She glanced up, and there he was, looking at her like she was the only thing in the room that mattered. It was the exact look she pretended not to notice in public—the one that made her whole world tip sideways.

"You know," he said, reaching out to tuck her hair behind her ear, his touch gentle…almost hesitant. "I keep thinking about Miller's Bluff."

So did she, even more than she wanted to admit.

His eyes went tender, and the memory of their first real date unspooled between them—the river, the fireflies, the way he'd put his jacket around her shoulders even though the night really hadn't been that cold.

"I think about it, too," she whispered, as if the admission was a secret, like everything else. "I think about it a lot."

"You're fond of me, Bailey Bear," he said quietly, like he still wasn't sure he was allowed to say it out loud.

Bailey bit back a smile. She liked the way he'd phrased it. *Fond* didn't even begin to cover it, but it sounded safer than the truth. She busied herself with folding a dish towel, then watched her hands smooth the same square twice. Secrets were simple until they weren't.

Until small kindnesses turned into something else.

Something meaningful.

"Tell me something," Cade said suddenly, echoing their conversation from the other night.

She looked up. "Right now?"

"Right now."

She thought for a moment. He hadn't said it needed to be something she wished for this time, so maybe a confession would count. "Okay. I once served Principal Dean decaf and told him it was regular because he was terrorizing the ninth graders."

Cade choked out a laugh. "Bailey, I'm pretty sure that violates some code of barista ethics."

She shrugged. "You can thank me later. That one cup of decaf probably saved you and Jackson an entire afternoon of grief, too. That man is seriously overcaffeinated. It was an act of service."

"No doubt," he said with a chuckle.

She shot him a curious glance. "Now, you tell me something."

He paused as the pad of his thumb traced the rim of his mug. When he looked at her again, his expression wasn't playful anymore. It was sincere. "I like being here more than I like being anywhere else on earth."

Bailey swallowed. Hard. This little game had suddenly become quite revealing. "Cade—"

"I get it," he said quickly and gave her a lopsided grin. But the sincerity in his gaze still lingered. "I know we agreed to keep things quiet, and I understand why. I still think it's a good idea. But sometimes I think about…not."

The thought of going public sent a low, bright flicker through her, along with a thread of alarm. Her heart kicked hard at the thought, equal parts exhilaration and dread.

"Sometimes I do, too," she said, so quietly she wasn't sure he even heard her.

Cade's shoulders eased as he exhaled the smallest of breaths. He'd heard, alright. Relief softened his handsome face. "We can table that for now. Nothing changes until we're both ready. Deal?"

She nodded. "Deal."

He took a step closer, and his mouth was suddenly so near that she could feel the warmth of his breath mingle with hers. His hand slid to her waist, fingers warm through the thin cotton of her Bulldogs T-shirt. "Shall we seal that promise with a kiss?"

She tipped up her face toward his, her breath catching as the moment stretched between them, sweet and inevitable. "Yes, please."

Then his lips skimmed hers in a quiet kiss that started with a smile against her lips and turned into something that made the lights seem softer, like the whole shop was wrapped in a golden glow. She tasted coffee, sugar and the hint of honey she'd sworn he'd love. He was so gentle, so sure, that it made her wonder if kissing him would always undo her this completely.

She hoped so. And for once, that hope didn't frighten her at all. It made her feel whole again, like the old Bailey Davis, who'd thrown herself into life without hesitation.

When they parted, he pressed a chaste kiss to her forehead and rubbed a thumb over her bottom lip with a wink. "Just checking to make sure I didn't leave behind any whipped cream."

"That's a pretty sweet way to check," she said, breathless.

"I aim to please," he said. Then he tipped his head toward the chalkboard, where she'd added the menu item for the Hail Mary. "Are you really going to leave that up there?"

"Maybe. Even Starbucks has a secret menu." She waggled her eyebrows. "It's high time we have a mystery drink, too. I won't tell anyone what's in it. They'll just have to guess once they taste it."

He took her hand and held it loosely as they leaned hip-to-hip against the counter, talking about nothing and everything—the scrimmage next week, Cade's latest visit with his grandmother and whether Dr. Dunne would recognize Bluebell if Bailey strolled into the veterinary clinic for the kitten's next round of vaccinations. He would, without a doubt.

When Cade finally reached for his hoodie and headed for the back door, Bailey walked alongside him with her fingers laced through his until the last possible moment. Bluebell padded after them, purring like a freight train. Cade squeezed her hand once, a silent good-night, and then brushed a kiss against her knuckles before he slipped out into the cool spring evening. Bailey jiggled the crooked bolt in place, leaned her forehead against the wood and smiled to herself like a girl with a secret worth keeping.

Then she scooped her kitty into her arms, returned to the counter to pick up the chalk and drew a little star beside the words *Hail Mary*. It wasn't a grand gesture, only a small, tender one. Just bright enough to light the way from here to wherever they were going.

Chapter Fourteen

Cade adjusted the brim of his cap and squinted into the glare of the afternoon sun as the Bulldogs jogged into position for the first drill of afternoon practice. A whistle shrieked, and the boys launched into the play.

Jackson stepped up beside him, arms folded tight across his chest. He always looked at home out here, like a man who'd been born with a whistle lanyard instead of an umbilical cord. He'd struggled to think of himself as a coach when he'd first arrived in Bishop Falls, but Cade had to admit, he'd grown into the part better than anyone had predicted. Jackson had been exactly what the town needed. The Bulldogs had their best season in over a decade last fall. Better yet, they'd won with grace and good sportsmanship.

Now, they just needed to do it again.

Bishop sprawled at Cade's feet, tongue lolling from the side of his broad mouth. Every now and then, his ears pricked at the shrill sound of a whistle or the chants coming from cheerleading practice on the sideline. The squad was warming up near the fifty-yard line, pompoms flashing as they rehearsed routines in between drills.

"Noah's still looking shaky," Jackson muttered, tracking the ball with sharp eyes as the quarterback launched a pass that sailed high over his receiver's head. The tight end cursed and jogged after it.

Cade blew out a breath. "Yeah, I see it. Honestly, I'm surprised. He's been sharper during the early practices we've been doing. The kid's got game, no question. He's a gifted player. Unfortunately, the arm that won us our championship at State isn't showing up very consistently nowadays."

They watched as Noah hustled back, helmet tilted just enough to show the frustration written on his face. Cade recognized the slump of the shoulders, the way the boy's mouth moved in silent self-recrimination. He'd seen it in plenty of athletes over the years. Pressure could be as brutal an opponent as anything across the line of scrimmage.

"It could be fatigue," Jackson said with a shrug. "He's got school, you've got him working at dawn and then he's back out here every afternoon. That would wear anyone down."

"Maybe." Cade rubbed at the back of his neck, eyes narrowing on the play unfolding in front of them. "But he's handling the morning stuff fine. He's sharper then. I'm not seeing mistakes like this before school starts. It's like a different player in the afternoons."

Jackson gave him a sideways glance. "Are you sure it isn't just nerves? The kid knows we're watching him close. He knows the scrimmage is coming up and how important that game is to the team. No one ever wants to lose to Rustwood. Now that Simmons is there, it's more than just bragging rights at stake. The whole thing feels personal for everyone on the team. He might be getting in his own head."

"Could be." Cade nodded, but he had a nagging feeling there was more to Noah's troubles than simple performance anxiety.

He cupped his hands and hollered encouragement toward Noah as the boy tried again. This time the pass was closer, but still a beat too late, forcing the receiver into an awkward stretch. Cade winced. Timing was everything, and Noah's was definitely off.

Jackson blew his whistle again. The players reset, helmets gleaming in the sun.

"Let's run it clean this time," Jackson barked. His voice snapped a few kids back to attention.

They watched another play unfold, sloppy but passable.

Cade narrowed his eyes at his quarterback. "He's rushing. His footwork's all over the place."

Another pass went off target, and Cade swore under his breath. He turned toward Jackson. "We'll fix it, Coach. Mornings are working. I've just got to figure out how to carry that success over to the afternoon."

Jackson's reply was cut short by a burst of laughter from the stands. Cade glanced up without thinking and spotted a small figure in the middle of the bleachers, legs tucked beneath her, a cardboard tray of four coffee cups balanced carefully in her lap.

Bailey.

He'd taken a bit of a risk inviting her to come watch practice. She wasn't technically supposed to be there. Practices were closed to the public now, thanks to the new rule Jackson had implemented last fall. The policy was designed to keep boosters and parents from crowding the sidelines and interfering with the team, but Bailey wasn't just anyone around here. She was football royalty, so she got a pass. Besides, on the rare occasion she'd popped by in the past, she slipped in under the radar and never disturbed anyone. The fact that she usually brought the coaches coffee didn't hurt, either.

Still, Cade's chest tightened the second he saw her.

She lifted her gaze from the tray of cardboard cups, and for the briefest second their eyes met. The noise of cleats on turf faded directly into the background. Bailey's lips curved into the smallest smile, not much more than a quirk at the corners of her mouth, but it was enough. Cade felt it like a jolt straight through him.

His hand flexed uselessly at his side. He'd been telling himself for weeks to get a handle on this, to stop letting every glance from her feel like a punch straight to the sternum. But here he was again, standing in the middle of a football field with fifty kids waiting on his direction, and all he could think about was the way the sunlight caught in Bailey's hair.

He did his best to school his expression and turned back to the field before Jackson noticed, but his heart hadn't gotten the message. It thudded hard against his ribs.

Noah fumbled the snap, jolting Cade out of his spell. The other players piled onto the loose ball as he ripped off his helmet and dragged a hand through his hair in frustration.

"It's okay, Noah. Just shake it off and concentrate on the next play," Cade shouted.

He tried to infuse the comment with enthusiasm, but his thoughts were still tangled in the bleachers.

Bishop hauled himself up off the turf and lumbered toward the bench, flopping down next to the equipment manager and the oversized Gatorade cooler every coach secretly feared in the final seconds of a victory. He panted in the shade, earning a chuckle and a quick pat on the head.

Jackson blew his whistle and waved the boys into formation again. As the team reset, he leaned closer, his voice pitched low. "Do you ever think maybe we're pushing him too hard?"

Cade dragged a hand down his face. "Every day. But if we don't, he won't be ready. Rustwood is not going to take it easy on him. He's got it in him. I just need him to believe it."

Across the field, the cheerleaders launched into another chant, their voices rising over the sound of pads colliding. Cade barely spared them a glance, too focused on Noah's shaky performance to notice the way the boy's helmet tilted ever so slightly in their direction.

The late-afternoon sun slanted across the bleachers, casting long shadows on the scuffed metal seats. Bailey tucked her cardigan tighter around her and slid into a spot halfway up the stands, her to-go carrier balanced carefully in one hand. Calla plopped down beside her a moment later, her ponytail swishing, curiosity practically radiating off her.

"I've got to say," Calla said, tugging off her sunglasses, "I'm surprised you wanted to come out here today. You never watch practice."

Bailey kept her gaze fixed on the field, where the Bulldogs were running drills. "That's because Jackson changed the rules, remember? Practices are closed."

Calla tipped her head, a sly smile playing on her mouth. "With a few exceptions," she teased, giving Bailey an exaggerated wink.

Bailey forced a laugh, though her stomach gave a nervous twist. *If you only knew.*

"Seriously, though," Calla persisted, turning toward her. "What are you doing here? You've never been much of a practice junkie."

Bailey hesitated, her fingers tightening around the cardboard cupholder. For one terrifying second, she thought she might actually spill the beans about Cade. Calla was her best friend. If anyone could handle the messy truth, it was her.

But then she pictured what would happen once word got around. There would be an instant whirlwind of questions, and the news would ripple through Bishop Falls like wildfire. Cade didn't need those kinds of distractions. He had far too much riding on the spring scrimmage. They weren't ready.

Bailey wasn't ready, and the scariest part was that she wasn't entirely sure why.

"I just felt like hanging out with my best friend. Is that allowed?" she said lightly.

Calla's grin softened. "Of course, it's allowed. I'll take all the Bailey time I can get." She pulled out one of the cups, popped the lid and inhaled dramatically. "And with a sugary latte bribe? You can sit with me anytime."

Bailey smiled, and a bit of the tension in her chest uncoiled. Sitting with Calla, sipping lattes and pretending everything was normal was familiar ground. Safe ground.

They turned their attention to the field, where drills had started in earnest. Cade's voice cut through the air, unmistakably familiar. Bailey's heart did its ridiculous lurch at the sound, and she quickly took another sip of coffee to cover it.

It didn't take long to notice something was off. Noah, usually quick on his feet, looked jittery. His passes wobbled. Twice in a row, he missed easy throws and smacked his helmet with the heel of his hand in frustration.

Beside her, Calla winced. "Yikes. He's way off today. Simmons and the Roosters are going to eat him alive if he's not careful."

Bailey bit her bottom lip. This wasn't looking good.

Calla sighed, absently swirling her drink. "There's so much at stake with this silly spring scrimmage now. Like suddenly it matters more than State."

Not just for the team, Bailey thought grimly. Cade's promotion, his raise and Granny's care all hinged on that scrimmage now. It didn't seem fair. Then again, history had proven that life wasn't always fair on the football field.

Calla frowned as Noah threw another misfire. "That's weird. Jackson said he's been looking a little better lately."

Bailey hesitated, debating whether she ought to admit how much she knew about the quarterback situation. Then she said, "Cade thought so, too. At their early morning practices this week, Noah's been looking great."

Calla's head swiveled. "You and Cade have been talking about Noah? He and Jackson have been so busy lately. I didn't realize you two had been hanging out."

Bailey's pulse hiccupped. She scrambled for a casual tone, waving a hand like it was nothing. "We haven't. He only mentioned it in passing. You know how it is. Coffee-shop chatter."

Calla's eyebrows drew together like she wasn't entirely convinced, but she let it slide and turned her attention back to the field.

A loud cheer erupted near the sidelines. Bailey glanced over just in time to see one of the new cheerleaders cupping her hands around her mouth. "It's okay, Noah! You've got this!"

The words were sweet and encouraging, but it wasn't the sentiment that made Bailey pause. It was the look.

Noah's head turned. His shoulders straightened. And even though he clearly tried to hide it, there was no mistaking the way his gaze snagged on the girl and held just a little too long. His next throw wobbled, nearly missing its mark entirely.

"Wait a minute." Bailey leaned forward and nudged Calla with her elbow. "Look. Is it just me, or do you see the way Noah and that cheerleader are looking at each other?"

Calla blinked, then shifted her gaze in the same direction as Bailey. The cheerleader, slim and bright-eyed with a ponytail that bounced as she moved, was still watching Noah with unmistakable fondness. And Noah? He was doing a terrible job of pretending not to notice.

Calla's mouth dropped open. "Oh, my word." She slapped a hand to her chest like she'd just witnessed something scandalous. "He's got a crush."

Bailey grinned despite herself. "That explains it. The nerves. The jitters. The sudden inability to throw a clean pass."

They both laughed, a ripple of relief cutting through the tension.

"No wonder Jackson's been baffled," Calla said, shaking her head. "He probably thought it was the pressure of living up to the big win at State. Meanwhile, poor Noah's just trying not to embarrass himself in front of…" She squinted. "What's her name again? Chloe? Clarissa?"

"Delaney. She's new. Her family moved here in January. She comes into Huddle Up sometimes with the other cheer girls. She's quiet, but sweet," Bailey said.

Calla let out a low whistle. "Well, quiet Delaney just knocked Noah off his game harder than Rustwood ever could."

Bailey's laughter bubbled up again, but it settled quickly into something else. Watching Noah steal another glance toward the cheerleader, she felt a pang of recognition. The way he fumbled, the way he came undone under the weight of someone's eyes…it was too familiar.

She knew exactly what that felt like. She'd been feeling it for months around Cade.

Calla nudged her shoulder. "You know, maybe this isn't the worst thing. Crushes can be motivating. If Jackson and Cade play this right, it could light a fire under Noah."

Bailey hummed noncommittally, her gaze drifting back to Cade where he stood on the field, his voice calm but firm as he corrected Noah's form. His patience, his steady belief in those boys—it lit a fire in her, too.

* * *

Cade lingered in the weight room the following morning, angling for a word with his quarterback in private. Most of the boys had cleared out after conditioning, but Noah lingered, slouched on a bench with his elbows braced on his knees.

Weight training during first period had been fine. But now that Bailey and Calla had clued him into what was going on, Cade had noticed Noah's head tilt toward the window more than once, like he expected someone to be standing outside on the sidewalk waving pom-poms and a sign with his name on it.

"Calla and I just figured out your quarterback problem. Noah's got a crush," Bailey had said as she'd handed Cade and Jackson their coffees after practice yesterday. "On Delaney, the cheerleader with the ponytail and the big green bow."

Jackson had let out an immediate snort, sounding eerily like Bishop. Sometimes Cade thought those two spent way too much time together. "That'll certainly do it."

Cade had simply gripped his coffee and pretended not to hear his own heart getting itself tangled up in the conversation. The irony wasn't lost on him. Here he was, doing his best to keep his own head down and his relationship with Bailey as invisible as fog, while coaching a teenager through that first rush of feeling that made everything else fade into oblivion.

Now, with the room mostly empty, Noah reracked a pair of dumbbells and wiped his palms on his shorts. He still had that baby-faced look around the eyes that made his opponents underestimate him until he zipped a thirty-yard pass through the seam. Dark hair, cowlick in the back he never remembered to flatten. And, under normal circumstances, a pair of hands most high-school quarterbacks would kill for.

"Hey, Q," Cade said in the least coachlike voice he could summon. "Got a minute?"

Noah glanced up, alert as always. "Yes, sir."

He crossed the room and stopped near the bench where Cade had tossed his clipboard. The kid's shoulders were broadening this year. Another ten pounds, and he'd look like a different person in his football uniform.

"Walk with me," Cade said.

He wanted to get as far away from the locker room as possible. The last thing he wanted to do was embarrass the boy in front of his teammates.

They wove through racks and benches until Cade leaned a shoulder against the wall and crossed his feet at the ankles. "Bailey mentioned something about you and one of the cheerleaders yesterday."

A red flush climbed up Noah's neck at the speed of light. "Ms. Davis? She knows about Delaney?"

"Relax, kid. She wasn't poking fun at you. She thought maybe I could help. So—" Cade lifted a single eyebrow "—are you going to confirm anything, or am I supposed to try and guess?"

Noah stared at the floor like maybe an answer had been chalked into the rubber-mat flooring somewhere between the jump rope and the medicine balls. When he lifted his head, the look in his eyes was exactly what Cade expected, a mixture of hopefulness, terror and stubbornness, all at once. Ah, to be sixteen again.

"I like her," Noah said, his voice barely audible above

the hum of the fluorescent lights. "I think she likes me, too. But I don't know for sure."

He swallowed, and his Adam's apple bobbed up and down his slender throat.

Cade nodded. "Alright, then. Delaney." He tested the name in his mouth and tried not to hear Bailey's name instead. "Tell me what you like about her."

Noah blinked, as if he hadn't considered putting his feelings into words before. The slowest smile in the world started in one corner of his mouth and worked its way across his face. "She's kind."

He looked down, then up again quickly, like he was afraid the concept of kindness might sound uncool. "Like, when the freshman girls miss a count, she doesn't roll her eyes. She helps them. And she volunteers at Dr. Dunne's pet clinic on the weekends, bottle-feeding kittens and walking dogs and stuff. Sometimes, she notices when someone's having a rough time, and she finds these quiet ways to make them feel better."

He made a helpless face. "This all sounds stupid, doesn't it?"

"It sounds exactly right," Cade said. He felt something in his chest go warm and a little sore, the way it always did when he thought about Bailey noticing him across a crowded room and knowing what he needed before he'd asked. The way she'd wordlessly slid a coffee into his hand yesterday and touched her fingers to the back of his knuckles, like they were passing a note in school. "So we've established you're not imagining things. You like her for reasons that matter."

Noah's shoulders eased a fraction. "Okay."

"Now, let me tell you what I saw yesterday," Cade

went on, slipping the coach voice back on like a jacket that had been hanging in his closet since high school. "I saw my quarterback repeatedly throw late because his head wasn't where his feet were. I saw you go deep when the read was shallow because your eyes were somewhere on the sidelines. Are you following me?"

Noah's flush deepened. He scrubbed a hand over the back of his neck. "Yes, sir."

"This isn't about getting on your case," Cade said, gently but firm enough so Noah knew he was serious. "This is about making you excellent at two things at once. Football and being a decent human being who knows how to talk about his feelings. You can handle both, but not if you keep trying to pretend one of them isn't happening."

Noah's mouth quirked into a lopsided grin. "So what should I do? Tell her? Just like that?"

Cade thought of the tightrope he and Bailey were walking—how they'd agreed to keep quiet about whatever was happening between them, both pretending it wasn't serious, even though he knew better, all the way down to his bones. He thought of the way a secret could make you feel like you were breathing through a straw.

"Pretty much," he said. "You need to let Delaney know how you feel. It doesn't have to be some big Shakespearean thing, but wouldn't you rather know for sure if she feels the same way?"

Trust me, kid. Knowing is better than guessing. Sometimes Cade wished he could see inside Bailey's head so he would know if a future together was even possible. Was a real relationship on the table, or was she going to run for the hills the moment he asked her to go public as a couple?

He knew it wasn't fair to think like that. After all, he'd been the first to suggest keeping things quiet. But he knew Bailey. He knew how deeply the past still weighed on her and how quick she was to brace for hurt. She'd always been cautious when it came to giving her heart again, and Cade couldn't blame her for it. If anything, it made him want to slow down and prove she didn't have to be afraid this time. He could be patient. However long it took, he'd wait.

Noah chewed on his bottom lip and heaved out a breath as he looked back up at Cade. "Junior prom is coming up. Do you think I should ask Delaney to go as my date?"

Cade felt the tide of the conversation turn, at long last. "Absolutely."

The teen's eyes lit up. "Really?"

"Prom is a ready-made excuse to let her know that you like her. That's the moment, Noah," Cade said.

"How, though?" Noah asked. The poor kid looked tortured. Bailey and Calla had been spot-on. If they could get this Delaney thing straightened out, Cade's quarterback might actually start playing like himself again. "You've seen the promposals going around. Guys are showing up with posters, balloons, even, like...livestock. Somebody brought a goat into the cafeteria yesterday. A goat, Coach. I can't compete with that."

"If you think Delaney wants a promposal, we'll give her one," Cade said.

But no goats. Cade had had his fill of farm animals after the rooster prank.

"What does Delaney like besides animals?" he asked.

"Well…" Noah shifted from one sneakered foot to the other. "She likes Taylor Swift."

Of course, she does. Cade crossed his arms and nodded. "This is good. We can work with this."

Noah's forehead furrowed. "We can?"

"Yes, and don't worry. I'll help you," Cade said. What was he getting himself into? Planning a promposal wasn't exactly in the job description. Still, if it got Noah's head back in the game, then that was what he'd do.

"You will?" Noah straightened. "I heard about the glitter-poster and boom-box thing that happened in your class the other day. The promposal that Trevor did for Kaylee? The whole school is talking about it."

Of course, Cade remembered Kaylee and Trevor. That song was still ringing in his ears, along with the stunned comment one of his students had made when the class found out he hadn't gone to his own prom. *But you were a football star*, the teen had blurted, like that alone should've guaranteed him a date and a crown.

Noah was a good kid. He was hard-working, humble and he liked a girl because she was kind and volunteered with animals. He didn't possess an ounce of Tyler Crenshaw's empty swagger. But a little confidence wouldn't hurt him either.

"You're QB one, Noah." Cade shot him a sidelong look and arched a single eyebrow. "I think we can do better than a goat and some glitter."

Chapter Fifteen

Bailey curled up with Cade in her apartment, the two of them stealing a quiet evening just a few days before the pep rally for the spring scrimmage. Warmth filled her chest at the sight of him on her couch with his long legs stretched out, socked feet crossed at the ankles and Bluebell tucked like a comma against his side. The remote rested loosely in his hand as he flipped through channels with the ease of someone who belonged there.

It felt natural, *dangerously* natural, as if her living room had been waiting for him all along.

"How's Noah doing?" Bailey asked as she plucked a piece of popcorn from the bowl in her lap.

Cade chuckled. "You and Calla were right. The kid's got it bad. I'm helping him plan a promposal for Delaney. Let's hope that once his feelings are out in the open, he can focus on his game."

A swell of affection softened the ache in Bailey's chest. "I think it's really nice that you're mentoring him like that. You're helping him with football, obviously, but you're also guiding him through his feelings. You're a really good coach, Cade. You deserve that promotion, and I know you're going to get it."

Cade gave a crooked grin, like he wasn't sure what to

do with praise. "Somebody's got to keep him from rent-ing barnyard animals."

Bailey laughed. "I heard about the goat. Seriously, though. You're not just a good coach. You're a good man."

A man I could really fall for.

Maybe she already had.

Her pulse skipped at the thought, startling in its hon-esty. She busied herself with stroking Bluebell's fur, hop-ing Cade wouldn't notice the heat rising in her cheeks. Cade glanced over, eyes fixed on hers for a beat too long. Something flickered in his gaze. Gratitude maybe, or the hint of something he wasn't ready to say out loud.

She nudged his foot with hers. "Tell me more about this promposal."

"Not a chance, Bailey Bear. It's a secret. Even you don't get spoilers. You'll just have to wait and see." Cade's eyes glinted with humor. "Let's just say the band director owes me a favor."

She tried to laugh, but something in her tightened at the words. "Do you ever wonder if these grand gestures set kids up for disappointment later on in life?"

Cade angled his head as he considered her question. "I don't know. I thought so at first, maybe. Helping Noah has given me a different perspective, though." He cleared his throat. "I'm starting to think that sometimes it's good to let people know how you feel in a way they'll never forget."

Bailey's gaze dropped to the bowl of popcorn in her hands, heart thudding harder than it should have. She wondered if he was still talking about Noah...

Or about them.

"Movie or sports?" Cade asked, aiming the remote at the television.

"Sports," Bailey said automatically.

He smirked. "You say that like it's not baseball season."

She wrinkled her nose. Somewhere, Coach Carter was probably dissecting batting averages with his lizard. "Valid. Those games drag on forever."

"If baseball is out, a movie it is." Cade flipped the channel again, and the swell of piano music filled the room. Onscreen, a couple kissed in the rain while the title *The Notebook* scrolled across the bottom.

Bailey rolled her eyes. "Hard pass. I've managed to avoid finishing this movie my entire life. I'm not starting now."

Cade gaped at her like she'd just admitted she hated coffee. "You're kidding. This is a classic. Don't tell me you've never seen it."

Bailey shook her head quickly, stroking Bluebell's ears to keep her hands busy. "Nope. Not the whole thing, only bits and pieces."

"What?" Cade sat up a little. "You own a coffee shop in a small town. I'm pretty sure you're the target demographic. They might revoke your latte license if you can't quote at least one Nicholas Sparks movie."

She gave him a faint smile. "I guess I missed that memo."

"I thought I knew all your secrets. Turns out you've been hiding the biggest one," he teased. "How did I not know this about you?"

Her throat tightened, but she tried to keep her tone light. Calla knew better than to suggest a rom-com or teary love story when they had a girls' night, but her reluctance to sit through other people's happily-ever-afters wasn't something she'd ever shared with Cade. She wasn't sure she could without exposing the ache that still lived too close to the surface. "Happy endings can be a little hard for me sometimes."

The humor faded from Cade's eyes. He didn't push or try to make her laugh it off. He simply slipped her hand in his and squeezed tight, as if doing so could keep her anchored in this present moment instead of the past. Bailey dropped her head onto his shoulder and let herself lean into his steady warmth and the silent promise that he wouldn't let her drift too far.

When Cade turned back to the TV, he flipped the channel to a ball game. Relief and regret tangled together in Bailey's chest. She didn't want to ruin the easy rhythm of their evening, but the truth was, watching people get forever still felt like pressing hard against a tender bruise.

They sat side by side, Bluebell's paws twitching in her sleep as she nestled between them. Cade poked fun at the slow pace of the game, and Bailey chuckled in the right places. Yet beneath the easy banter, something unspoken tugged between them. It was sweet, but it ached around the edges, like they were both reaching for more and holding back at the same time.

"I should probably go," Cade finally said, standing up with a stretch. "Morning workouts with Noah start before the sun, and the kid's already got more energy than I know what to do with."

"Thanks for coming over," Bailey said, and her voice came out brighter than she intended.

He leaned down and pressed a quick kiss to her forehead, his hand warm on her cheek. "Make sure you lock up downstairs after I go, okay?"

She nodded. "I will."

Silence rushed in as soon as the door closed behind him. Bailey collected the popcorn bowl and their empty wineglasses, then carried them into the kitchen and rinsed them in the sink. The rhythm of the water soothed her nerves for a moment, until she returned to the living room and froze.

Bluebell had relocated to a side chair by the window, curled into a ball on a green-and-white bundle that Bailey hadn't even realized was there—Ethan's old letterman jacket. The number patch glowed faintly in the lamplight, the fabric worn soft from years of use.

Her heart clenched. She thought she'd shoved that jacket into the back of the closet months ago, reluctant to completely get rid of it. Somehow it had made its way back into the living room, and now, her kitten was nestled in it like it was just another blanket.

She moved to scoop up Bluebell, her fingers brushing the familiar fabric. The ache came fast and sharp, grief layered with guilt. Ethan's world had ended too soon, and sometimes she still felt like hers had ended with it.

"Bails?"

Her head snapped up. Cade was back in the doorway with his own Bulldogs sweatshirt slung over his arm.

"Sorry," he said quietly. "I almost walked out without my hoodie."

His gaze moved past her until it landed on the letter jacket on the chair and Bluebell curled so innocently against Ethan's number. Cade, of course, recognized it instantly. He had one just like it tucked away in his own closet, the same Bulldogs colors, the same stitched letters marking a different time.

Guilt rooted Bailey to the spot. Cade's eyes lifted back to hers, but his expression wasn't sharp or accusing. Only bittersweet.

"You don't have to hide that from me," he said gently.

Her throat tightened. "I wasn't—"

"Bails." His voice softened even further. "It's part of you. I know that. I just... I don't ever want you to think you've got to pretend with me."

She wanted to thank him, to admit how much it meant that he hadn't flinched at the sight of Ethan's jacket or at the jagged pieces of her heart it represented. But the words wouldn't come. Her throat was too tight, and her voice was too fragile. So she nodded instead, the only answer she could manage without shattering wide open.

Cade lingered just long enough for his eyes to steady on hers again, his gaze calm in a way that grounded her even as it undid her. Then, with a tender smile, he turned and slipped out the door again.

Silence settled in his wake, and Bailey stood there beneath the lamplight and reached instinctively for the jacket. She pressed the fabric against her cheek like a memory she hadn't meant to summon, soft and worn and unbearably familiar.

Gratitude and guilt tore through her in equal measure. Because even as part of her clung to the past stitched into Ethan's number, another part of her was reaching, quietly, dangerously, toward the future that had just walked out her door.

* * *

Cade pushed open the heavy glass door of the hardware store and blinked against the sudden shift from spring sunlight to fluorescent glow. The place smelled like sawdust and fertilizer, same as it always did, and the aisles were cluttered with everything from extension cords to fishing tackle. He'd come in for light bulbs. Principal Dean had told him to track some down for his classroom after the janitor grumbled about the supply closet being cleaned out again. Cade wasn't sure when teaching had started to include maintenance runs, but apparently it did.

Such was life in a small town. Yet another reason to snag that promotion.

"Afternoon, Coach." Earl Whitaker met him halfway down the lighting aisle, reading glasses perched halfway down his nose and dressed in full head-to-toe Bulldogs gear. As per usual.

"Hey there, Earl," Cade said.

Earl was one of those men who seemed like he'd been old since Cade was in diapers, as sturdy as the live oak trees that shaded Bulldog Avenue. He waved a hand toward the shelves, packed with boxes of light bulbs. "Don't tell me they've got you fixing the scoreboard yourself again."

Cade chuckled. "Not this time. I'm replacing the ones in my classroom. The kids keep complaining that it's too dark in the back row."

"Too dark to learn about dead presidents, huh?" The Victory Club president smirked. "Back in my day, teachers let us squint."

Earl shifted aside his cart to let a woman pass, then

leaned back on it like he had all the time in the world. "Speaking of squinting, how're things looking for the spring scrimmage? Folks are already buzzing. You know how it is. Half the boosters are nervous wrecks, and the other half are acting like it's in the bag."

Cade nodded. He did, indeed, know how it was.

Earl's forehead furrowed. "So which is it? Tell me it's in the bag."

"It's just a scrimmage, Earl. It doesn't even count," Cade said with a wry smile. It *shouldn't* count, anyway.

"Oh, it counts. Stats aren't everything. Pride is equally important, especially since Bob Simmons up and betrayed us," Earl retorted, eyes sharp beneath the brim of his Bulldogs cap. "Rustwood can't win. They just can't. But don't worry. As long as Bishop Falls comes out on top, you'll keep the town behind you. That assistant-coaching job's yours to lose, you know."

As if Cade could forget.

"You'd be really great at it. You've got the kids' respect, and you've been proving yourself for years," Earl said.

Just not enough for me to get the job without one final, excruciating test. Understood.

"Thanks again," Cade muttered. He knew Earl was trying to be nice, inasmuch as Earl Whitaker knew how. Support always came with a scoreboard attached.

It didn't matter much, though. Compliments sometimes felt too tight on Cade, like a shirt a size too small, especially when they had to do with football.

Or with Ethan.

Everything seemed to have a way of circling back to his late best friend.

Ethan had been the golden boy, the one people still talked about like he'd only just stepped off the field yesterday. Cade could win games, he could earn the kids' respect, but there would always be whispers comparing him to Bishop Falls's fallen hero.

Ethan would've been head coach of the Bulldogs by now. Ethan wouldn't have to prove himself over and over. Ethan had never worn praise like it was ill-fitting.

And Ethan would still be with Bailey. Cade knew that as surely as he knew the weight of a football in his hands. He didn't resent it for a second. He understood, and a part of him loved her even more for her devotion. He only hoped, in time, she might let a little space open for him, too.

Right on cue, Earl cleared his throat. "You know, Ethan Dunne is up in heaven looking down at you, and he's got a smile on his face that's a mile wide. He wanted everything you've got now, and the poor kid just didn't live long enough to see it. You're living the dream the two of you used to talk about all the time."

Cade's jaw tightened, but he forced a polite smile. He didn't doubt Earl meant it as a compliment, the kind of blessing small towns handed out when they weren't sure what else to say. But the words scraped raw all the same.

Ethan *had* wanted this. Every single bit of it. So had Cade, but sometimes he still felt like an imposter. Or worse, like he was stealing something that didn't really belong to him. Most of all, Bailey. Ethan had loved her first, and the whole town knew it. Some days Cade wondered if he was allowed to love her at all, or if he was just trespassing in a life that was never meant to be his.

Cade forced a swallow. "Yeah, I am," he said quietly.

An awkward beat of silence passed. Earl, never short on words, seemed to have run out of them.

"I still miss him, you know. Every damn day," Cade added, more for his own benefit than for Earl's.

Earl patted his shoulder, the kind of rough, awkward comfort men in Bishop Falls offered when the subject of conversation strayed too far away from football. "You'll do right by him. You always have."

Cade nodded, but the guilt coiled low in his stomach, sour and sharp. He knew Earl was talking about winning the scrimmage and keeping the town's pride intact. But the words sank deeper, brushing against places Cade didn't like to touch.

Doing right by Ethan wasn't just about football, and he knew it.

Earl asked after Granny, and then they exchanged an awkward goodbye. Cade grabbed a box of light bulbs, slipped a few dollar bills from his wallet and pushed them across the counter toward Todd, who was drinking coffee from his pig mug. Then he stepped outside with the bag from the hardware store swinging uselessly at his side. The sidewalk hummed with the slow rhythm of life in Bishop Falls. Shop doors were propped open, a shaggy dog sat tied to a park bench outside the diner and an old Johnny Cash song spilled from the radio of a passing truck. All of it was familiar, straight out of a page from Cade's childhood. And yet, he felt off balance, like the ground had just tilted under his feet.

Ethan had wanted all of this. The team. The chance to lead. The girl.

And Cade was the one who had it.

He crossed the street, heading toward the empty

bleachers at the practice field. He sat on the bottom row, dropped the bag beside him and scrubbed a hand over his face. He hadn't asked for this. He'd never once asked to inherit the future Ethan had sketched out in bright, certain lines. But still, here he was, holding pieces his best friend had never lived long enough to keep.

His mind flashed back to Bailey's living room two nights ago. Bluebell curled in Ethan's letterman jacket, her small body rising and falling against the bright green fabric. The way Bailey's hands had trembled when she touched it. Cade had told her she didn't need to hide it from him, and he'd meant it. But afterward, lying awake, he'd wondered if he was lying to himself.

Because sometimes it felt like Ethan's shadow covered everything.

The letterman jacket. The portrait hanging at Huddle Up, frozen in time with that easy smile. The way half the town still referred to Bailey as Ethan's Bailey, like the girl he'd left behind belonged to no one else, not even herself.

Cade exhaled hard, elbows braced on his knees. Was that what this was destined to be? Was he always destined to be measured against the ghost of a boy who hadn't lived to see twenty-three? Bailey forever caught between the girl she'd been and the woman she was trying to become?

Was there room in that shadow for both of them to breathe?

He hoped so. Oh, how he hoped.

The memory of Bailey storming into his house after her ill-fated date with Carter McGraw came back to him, fast and hard. She'd been so furious, demanding to know

why he'd gone behind her back to set her up with someone else. And he'd finally admitted the truth he'd been
holding back for months…years…

I'd do anything to see you happy. He loved her from
the bottom of his soul, and that feeling had nothing at
all to do with Ethan. It was all her.

Cade had asked her if Carter made her happy, and the
instant her eyes had gone shiny, he knew she loved him,
too. Whether she realized it yet or not, it was as plain as
the sprinkle of freckles across her upturned nose.

It's you, she'd said, and then she'd kissed him like
she'd been holding her breath for years and finally let
go. That moment had felt like sunlight breaking through
clouds. Even now, the memory steadied him, a reminder
that some things were worth the risk. Most of all, Bailey.

Cade stared at the stretch of grass in front of him,
where kids would soon be running spring drills. He
wanted the assistant-coaching job. Wanted it badly. Heck,
he *needed* it.

But Earl's words gnawed at him. *You'll do right by
him. You always have.* As if the job wasn't about Cade
at all, but about carrying on for Ethan. Maybe that was
what the whole town thought—that Cade Montgomery
was only ever filling in the blanks Ethan had left behind.

The guilt pressed harder. Cade had the career Ethan
wanted. He had the team. He had Bailey, in secret at least.
Ethan had the portrait at Huddle Up, the memories, the
legacy…but Cade had the life.

And what if living that life meant Bailey could never
be free of the past?

A group of elementary-school kids rode by on bikes,
laughing, and the sound jolted Cade out of his spiral.

He leaned back against the bleacher, tipping his head to the sky. Clouds drifted slowly across the blue. He took a deep breath, trying to steady himself.

He couldn't change the past or rewrite his best friend's ending. All he could do was honor it, and hope Bailey understood that wanting her, wanting a future, wasn't betrayal. It was survival.

He picked up the bag of light bulbs, squared his shoulders and headed toward the school building. Maybe he'd never outrun Ethan's shadow. But maybe, just maybe, he could build something that honored it without being swallowed whole.

Because Bailey deserved more than a ghost. And if there was any way to give her that, Cade was determined to try.

Chapter Sixteen

The pep rally was held the day before the spring scrimmage, and Bailey wasn't sure she'd ever seen the high-school gymnasium so completely draped in green and white. Streamers crisscrossed the rafters, the cheerleaders lined the court with their pom-poms flashing and the marching band blasted "Eye of the Tiger" loud enough to rattle the bleachers.

Bailey sat at the raffle table with Calla, the two of them side by side as they traded dollar bills for long strings of green tickets. Volunteering for alumni events was second nature by now. Between the two of them, they'd worked every bake sale, car wash and raffle the Bulldogs boosters had ever dreamed up. This afternoon was no different. With the sleeves of her green gingham Bulldogs shirt rolled up, Bailey kept the line moving, smiling until her cheeks ached. Across the gym, the football team filled an entire block of bleachers. Cade, Jackson and the rest of the coaching staff stood close by, keeping an eye on their players as the band thundered out another fight song.

Cade glanced her way, and their eyes met across the chaos. Bailey's smile shifted from polite to genuine before she could help herself. He tipped his chin in the smallest nod, like the two of them were in on some inside joke no one else knew about. Heat fizzed in her chest, equal parts amusement and awareness.

"I'm running to grab us some popcorn and sodas before the concession-stand line gets insane," Calla said, already pushing her chair back. Bailey rolled her eyes with a chuckle. Classic Calla—abandoning her post the second snacks were involved.

Left on her own, Bailey risked another look across the gym. Cade was still watching her with the hint of a grin tugging at his mouth, a silent exchange that made the rest of the noise fade into the background.

The moment popped like a balloon when someone stepped up to her table. Bailey blinked, startled, as Lauren Jennings—the town librarian and, more to the point, Cade's most recent ex-girlfriend—slid a dollar bill across the surface. Her bright red lipstick was perfect, her ponytail as sleek as silk and her Bulldogs T-shirt was knotted at the waist and just a smidge more fitted than Bailey would have dared to wear.

"One ticket, please," Lauren said brightly, though her eyes flicked in Cade's direction before landing on Bailey again.

A flicker of heat rose to Bailey's cheeks before she could stop it. Fantastic. The last time she'd let jealousy get the better of her, she'd nearly made a public spectacle of herself at a chili cook-off.

"Hi, Lauren," Bailey said politely as she handed her a ticket. "Thanks so much for supporting the team today."

"Of course." Lauren's smile was warm, though there was a knowing glimmer in her eyes. "I'll always support the Bulldogs, especially with Cade coaching. He and I used to date, you know."

Bailey forced another smile, the roll of tickets warm against her palms. "Right. I remember."

Lauren's gaze drifted toward the far side of the gym, where Cade stood with a knot of players, his head bent as he explained something with his hands. He was laughing at something one of the boys said.

"If only he'd been willing to be my date for the library black-tie gala." Lauren sighed. "It's the biggest night of the year for the library. I worked really hard on that party. I needed him there."

"Wasn't it the same night as one of the district playoff games?" Bailey said, remembering what Cade had told her at the chili cook-off.

Lauren's eyebrows lifted. "Playoffs? No, the gala's always in September. Weeks before playoffs start. Last year, it was on the twentieth. I remember because we had a board meeting the very next day. Plus, it was the day we broke up, so…"

September twentieth.

Bailey's breath caught. Her birthday.

The memory surfaced so vividly she could almost taste the salt of the sweet-potato fries and the sweetness of the cupcakes Cade had brought her that night. She'd told Calla she wanted to spend the evening by herself, not because she dreaded birthdays, exactly, but because they always felt complicated. Getting older seemed strange when Ethan would forever be frozen at twenty-two.

But Cade hadn't let her hide away, all alone. He'd shown up at Huddle Up just as she was flipping the sign on the door to Closed. He'd had takeout from Hal's Diner in one hand and a single chocolate cupcake with a pink candle stuck right in its center in the other. They'd sat together under the stars on her apartment balcony with Cade's jacket draped over her shoulders, eating greasy food straight out of the bag. He'd let her talk when she felt like talking and sat beside her in silence when she'd gone quiet. That was Cade—never pushy, never filling the moment with empty words. He was always there for her, steady and true. And somehow, by the end of the night, she'd laughed for the first time in weeks. It had been one of her best birthdays since Ethan passed. Maybe one of her best birthdays ever.

And she'd never realized what it had cost him.

"Oh," Bailey said faintly, grasping for composure. "I must've gotten the timing mixed up."

Lauren tilted her head and seemed to be studying Bailey carefully. "Cade's a good guy. I liked him a lot, but if I'm really being honest…"

Bailey fidgeted with the tickets, unsure where this was going. Wherever it was almost felt like stepping onto thin ice.

Lauren hesitated, then let out a breath. "We never would've worked. I always had the nagging feeling that he wasn't really mine—like he couldn't fall for me because his heart belonged someplace else." Her eyes met Bailey's, searching. "Maybe with you, actually."

Bailey's stomach lurched. Her first instinct was denial, and the words tumbled out automatically. "Cade and I are just friends."

Lauren gave her a faint smile. "If you say so."

"I…" Bailey began, but what else was there to say?

Lauren tucked her raffle ticket into her purse. "Anyway, thanks for the ticket. That raffle basket is really something. I hope I win. Go Bulldogs!"

"Go Bulldogs," Bailey echoed, somehow getting out the words.

"It was good seeing you, Bailey."

"You, too," she murmured, though her throat felt too tight for words.

Lauren drifted away, leaving Bailey rooted to her chair. Her chest ached with a thousand conflicting feelings. Gratitude for that birthday last September... Guilt for never realizing what Cade had sacrificed to be with her that night... Fear at the idea that Lauren might be right.

She thought Cade was in love with her. That much was clear. The idea of Cade having real feelings for her was terrifying and wonderful, all at the same time. But the thought that he'd been quietly loving her for longer than she realized made her pulse stutter.

What if he's been in love with me all this time?

She'd always believed she was the one inching forward, the one testing the waters and deciding how far to let things go. The idea that Cade had already been standing there, waiting for her, changed everything. It meant this wasn't just a sweet distraction, a secret she could keep tucked away until she was ready. It meant his feelings weren't new or fragile. They were deep, rooted and real.

And that meant this secret relationship had the potential to break her heart in ways she hadn't dared to imagine.

Bailey's fingers tightened on the roll of tickets in her lap. For so long she'd told herself she was safe because

she was the one in control. But if Cade had been loving her all along…then maybe she wasn't steering this
at all. Maybe she was already in far deeper than she'd
been prepared for.

She glanced toward Cade across the gym. He was still
with his players, demonstrating a passing drill with exaggerated motions, utterly focused. He was the same Cade
she'd known since they were kids, always as steady as a
stone. But now, she saw him in a different light. He hadn't
skipped that gala for football. He'd skipped it for her.

Her fingers trembled as she tore off raffle stubs for a
woman in a green Bulldogs sweatshirt, and she tried to
tell herself it didn't mean anything, that he'd only done
it to be nice. But the truth pressed against her ribs, impossible to ignore. That night had mattered to him as
much as it had to her.

We're just friends. She'd said it out loud, but even as
she thought it now, she knew it was a lie. Maybe it had
been a lie for a long, long time.

"Hey," Cade said, suddenly at her table before she
had time to school her features. He held a roll of raffle
tickets in one hand, his Bulldogs cap shoved backward
on his head. His hair stuck out in ridiculous tufts, and
Bailey's heart ached at how ordinary and familiar—and
utterly irresistible—he looked.

"Are you okay?" he asked, tilting his head in that way
he always did when he was trying to read her.

She managed a small nod, hoping it didn't look as brit-
tle as it felt. "I'm fine. Just keeping the raffle moving."

His eyes flicked to the overflowing raffle basket on
the table, then back to her. He didn't call her out on the
way her hands were shaking. Instead, he leaned closer,

his voice dropping so only she could hear. "You don't have to do this, you know. The boosters would survive without you."

Bailey swallowed hard. "I don't mind. I like to help."

Cade studied her a moment longer, as though he could see the storm behind her eyes. And maybe he could. He always had a way of noticing more than she wanted him to.

"Thanks," he said softly. "For being here, I mean."

Something in his tone undid her. It was his quiet sincerity and the weight beneath his words. She knew he was anxious about the scrimmage tomorrow, which was half the reason she'd volunteered to be here at the pep rally. He knew it, too, without her having to say it.

It was all too much—the crush of the gym, the rhythmic chants of the cheerleaders, the green-and-white streamers everywhere she looked. None of it mattered compared to the way Cade was looking at her now. Like her very presence calmed him. Like she was the reason he could breathe when the rest of the world was pressing down on his shoulders.

"I wouldn't be anywhere else," she said quietly.

She stilled at her own words, wondering if she'd revealed more than she meant to. Cade's eyes, warm and a little unguarded, softened, as if her being there mattered more than anything else.

Then he tipped his chin toward the raffle basket. "Make sure Earl Whitaker doesn't win again. He cheats."

Bailey let out a shaky laugh, and Cade's mouth curved in that half smile that always made her stomach swoop. Then he headed back across the gym, leaving her clutching the roll of tickets, her heart pounding.

She took a deep breath as Lauren's words echoed in her head. *I always had the nagging feeling that he wasn't really mine—like he couldn't fall for me because his heart belonged someplace else.*

Bailey's chest gave a painful little squeeze. Maybe it had always been her.

Cade lingered near the edge of the bleachers with his players, but his attention kept drifting back to the raffle table. Bailey had laughed at his joke, but something about her smile hadn't rung true. She'd looked a little rattled, though for the life of him he couldn't figure out why. Maybe the noise was getting to her, or maybe she'd just had her fill of booster duties. Either way, he wished he could've stayed by her side a little longer instead of walking away.

"Coach Montgomery." Jackson's voice cut through the din of the pep rally, and Cade turned to see his friend muscling through the press of kids with Bishop waddling at his side. The dog sported a green Bulldogs bandana tied around his neck and a paw-print sticker stuck to his flank, which appeared to be hanging on for dear life. Bishop hated any form of dressing up, but he had a little spring in his step today. He might technically belong to Jackson now, but he was still the school mascot, and a pep rally was his moment to shine.

"Yeah?" Cade said with a glance at Jackson.

"Eyes front," he said. "It's showtime."

Cade blinked. "Showtime?"

Jackson tipped his chin toward the marching band. The drummers were on their feet now with their sticks poised above their instruments. The rest of the band shifted forward, whispering with anticipation.

Cade's heart gave a solid thud. This was it. Noah's big swing.

He spotted the boy pacing behind the baseline in his Bulldogs jersey, trying and failing to look casual. His hands wouldn't stay in his pockets, and every few seconds he glanced at Delaney like he thought he might be sick.

Cade pushed through the cluster of players until he reached him. He clapped a hand on Noah's shoulder, leaned in.

"You've got this," he said, his voice low and certain.

Noah's throat bobbed. "Coach…"

"You've *got* this," Cade repeated, his grip steady on the boy's shoulder. "She's going to love it."

The words came easily, but the truth was, he knew just how Noah felt. He remembered what it was like to be that age. Every feeling seemed larger than life. It was a kind of pressure football didn't teach you how to handle. At least on the field, you had a playbook. Out here, all Noah had was a shaky plan and the hope that the girl he liked felt the same way.

Cade had seen the way Noah had unraveled these past few weeks, his focus slipping, his confidence gone. The kid who once launched passes with fire in his eyes now looked like he didn't know if he should throw or run or hide under the bleachers. Delaney was part of that, sure. But it wasn't just about a girl. It was about Noah believing in himself again.

These boys needed more than practice drills and film sessions. They needed someone to care about the things that kept them up at night, the things that made them stumble. Football was only part of the story. Growing into the kind of men who knew how to show up for someone they cared about…that was just as important. Maybe more.

So, yeah, this wasn't exactly in Cade's job description. He wasn't supposed to be plotting out glitter letters and band cues like it was the Super Bowl halftime show. But this just might be what Cade loved best about coaching.

He gave Noah's shoulder another squeeze, the kind of reassuring touch he wished someone had given him back when he was seventeen and floundering during the last half of his senior year. There were no guarantees in football, or life, or love. But you didn't get anywhere by playing it safe. If Noah could learn that lesson here, in the middle of a packed gym with a marching band at his back, then he'd come out of this stronger, not just as a quarterback, but as the kind of young man Cade wanted all his players to become.

For a second, Noah looked about twelve years old, wide-eyed and terrified. Then his jaw firmed, and Cade saw the quarterback in him come to life. He straightened his spine, squared his shoulders and transformed into a different person.

"Okay," Noah breathed. "Okay. Game time."

Cade gave him a quick nod and stepped back just as the snare drums burst to life.

The gym hushed. Then, with a blast of trumpets, the band launched into Taylor Swift's "You Belong with Me." The opening riff soared over the crowd with a hook everybody recognized in the first two beats. A ripple of shrieks ran through the bleachers as hands shot up, clapping in time.

Cade felt his own grin spread. Beside him, Jackson shook his head a little, like he couldn't believe what he was seeing. But Cade recognized the pride in his eyes all the same. Not just for Noah potentially pulling this off, but for Cade, too, for finding a way to reach the kid when he needed it most.

Five Bulldogs jogged out from the sidelines and lined up shoulder-to-shoulder in the center of the court. They were linemen mostly, big guys who made the sparkly painted letters taped to their backs impossible to miss. For the moment, though, their fronts faced the bleachers and the cheerleaders lined up along the baseline, and the crowd leaned forward in confusion.

The drummers hammered out the beat and the brass blared the chorus as Noah stepped forward, heading straight for Delaney.

The whole gym seemed to hold its breath.

On the downbeat, the five players turned around in unison.

P—R—O—M—?

The letters sparkled in green glitter paint, catching the light as the boys lifted their arms theatrically, shoulders back like they were spelling it out for the whole world. Noah stopped in front of Delaney, hands spread wide like the question was hers to answer.

Her hands flew to her mouth, her eyes wide, cheeks flushed bright pink. For a heartbeat she just stared, stunned. Then she nodded—once, twice, fast enough to make her ponytail bob up and down. She threw her arms around Noah's neck, laughing into his shoulder as he stumbled backward in surprise.

Screams bounced off the rafters.

"She said yes!" someone shouted.

The rest of the cheer squad ran forward, squealing as they surrounded Delaney in a sea of green-and-white pom-poms. Noah looked dazed, thrilled, happier than Cade had ever seen him.

Cade clapped hard, his palms stinging as a swell of pride caught him off guard. He caught Jackson's eye just as his friend shook his head with a low whistle.

"Well, there it is," Jackson said, folding his arms. "Look at you, Coach. Now that you've got your quarterback's love life in order, maybe Noah can keep his eyes on the field instead of Delaney's ponytail."

Cade chuckled, shaking his head. He let the crowd's jubilant reaction to the promposal wash over him for a moment before his gaze sought out Bailey again.

She was still at the raffle table with Calla back at her side, holding two sodas. Bailey's hands were both pressed to her heart as she grinned at Noah and Delaney in the center of the court. He watched her for a second, just to memorize the way happiness softened her whole face. Then her gaze lifted and found his across the gym.

Her lips parted slightly. Her eyes held his like a secret question, one she didn't dare voice. Cade's chest ached. He wanted to stalk across the gym and tell her that if a whole marching band could play for a promposal, then maybe it was time they stopped pretending, too. The urge clawed at him, wild and reckless, to close the space and let the world see what he felt. To take her hand and tell her that secrecy wasn't enough anymore, but everything would still be okay.

Better than okay.

But he stayed rooted in place, the roar of the crowd rising up between them. Charging across the court would only draw every set of eyes in the gym straight to them, and whatever was happening here wasn't meant for an audience. Yet. Sooner or later, though, if this thing between them was real, it deserved to thrive out in the open.

He forced himself to look away, but the moment clung to him like static. And the image of Bailey's eyes, uncertain and shadowed, lingered with him long after the music ended.

Chapter Seventeen

The bell over the door stayed silent in the empty coffee shop, but the last traces of the pep rally still buzzed in Bailey's veins as she moved through the quiet space. Huddle Up had just closed, and she had no idea if Cade was going to surprise her again tonight, or if he and Jackson were too busy with final preparations for the scrimmage tomorrow. With a soft click, she opened the door to the storage room, and Bluebell padded out, stretching luxuriously before twining around her ankles.

Bailey bent to scoop the kitten into her arms, pressing her cheek against the soft fur as if the tiny cat could absorb the whirl of thoughts spinning wildly through her mind.

She couldn't shake the things Lauren had said to her earlier, nor could she tamp down the spark of elation she'd felt when she realized Cade might actually love her. As frightening as that prospect was, it lit something inside her she hadn't dared hope for—a future that wasn't defined by loss, but by the chance to love and be loved again.

She shifted Bluebell higher in her arms and turned toward the counter, her gaze snagging on the familiar portrait of Ethan hanging on the wall. His smile met hers the way it always had, as faithful as the sunrise.

Her chest tightened. Loving Cade felt like standing on the edge of a precipice with the ground crumbling beneath her toes. What if she gave in only to lose everything again? What if she opened herself completely and the pain came back, sharper than before? She wasn't sure she could survive another hollowed-out ache, another gaping absence she couldn't fix.

And yet, somewhere between the stolen glances and the secret knocks at the back door, her heart just might have made its choice without asking her permission.

Bailey shivered, replaying the moment in the gym when their eyes had met across the noise and color. She'd tried so hard to keep things contained, to let herself believe she was the one deciding how far to let this go. But then came the promposal, and when the whole school had erupted when Delaney threw her arms around Noah, the thunder of cheers had rolled over her like a wave. She'd wanted to laugh with them, to cry with them, to let herself believe in a love that bold and fearless. And suddenly it was impossible not to compare her hidden glances with Cade against Noah's public declaration.

There was power in a declaration like that. It made secrets feel small…

And wrong.

If she really cared about Cade, she couldn't keep drifting in this halfway place between hiding and hoping. She needed to decide if she was brave enough to give her heart completely or risk losing what was already slipping through her fingers.

Bluebell wriggled free, landing with a soft thud before

scampering across the floor as Bailey sank into one of the window seats. She pressed her palms over her eyes. Her pulse was too fast, and her chest too tight. She felt like she couldn't breathe. Lauren and that promposal had cracked something open inside her, and now, she couldn't force it closed again. She was barely aware of Bluebell darting happily around the shop, batting at a stray sugar packet and chasing shadows cast by the lamplights that lined Bulldog Avenue.

But then a sudden scrape startled her. Her eyes flew open, and she looked up just in time to see the door to the alley creak open, the faulty latch giving way once more. In the sliver of light, a streak of cream-and-chocolate fur slipped through.

"Bluebell!"

Bailey scrambled to her feet. The door swung wider, and by the time she stumbled into the alley, the kitten was halfway down the block. She caught a glimpse of Bluebell beneath a streetlight, a flicker of cream-and-chocolate fur, before she vanished into the dark.

Her heart leaped to her throat. "Bluebell!"

The night air was sharp and cool against her cheeks as she ran, boots slapping against the pavement. Panic clawed its way up her chest. The alley opened to the street farther down, spilling into the glow of passing traffic. Headlights flickered in the distance, and Bailey pictured the cat's tiny body darting under someone's tires.

"No, no, no—" Her voice cracked as she ran harder, her lungs burning. "Bluebell!"

The kitten darted toward a patch of grass near a trash can, chasing a moth that danced in the glow of a streetlamp.

Bailey's legs wobbled, fear blurring her vision. What if she couldn't reach her in time? What if Bluebell slipped away into the dark? Maybe that was only fair. The kitten wasn't really hers, not any more than Cade was. Holding on to either of them felt like tempting fate, and fate had already shown her how easily it could take everything away.

She stumbled to her knees, scraping her palms against the pavement as a sob broke free. Then, strong arms caught her before she could crumble.

"Bailey." Cade's voice, firm but gentle, wrapped around her like a lifeline. "Bluebell's fine. Look."

She blinked, breath jagged, and followed the line of his hand. There, just ten feet away, sat Bluebell, crouched in the grass, batting playfully at the moth as if none of this mattered. As if her antics hadn't just unraveled Bailey from the inside out.

Cade crouched low, his voice calm as he murmured something Bailey couldn't hear. He moved gingerly, easily scooping the kitten into one of his big palms. Bluebell wriggled once before curling into the cradle of his arm, purring like the great escape had never happened and Cade's arms had been the destination all along.

Bailey pressed a trembling hand to her mouth, her heart battering her ribs. Relief hit her hard enough to hurt.

"She's okay," Cade said softly, stepping closer. He held Bluebell out, but Bailey couldn't bring herself to take her. Her hands shook too hard.

"She could've been gone," Bailey whispered, her voice ragged. "I thought I lost her."

"But you didn't." Cade rubbed his thumb behind the

kitten's ears, just the way she liked it. "She's right here, sweetheart. Everything is okay."

Bailey finally reached for the kitten, gathering her against her chest, burying her face in the warm fur. Bluebell purred, completely content, but Bailey's tears slipped hot and unchecked down her cheeks.

The relief didn't soothe her. It terrified her, all the way down to her soul.

If she could fall apart like this over almost losing a cat, if her world could tilt so violently in the space of a few heartbeats, what would happen if it was Cade? What if she gave him her heart, fully and completely, and something happened to him? Bailey knew what it was like to lose someone she loved. She'd clawed her way out of that darkness once already. She couldn't do it again.

She couldn't survive it.

Cade must've seen some telltale hint of her panic in her expression, because his brow furrowed. "Bailey Bear, you're shaking. Let's go inside and sit down."

He wrapped a strong arm around her shoulders and angled his body toward Huddle Up, guiding her back toward the coffee shop gently but firmly. She stiffened for the first few steps and then fell in step beside him, eventually letting herself be steered back through the door. Once they were inside, she stood frozen in the middle of the shop clutching Bluebell while he jammed the door locked.

Cade turned toward her, and the tenderness in his eyes was suddenly too much. *All of this* was too much.

She shook her head and took a shaky backward step. He lifted his arms, reaching for her as if he could steady her with just his touch.

"Don't. Please." She sniffed. When had she started crying again? "I can't."

He took a careful step closer, unwilling to let the space widen between them, and she shook her head.

When she tried to speak again, her voice broke. She was falling apart, and it showed. Couldn't he see that? "I can't do this, Cade."

His expression sobered, confusion flickering in his eyes. "Can't do what?"

"This." She waved a trembling hand between them. "Us. Whatever this is."

He froze at first, like the words didn't make sense. Then his jaw tightened, not in anger but in hurt. "Where is this coming from?"

Bailey's chest heaved and the words came tumbling out in a rush. "It's too much. Too serious. I thought I could handle it, but I just can't. Tonight made that all too clear. I'm not ready. I don't think I'll ever be ready."

She couldn't even handle loving a pet. How on earth had she thought she could handle loving Cade?

He stared at her for a long, silent moment, searching her face as if he could will her to take it back. "Bailey—"

She cut him off, desperate to put an end to things once and for all, before her courage failed. "You deserve someone who isn't broken, Cade. Someone who could actually give you all the pieces of her heart without fearing they'd shatter in your hands. You deserve better than me."

He inhaled sharply, like the words had knocked the wind from him. The ache in his eyes made her want to crumble.

When he finally spoke, his voice came out low and rough-edged. "Don't you know by now? I don't want better. I want you. It's always been you."

Her throat burned. Hot tears slid down her cheeks. She hugged Bluebell tighter, clinging to the only thing keeping her from collapsing entirely.

Her eyes darted to Ethan's portrait and then back to Cade. His gaze followed hers, and when it returned to her, his eyes were raw...haunted.

"I can't risk it. I'm better off by myself. If I let myself love you and something happens, I wouldn't survive it. You know I wouldn't." Her voice cracked, the confession spilling out like a wound she couldn't hide.

Cade had been with her every step of the way. He'd seen her grief up close, and he'd experienced it himself, too. He'd loved Ethan like a brother. How could he possibly think she had the strength to risk that kind of pain again, when even he knew how deep it cut?

Silence stretched between them, heavy as stone.

"You're not going to lose me, Bails," he said quietly.

She longed to believe him, but the ache in her chest screamed louder than his promise. "You don't know that. You can't make me a promise that you know you can't keep."

Her words came out sharp, defensive, even though a part of her wanted to reach for him instead of pushing him away.

Why does this have to be so complicated?

But she already knew the answer. It wasn't Cade or fate or the past making things complicated.

It was her.

Cade's chest ached like someone had driven a fist straight through him. He wanted to shake her, to beg her, to do anything but stand here while she convinced herself she wasn't worthy of what he already knew to be true. Every second she pushed him away, he felt the ground shift under his feet, like the whole foundation he'd been building with her was giving way.

"Bailey," he said, his voice rougher than he intended. "You're wrong. This—us—it doesn't have to be this hard. You'll feel better when we're not hiding anymore. That's what's tearing you apart, all this sneaking around like we've got something to be ashamed of. We don't. We never did. I should've never suggested it."

He'd thought keeping things quiet would protect her from town gossip, from pressure and from the endless comparisons to Ethan. But all he'd really done was plant the idea that what they had wasn't strong enough to stand in the light.

Her eyes widened, then shuttered, that guarded look he hated sliding into place. "Cade, don't—"

"No." He shook his head, heat crawling up the back of his neck. He'd kept quiet and let her run circles around her fears long enough. "I mean it. I thought I was protecting you, but all I did was make things worse. You think this is too much? You think it's too serious? Then let's stop pretending it's anything less. Let's stop acting like we're not already in the middle of it."

Her lips trembled, like she wanted to argue but couldn't quite find the words. Bluebell stirred in her arms, blinking her bright blue eyes as if nothing in the world was wrong, while Cade's heart cracked wide open.

"Do you hear yourself?" Bailey whispered finally. "You make it sound so simple."

"Because it is," he said, his voice breaking. He dragged a hand over his jaw, fighting to keep his composure. "I love being with you. You're the only thing that feels right in my life right now, and you look at me like you feel it, too. So stop pretending you don't."

Her breath hitched, her lashes wet, but still she shook her head. "We shouldn't even be talking about this. You've got your big scrimmage tomorrow, and you—"

"Don't," he interrupted, frustration sharpening his tone. "Don't throw the game at me like it matters more than this. You matter more than any of it. I'd give it all up if it meant you'd let me in."

The words hung between them, raw and unpolished, his whole heart laid bare. He swallowed hard, throat dry, then said the thing he'd been carrying for weeks. "I love you, Bailey. I love you, and I'm done hiding it."

He hadn't planned on telling her like this. He'd wanted the moment to be special, and instead, he'd blurted it out like a confession in full view of Ethan's portrait. But, of course, it would happen this way. Ethan had been standing between them all along. Cade loved his best friend. He always had, and he always would. But it was time to let go. Ethan wouldn't have wanted this for Bailey. He'd want her to be happy again, to find joy, even if it came in Cade's arms.

Bailey sucked in a breath as if the force of hearing "I love you" might knock her over. For a second, just one agonizing second, he thought she might let herself fall. But then she squeezed her eyes shut and clutched Bluebell tighter, like the kitten could shield her from him and the force of his feelings.

"Don't you get it?" she whispered. "I can't love you back."

Can't...or don't? Cade's jaw clenched. Which was it? There was an awfully big difference.

His gaze dropped to the little cat pressed against her chest, purring like she didn't know she was only temporary. Bailey hadn't even found the strength to claim Bluebell as her own, to give the kitten a real place in her life. She could have gone to the mayor and admitted the truth out loud—that the cat was safe with her and she wanted to keep her. She could have fought for Bluebell, but she hadn't. She'd kept the sweet kitty tucked away, just like she kept her real feelings hidden behind closed doors, never letting them see the light of day. If she couldn't risk that small kind of love, why had he ever believed she'd let him all the way in?

He wanted to argue, to tell her he wasn't Ethan, and he wasn't going anywhere. He wanted to swear he'd fight every single day to be the man she needed. But the haunted look in her eyes told him there was nothing he could say that would reach her tonight.

"Bailey..." His voice cracked despite his effort to hold it steady. He reached for her again, desperate to bridge the space between them, but she shook her head as her tears spilled faster.

Her eyes squeezed shut, and then she turned her face toward the floor as if she couldn't bear to look at him. "Please, Cade. Just go."

The words hit harder than any tackle he'd ever taken. For a long moment, he couldn't move. His legs refused to work, and his heart refused to accept what his mind already knew—that there wasn't a thing he could say or do to convince her to let him stay. Finally, he drew in a sharp breath, squared his shoulders and forced his body to obey.

"Alright," he said quietly, his voice raw with defeat.

He memorized her face in the dim light of the shop, every tear, every tremor, every piece of her that still felt like home. Then he turned and walked out the door he'd slipped through night after night, the door that had always felt like the beginning of something tender and new. Now, it felt like goodbye, and the weight of Ethan's eyes on him from the portrait made the leaving ache all the more.

He didn't look back.

Chapter Eighteen

The morning light felt harsher than it should have as it streamed through Bailey's apartment windows. She moved stiffly, hollowed out from a night of zero sleep, her chest still raw from the painful ending with Cade. She'd done the hard thing, though. She'd told him goodbye before fear could swallow her whole. It had nearly broken her, but she'd done it.

Now, there was one more hard thing left. This time, it fit inside a box.

Her fingers tightened on the cardboard carton in her arms until the edges bit into her palms. The faint smell of roasted coffee beans clung to the stiff flaps, a reminder of where the box had come from, and where Bluebell had been hiding for all the months she'd been missing. Inside, the kitten gave a plaintive mew, the sound muffled by the cardboard but piercing all the same, nearly cracking Bailey's resolve. She drew in a shaky breath, squared her shoulders and stepped onto Bulldog Avenue. She'd let Cade go. Now she had to let the cat go, too. Neither of them had ever really belonged to her, no matter how much her heart wanted otherwise.

Bailey forced her feet to keep moving toward the water

tower and the town green, past the hardware-store window with the missing-cat poster still taped to the glass.

Her throat ached at the sight.

Missing: Beloved Ragdoll kitten. Responds to the name Baby.

She didn't have to read the words. She'd known them by heart for months. Every time she saw one of those flyers, guilt had gnawed at her like a living thing. It didn't matter that Bluebell had all but chosen her, wandering into her life and curling into her lap as if she belonged there. The truth was simple: she belonged to someone else. And Bailey had reached the point where she couldn't carry another secret, not with Cade gone and her heart aching like it had been torn in two.

The mayor's house sat at the end of a quiet street shaded by live oak trees, their limbs sprawling like arms across the cracked sidewalk. Bailey paused at the white picket fence, her chest tight, then she made herself push open the gate. She walked up the path slowly, her sneakers crunching against the gravel, and tried her best not to cry. She wasn't here for herself. She was here to do the right thing.

She raised her hand and knocked.

The door swung open, and Mayor Pearl filled the doorway, a floral-print blouse bright against her ample frame. Her gray hair was swept back with a sparkly barrette, and her lipstick was a shade too pink, but her eyes softened the second they landed on the box in Bailey's arms. Behind her, cats flickered in and out of sight. A tabby darted down the hallway, a calico stretched lazily on the back of the sofa and a pair of curious green eyes peeked at Bailey from behind a curtain.

"Well, if it isn't Bailey Davis," Pearl said warmly. Her gaze dropped to the cardboard box in Bailey's arms, where Bluebell's little nose poked against the narrow gap in the flaps, a plaintive mew slipping out. "And, good heavens, Baby?"

Bailey's throat closed. She nodded, fumbling her words. "I—I'm so sorry, Mayor. I should've come sooner. Sh-she showed up at the coffee shop weeks ago, and I didn't know what to do. I saw the posters, but she was just so sweet, and I really enjoyed her company. I know it was wrong to keep her this long, but I just couldn't make myself let her go."

She needed to stop talking. The excuses sounded hollow, even to her own ears.

Pearl bent closer, her smile trembling as she peered in at the kitten. Bluebell let out a meow and poked a paw through the box's opening, earning a chuckle from the mayor. "Oh, Baby. Always wandering where you don't belong."

Bailey's chest squeezed tighter. "I brought her back. She's yours. I know I can't keep her."

"Come inside," Pearl said, ushering her in before Bailey could change her mind.

The mayor's house was cozy but cluttered. Every available surface was claimed by either a cat or something cat-shaped. Figurines lined the shelves, pillows with embroidered whiskers covered the sofa and the real thing sprawled across every spare patch of furniture. A tuxedo cat blinked at her from the mantel, tail twitching.

Bluebell poked her head out of the box, her blue eyes tracking the cats scattered around the room.

She belongs here, Bailey told herself. *Not with me.* What kitten wouldn't love this feline playground? It was like Disneyland for cats.

Pearl led her into the sitting room and motioned for Bailey to set the cardboard box on the coffee table. With careful fingers, the mayor pried open the flaps, and Bluebell bounded out, tail high, and immediately launched herself onto Bailey's lap.

Bailey's throat burned. This was it—the moment she had dreaded and prepared for all morning. Slowly, she reached out and guided Bluebell from her lap into Pearl's waiting arms. The kitten emitted a baffled meow before giving in and curling against the mayor's blouse as though it was the most natural thing in the world. Bailey's fingers lingered in the kitten's fur for half a heartbeat before she pulled them back, empty.

Letting go of Cade had hollowed her out, but this—this felt like pressing the bruise all over again.

"Well, hello, sweetheart," Pearl murmured, rubbing her cheek against Bluebell's tiny face. "I did miss you."

Bailey clasped her hands in front of her, nails digging into her palms. "She's been with me this whole time. I fed her, played with her and even bought her toys. But she's yours, and I had no right to keep her. I'll bring her things by later, if that's okay."

Pearl looked up then, her expression kind. "Bailey, sweet girl, do you think I don't know how much love you've given her? Just look at her."

She held Bluebell up for emphasis, the kitten sleek and bright-eyed, her coat brushed as soft as silk. "This is not a cat who's been neglected. This is a cat who's been adored."

Tears burned Bailey's eyes. "But she was missing. Everyone in town was looking for her, and I never said anything. I even let you put missing posters in Huddle Up."

Pearl stroked Bluebell's head, her own gaze softening. "I know, dear."

Bailey blinked. "What do you mean, you know? You're not surprised that I had her all along?"

The mayor shook her head. "No, honey. Because Cade Montgomery was here earlier this morning, and he told me the entire story. He explained everything—how Baby showed up at your door and that you'd taken her in and cared for her like she was your own. He even offered to buy her for you."

Bailey's breath caught in her throat. Cade had done *what*?

After everything she'd said to him last night, after she'd torn his heart to pieces, he'd still come here and fought for her to have this one small piece of love? Her vision blurred, fresh tears spilling. Even if Cade couldn't be the one holding her, he'd wanted to make sure she never felt alone.

Pearl went on, her voice quieter now. "You know, people ask me all the time why I have so many cats. Eight's an awful lot, even for a woman living alone. I could tell them it's because the house feels too quiet, or because Bishop Falls has more strays than it knows what to do with. But the truth is much simpler than that."

She paused and offered Bailey a watery smile. "My late husband gave me my very first kitten. She was a calico named Miss Patches. We were just kids ourselves back then, and he showed up at my door with that little bundle of fur, grinning like he'd handed me the moon. After he died, I found myself reaching for that comfort again. Each cat I've taken in since has been my way of holding on to his memory. My house may be full, Bailey, but it's still empty without him."

Bailey pressed a trembling hand to her mouth. She knew what it meant to try and fill a silence so vast that it swallowed you whole. She'd filled hers with the clatter of espresso cups, with the bustle of customers, with volunteering for every booster event under the sun—anything that kept her from feeling her own loneliness too clearly.

"I didn't know," she whispered.

Pearl smiled gently. "I don't talk about it often. But I see it in you, child. The way you cling to that little shop of yours, the way you put on a brave face for the entire town. You've been through loss, too. You and I, we're more alike than you think."

Bluebell squirmed then, leaping from Pearl's lap and scampering back to Bailey. She batted at the hem of her jeans as if declaring her allegiance. Bailey bent, scooped the kitten into her arms and buried her face in the warm fur. Tears slipped free before she could stop them.

"I don't want to give her up," she admitted brokenly.

Pearl reached out and put a warm, steady hand over Bailey's. "Or maybe she's yours now. Did you ever think of that? Cats have a funny way of choosing their people. Maybe Baby found you because you needed her more than I do. Lord knows I've got enough to keep me company."

Bailey blinked at her, startled. "You—you mean you'd let me keep her?"

"Of course, I would," Pearl said firmly. "I told Cade so this morning. I wouldn't take a dime from that lovely man, and believe me, he didn't want to take no for an answer. I may have plenty of cats, but I only have one heart. And I can see plain as day that little rascal has wrapped herself right around yours."

She still couldn't believe Cade had come here. He was still finding ways to take care of her, even when she'd made it clear she couldn't give anything back.

Pearl gave Bailey's hand a squeeze. "Don't let go of something good just because it came to you unexpectedly. Sometimes that's how the best blessings arrive. Life doesn't always give us neat, tidy packages. Sometimes it drops love on our doorstep when we're not looking for it. That can feel frightening, like it's too much, too soon. But if you close your hands to it, you risk closing your heart right along with them."

Bailey's chest stretched with something too big to contain, grief and gratitude tangling together. Pearl's words pressed against the rawest parts of her, echoing truths she hadn't wanted to face. Maybe she'd been so afraid of losing again that she'd mistaken every gift for a threat. Maybe love wasn't something to guard against at all, but something to be received, even when it terrified her.

The older woman leaned back in her chair, her eyes glimmering. "Love isn't a betrayal, Bailey. It's a blessing. Don't be afraid to let yourself have it again."

Bailey clutched Bluebell closer, the kitten's purr vibrating against her ribs like a second heartbeat. She didn't answer right away, but the thought pressed sharp and certain through her fear…

Maybe it really was time.

* * *

The day of the spring scrimmage dawned bright, but Cade felt anything but. Tonight, the Bulldogs would take the field against Rustwood. The entire town would pack the stands, the boosters would all be on edge and every ounce of pressure to win would land on Cade's shoulders. It should've been the only thing on his mind, but instead his thoughts kept circling back to Bailey's tears, the way she'd pulled away and the finality in her voice when she told him she couldn't risk loving him.

He'd driven toward the water tower at first light, restless after a night of broken sleep. Somehow his truck had carried him to Mayor Pearl's house, like it had made the decision for him. He hadn't been able to stand the thought of Bailey facing the mayor alone with that little cat in her arms, weighed down by guilt. If he hadn't stepped in, she might have carried that secret forever, punishing herself long after the truth could've set her free. Enough with the secrets. They'd already cost them both too much.

So he'd knocked on Pearl's door and explained how Bluebell—Baby, rather—had made her way to Huddle Up and how Bailey had cared for her like her own. He'd even offered to pay for the kitten if it would make Pearl let Bailey keep her. Pearl had listened, kind-eyed and patient, before patting his arm and refusing the money.

"That girl's already paid enough," she'd said.

The memory stayed with him as he drove the familiar road to Maplewood. He told himself he was just going to see Granny, like he always did on Saturday mornings, but the truth was harder to swallow. He needed her wisdom more than ever. He needed someone to tell him he wasn't crazy for still believing in Bailey when she'd made it so clear she was terrified of him.

The halls of Maplewood stretched long and familiar, their stillness broken only by the distant squeak of a medical cart. The weekend receptionist at the front desk waved him through, and Cade's boots echoed down the corridor toward Granny's room.

His grandmother was in her chair by the window with a quilt draped over her knees when he entered. A vase of yellow daffodils sat on the side table beside her crossword puzzle, their soft petals tilted toward the window's light. The sight of the flowers stirred something sharp in his chest, because he couldn't see daffodils without seeing Bailey.

"Well, if it isn't my state champion," Granny said, her voice warm and teasing. "Did you come to see if I'll say a prayer for the game tonight?"

Cade bent to kiss her cheek. "I'll take all the prayers you've got."

She patted his hand, and though her memory faltered at times, her eyes in that moment seemed to see too much. "It's not just the game weighing on you, is it?"

Cade pulled the other chair closer and sank into it, bracing his elbows on his knees. His voice came out low, rough. "You always seem to know."

"I've had a lot of years to practice," she said gently.

For a moment he stayed quiet, watching the light slant across the daffodils. They were so bright, so stubbornly alive against the stillness of the room. His throat thickened.

"Bailey loves those," he said quietly, more to himself than to Granny.

A flicker of recognition crossed her face. "Ethan's Bailey?"

For a beat, Cade couldn't breathe.

"Yeah," he said in a rough voice. "Ethan's Bailey. Except, not anymore. Ethan's gone, Granny. Now, she's just... Bailey."

He couldn't do it anymore. The pretense was killing him. He loved his grandmother with his whole heart, and maybe someday he'd be able to walk back in here and pretend that Ethan was still alive and well, Bailey was the head cheerleader and they still called themselves the Three Musketeers. But today wasn't that day.

He lifted his gaze to Granny's and braced for more questions. By some miracle, she didn't press for details. She only studied him with quiet sympathy.

Cade's throat worked as he forced himself to spill the rest of the truth. "And I—I've been seeing her, actually."

Granny's eyes warmed with a quiet understanding born of decades of knowing more than she ever said aloud. She didn't look shocked. She didn't scold. She only gave the smallest nod, like she'd been expecting him to admit it all along.

He didn't know if she fully grasped anything he was saying or if she simply understood the shape of his heart. Either way, the weight pressing down on him seemed lighter now that the truth was out in the open, spoken here in this room where the gossamer-thin line between past and present was as fragile as ever.

Granny tilted her head. "And she likes daffodils?"

"Yeah. They're Bailey's favorite flower." His chest tightened around her name. "Not roses or peonies like most women. For her, it's always been daffodils."

Granny's hand smoothed the quilt in a slow, thoughtful motion. "Has anyone ever told you what daffodils symbolize?"

Cade shook his head. He knew roses stood for love and romance, lilies for mourning and tulips for spring. He'd never realized daffodils had meaning, too. He'd only ever known them as Bailey's favorite.

"They're the first flowers to bloom after winter. Daffodils come early, always pushing up through the frost, even when nothing else will grow. Folks say they're a sign of new beginnings."

"New beginnings," he echoed with a pang in his chest.

At least his grandmother was having a good day, and he was thankful for that small mercy. He held on to it, knowing her clarity might slip away at any moment, the way it sometimes did.

Granny nodded. "I used to plant them every spring after your granddaddy passed. I thought maybe I wouldn't make it through that first year without him. But those flowers came back, as bright as the sun, reminding me that I was still standing... Reminding me that there's life after loss if you're brave enough to take hold of it."

Cade swallowed hard, his throat burning. Bailey's face flashed in his mind—her laughter, her jealous indignation at the chili cook-off, the press of her lips against his the night of the ring ceremony. That kiss had been the start of something, whether he'd realized it then or not. He wasn't ready for it to end, because Bailey was worth holding on to.

What if Granny was right? What if Bailey's fear last night wasn't the end at all, but only the last breath of winter before something new could finally bloom?

"I'm in love with her, but she said she can't do it. She thinks she's broken and that I deserve better." Cade scrubbed a hand over his face. He felt like a kid again, pouring his heart out to his grandmother.

Except he hadn't actually done that back then, had he? After Ethan's accident, he'd shouldered on in silence, carrying the weight alone because somebody had to. He'd wanted to be strong for the Dunnes. For the team. Most of all, for Bailey. Maybe if he had let himself lean on Granny, on *anyone*, the grief wouldn't have settled so deep into his bones.

He and Bailey had both made their fair share of mistakes. They'd been so young, though—kids trying to play at being adults, fumbling their way through heartache without knowing what to do with it. This time could be their chance to finally get it right.

Granny touched his arm. "You've been carrying something heavy, son. Don't let it make you forget who you are. Or what love can be."

He blinked fast, dragging a hand down his face. "She doesn't want me, Granny. She said as much."

"Did she say she didn't care for you?"

"No," Cade admitted, his chest aching with the memory. She hadn't said that. She'd said she couldn't risk it. That she'd break him. That she wasn't ready.

But she'd never once said she didn't love him.

Granny smiled knowingly. "Then it sounds to me like fear talking, not the truth. Fear makes folks run. But it doesn't mean they don't love what they're running from."

Cade stared at the daffodils again, their petals glowing gold in the light.

New beginnings.

Bailey's favorite flower.

She had to know what they meant, didn't she?

A glimmer of hope stirred low in his chest, faint but insistent. "I don't know how to fix it."

"Maybe you don't have to," Granny said simply. "Maybe you just have to be patient and true until she finds her way back."

Cade sat back, the knot in his chest easing just enough for him to breathe. Granny's words didn't erase the hurt, but they gave him something to hold on to. He could do patient. He could do true. He'd been faithful all his life.

He leaned over and kissed her cheek again. "Thanks, Granny."

She patted his hand, her eyes bright. "Now, go beat Rustwood tonight. Go, Bulldogs."

"Yes, ma'am." He chuckled, lifting his fist in the only answer that felt right. "Go, Bulldogs."

He stood to go. He still had a football game to win, a job to secure and a heart on the line. Nothing had actually changed since he'd walked through Granny's door. But when he glanced back at the daffodils, his smile settled into something deeper. For the first time since Bailey had pushed him away, he felt the faintest flicker of belief that maybe she wasn't gone for good.

Maybe this wasn't the end. Maybe it was the beginning.

Even if it meant finally laying his best friend to rest in his heart.

The high-school stadium sat in half shadow, caught between daylight and darkness. The game wouldn't start for a couple of hours yet, but the floodlights were already blazing, casting long beams across the empty field. Soon the stands would be packed, the band blaring, the whole place loud and alive.

For now, though, the silence held—the calm before the storm.

Cade stepped through the stadium gates alone. Empty bleachers rose on either side of him, their rows of metal seats waiting for the crowd that would soon rattle them with cheers. The faint buzz of the lights hung overhead, while his own footsteps echoed against the pavement like he didn't quite belong here. He bit down hard as he crossed midfield, drawn toward the spot he'd been avoiding for weeks.

The thirty-yard line.

The memorial logo spanned at least five yards, painted in green and white with Ethan Dunne's name stenciled clean in block lettering. Cade stared at it, the weight in his chest pressing harder. He only just realized now that he hadn't set foot on this spot since the night he first kissed Bailey. Maybe he'd been avoiding more than the paint on the turf. Maybe he'd been avoiding everything it stirred up—guilt, longing, the sharp edge of wanting something that had once belonged to Ethan.

"Hey," he said, his voice sounding too loud in the emptiness. He tried again, softer this time. "Hey, Ethan."

The words felt clumsy, but once they started, they wouldn't stop.

"I don't even know what I'm doing here. I just... needed to talk. And maybe, if there's anywhere I can still reach you, it's here. Calla comes out sometimes, I know that. She says it helps." He huffed a humorless laugh. "I've been stubborn. I told myself I didn't need it. That I could just keep moving forward, same as always."

His boots shifted against the turf. The silence pressed back.

"But the truth is, I think about you constantly. It feels like I'm walking through the life that was meant for you—hearing the kids call me 'Coach,' chasing victories that should've been yours...even Bailey." Cade swallowed hard. "Especially Bailey."

The only answer came from the hum of the floodlights overhead. Cade rubbed a hand over the back of his neck.

"She asked me a while back if I ever feel guilty." His voice cracked, and he had to steady himself before going on. "And I do, man. Of course, I do. Because you should be here. You should've been the one leading the team at State, not me. You should've been the one kissing her after the ring ceremony, instead of me, wondering if I even belonged in that moment at all."

He lowered himself to the turf, sitting cross-legged at the edge of the logo. For a long time he just stared at Ethan's name painted bold under the stadium lights.

"I don't want to hurt her," he whispered. "She's been through enough. But I... I can't stop wanting her, either. I've tried. You know I have." His laugh was raw. "Spoiler alert—it didn't work. I guess some things are bigger than us."

The field stretched quiet around him, heavy with memories. Ethan throwing touchdowns. Ethan's grin in the huddle. Ethan's laugh when Cade flubbed a drill. Cade pressed his palms together, leaning forward until his elbows dug into his knees.

"I'm not trying to take your place. You need to know

that. Nobody could." His eyes burned, but he kept talking. "I just want to build something that's mine with her. Something that honors what you two had, but doesn't get swallowed by it, either...if that's even possible."

A breeze stirred, carrying the faint scent of spring blossoms from beyond the bleachers. Cade let out a shaky breath.

"Maybe it's selfish. Wanting her. Wanting this job. Wanting to keep moving like the world didn't fall apart when you got hurt. But the thing is, Ethan..." He scrubbed a hand down his face. "The thing is, I think she wants it, too. Wants me. And that scares her as much as it scares me."

For a while he didn't move. He just sat there with Ethan's name spelled out beneath him, letting the silence close in until his chest ached.

Finally, he pulled his state championship ring from his pocket. He'd taken it off weeks ago and never had the heart to put it back on. Now, he turned it over in his hand, the gold glinting faintly in the twilight. The boys had been so proud, shouting and laughing when they won. Cade had smiled with them, but even then, a hollow had opened somewhere deep inside.

"This was supposed to be yours," he said softly. "You should've won it that night our senior year instead of lying on the field hurt while everything changed. It almost feels like I stole it from you. I don't even know what I'm doing half the time. Just trying to keep the pieces together."

He set the ring down on the painted turf, right where Ethan's name curved across the thirty-yard line. The sight of it there twisted something deep in Cade's chest.

"I wish I could give it to you, man. I wish you'd gotten to see it, to feel it. But since you can't…" His voice broke, and he swallowed hard. "Since you can't, I'll leave it here. It feels like the only thing that makes sense."

He stayed there a long time, his hand resting against the cool turf, the ring glinting faintly in the floodlights. Eventually he pushed himself to his feet, staring down at the memorial one last time.

"Take care of her, alright? I think it might always be you," he whispered. "Because I'm trying to believe she could still choose me, but God help me, I don't know if I'll ever be enough."

Then he walked off the field, the echo of his steps trailing behind him as the ring rested heavy against Ethan's name.

Chapter Nineteen

Bailey slipped through the gate on the home team's side, the cool metal rattling shut behind her as she squinted against the stadium lights. She was late. The game had already begun, but she didn't stop to explain or apologize. She simply pushed up the sleeves of her Bulldogs shirt, lifted her chin and started up the bleachers.

Across the way, the visitor stands were awash in red and gold. Rustwood fans packed the benches, and when their star quarterback passed for a first down, a knot of students with painted faces leaped up and crowed like roosters, their voices carrying clear across the field.

The home team's side was no quieter. Families waved foam paws, students leaned over the rails shouting encouragement and boosters filled entire rows with their Bulldogs jackets and caps. Bailey spotted Calla halfway up the stands, one arm lifted as she waved her down. Dr. Dunne sat beside her, of course. The three of them had been attending football games together since graduation, ever since Bailey hung up her cheerleading uniform and traded the sidelines for a spot in the stands.

"Come sit down!" Calla called, her blond curls spilling from beneath one of Jackson's Bulldogs caps.

Bailey threaded her way across laps and knees until

she dropped into the empty spot between the Dunnes. Then her breath caught in her throat, not from the climb, but from what she saw the moment she looked down at the field.

Cade.

He stood near the forty-yard line with his arms folded over his chest as he watched every movement on the turf. The hard lines of his jaw were set, and his whole frame thrummed with focus. He looked every inch the coach—commanding, steady, in control—and Bailey's chest tightened. She wanted him to see her and know she was here, watching him, standing with him in her own small way.

But his eyes never strayed from the field.

A whistle blew, and she forced herself to focus on the action, eyes following the line of scrimmage as the Bishop Falls defense bent low into formation. Rustwood had the ball.

The first snap was crisp. Tyler Crenshaw, the quarterback who'd followed Bob Simmons to Rustwood, stepped back and fired the ball clean down the middle of the field. His receiver caught it easily and took off downfield thirty yards before a Bulldogs safety dragged him out of bounds.

The Rustwood stands thundered with approval, and their band launched into a fight song.

Calla exhaled a sharp breath beside Bailey. "Unbelievable. That kid looks like he's already got scouts in the stands."

Bailey's stomach knotted. She forced her gaze away from Cade again, away from the sideline, where she wanted to read his reaction, and fixed it on the line of scrimmage. The Bulldogs set again, ready for the next play.

It was only the first quarter, she reminded herself. And she believed in them.

Rustwood pushed hard on that opening drive, their quarterback slinging passes like he had ice in his veins. Each completion left him strutting a little taller, chin tipped toward the home stands as if daring them to doubt him. By the time they crossed midfield, only four plays in, he wore a smirk like the game already belonged to him. He capped the series with a laser to the corner of the end zone, jogging off the field with his pointer finger raised to the sky. Touchdown, Roosters.

On the opposite sideline, Bob Simmons pumped both fists in the air, his gaudy red-and-gold Roosters jacket loud enough to match his gloating grin. He clapped hard, then turned deliberately toward the Bulldogs's bench as if to rub salt in the wound. The sight made Bailey's stomach knot, her fingernails digging into her palms.

Calla let out a sharp, furious sound beside her. "Can you believe him? He wouldn't even have a coaching career if it weren't for this program, and now he's standing over there cheering against us like he's not wearing a Bulldogs championship ring on one of his sausage fingers."

Dr. Dunne shifted in his seat, his calm a quiet counterpoint to Calla's fire. "Easy now. Let's just keep the faith. Jackson, Cade and the rest of our coaches have got this under control. One play doesn't decide a game."

Calla huffed, crossing her arms tight over her chest, though her eyes stayed locked on the field like she might set Simmons on fire with sheer indignation.

Bailey couldn't help it...her lips twitched. "When you decide to become a sports fan, Calla, you really go all in."

Calla shot her a look, but the corners of her mouth betrayed a reluctant smile as the Bulldogs offense jogged onto the field with Noah Weaver at the helm.

Bailey leaned forward. "Come on, Noah."

The sophomore quarterback moved like he belonged there, shoulders squared as he clapped his hands for the snap. His frame carried none of the nerves she'd seen in him at practice a few days ago. According to Cade, he'd hardly been able to string a sentence together in front of a girl, much less throw a football. Yesterday's promposal at the pep rally had clearly changed something, though.

"Look at him." Calla gave Bailey a gentle shoulder bump. "Cade did that, you know."

Bailey's throat tightened. She didn't doubt it. Cade had a way of steadying people, of giving them room to grow until they realized they were stronger than they thought. It was written all over Noah now—in the set of his shoulders, the confidence in his step, the way he called out the cadence loud enough for the whole stadium to hear.

The snap came, the ball sailed and Noah's receiver pulled it in clean for an easy first down. The crowd roared, but Bailey's gaze lingered on the sideline, searching for the man who'd made it possible.

Cade didn't strut or fist pump like Simmons. He just clapped Noah on the shoulder when he returned to the sidelines, as if he'd never doubted the boy could do it. That quiet confidence was Cade's gift. He believed in people until they couldn't help believing in themselves.

The game became a tug-of-war after that. Rustwood's showboating quarterback answered every challenge with another precise throw and another touchdown march. But Noah held his ground. He delivered short, sharp passes, then took a deep shot that soared down the sideline into his receiver's arms. The Bulldogs struck back, possession after possession.

The scoreboard ticked upward: 7–7. Then 14–14.

Every play ratcheted the tension higher. Around Bailey, the Bulldogs fans cupped their hands around their mouths and shouted themselves hoarse. Dr. Dunne nodded in steady approval each time the boys executed a clean play. Calla was the opposite—up and down with every snap, pumping her fist at completions, groaning at dropped passes, muttering threats under her breath whenever Simmons paced too close to midfield.

Bailey hid a smile. Calla had never done anything halfway, and football fandom was no exception. Her WAG era was truly something to behold.

All the while, Bob Simmons prowled like a wolf, barking across the field. "That's how it's done, boys! The Bulldogs can't stop you!"

His voice carried even over the roar of the crowd, and through it all, Bailey kept wanting Cade to look up, just once. To know she was here.

But he didn't. His focus stayed locked on his team.

She hugged her knees for a moment, feeling the restless hum in the stands vibrate straight through her bones. Everyone else was swept up in the game, but she was caught between doubt and longing, wishing for something she wasn't sure Cade even wanted anymore.

And then, finally, he looked up.

Their eyes met across the distance, and for a fleeting moment, Bailey thought she saw a flicker at the corner of his mouth, the barest hint of a smile. It wasn't much, but it was enough to steady the ache inside her. Enough to give her hope.

She pressed a hand against her racing heart. She was here. She hadn't let fear chase her off, and now Cade knew it.

With a long blast from the referee's whistle, the first half of the game came to a close. The players jogged toward their locker rooms in jerseys streaked with sweat and grass. Bishop bounded onto the field at the end of a leash held by the equipment manager, his nub of a tail wagging like he'd earned every yard himself. The scoreboard glowed bright: Bulldogs 21, Roosters 21.

It was a tie game, and the whole stadium buzzed with anticipation for what the second half might bring.

Bailey sat wedged between Calla and Dr. Dunne with her hands clasped tight in her lap, her sweatshirt warm around her shoulders and her heart hammering with something that had nothing to do with football. She hadn't come here tonight just to watch a game. She hadn't come only to cheer.

By the end of this night, town sweetheart Bailey Davis wasn't going to sit on the sidelines of her own life anymore.

The second half opened under lights that burned white against the velvet night. The teams burst from their locker rooms with fresh energy, the Roosters all swagger and strut, the Bulldogs taut with determination.

Cade stood just behind the line of coaches with his arms folded. He'd never admit it out loud, but his chest swelled with hope, despite the numbers on the scoreboard. Games like this weren't won by talent alone. They were won by grit. By kids who found a way to believe in the impossible.

He knew belief when he saw it, and right now, Noah had it written all over him. The boy jogged to the huddle, clapping his teammates on the shoulders, his voice carrying even over the pounding brass of the Rustwood band. A week ago, Noah had barely been able to look Cade in the eye without stammering. Tonight, he was commanding the field.

Cade's gaze flickered instinctively toward the stands. He didn't mean to, but his eyes searched until they found her. And there Bailey was, sandwiched between Calla and Dr. Dunne. Her hands were knotted together in her lap, her posture taut with hope and nerves.

For a split second, his heart soared. She was here. He hadn't known if she'd come tonight, hadn't known if she'd want to after the painful events of last night, but she had.

And then the whistle shrieked, snapping him back to the present.

The third quarter swung hard in both directions. The Bulldogs's defense dug deep, stuffing Rustwood at the line of scrimmage, only to be burned a series later by another of Crenshaw's laser throws. Every time Cade's offense clawed back, Rustwood answered. The scoreboard seesawed: 28–28. Then 35–35.

Across the field, Bob Simmons strutted in his Rooster red like he'd already won. Each time Rustwood found the end zone, he bellowed and threw a smirk deliberately toward Jackson and Cade. Cade's jaw tightened every time, his blood running hot, but he kept his arms folded and his eyes on his own boys. Let Simmons preen. The scoreboard would be the only answer that mattered.

The crowd lived and died with every play. Cade could feel the pulse of the town in every roar of approval and every groan of frustration. Calla leaped to her feet so often he could see her blond curls bouncing even from field level. Dr. Dunne didn't shout or pump his fists, but his calm applause carried a weight Cade felt in his bones. It was the same reassuring presence that made him such a great veterinarian. And Bailey... Every time Cade let his gaze stray, she was there, leaning forward, her whole body alive with belief.

It rattled him more than he wanted to admit. Because once upon a time, she'd looked at him the same way— back when he was just a boy throwing a football, not a coach trying to prove himself. Back when he'd been too tangled up in loyalty to even think about what he wanted. That look—hope, pride, something more—was seared into him, and seeing it again tonight, even from a distance, twisted him up inside.

It was impossible not to feel it. Impossible not to remember how she'd looked at him once, long before fear and grief and the weight of a whole town had settled between them.

The fourth quarter loomed, and Cade knew they were running out of time. Rustwood had swagger, but Bishop Falls had heart. Heart, and Noah Weaver.

The sophomore took the field for what everyone knew could be the final drive. The Bulldogs were pinned deep in their own territory with the roar of the Roosters fans loud in their ears. Cade crouched low on the sideline, watching, silently urging Noah to keep his composure.

And he did. Snap after snap, the boy threaded passes, short and safe, inching them forward. The clock bled precious seconds, but Noah's shoulders never slumped. The team rallied around him, the line holding firm, receivers stretching their fingertips to pull in every ball.

Still, they were too far. With only forty seconds left in a tie game, they were still stuck well outside of field-goal distance.

Cade's heart hammered, but he forced his face to stay composed. He wanted this win. Not for himself, not even for the assistant-coach promotion dangling like a carrot, but for these kids. For Noah. For the town that showed up every Friday night during football season, win or lose.

And, yes, deep down, he wanted it for Bailey, too. For the woman who still made him hope for more than football could ever give him. He wanted her to see what he was fighting for—not glory, not revenge against Simmons, but the belief that broken things could still be rebuilt. That people could stumble, fall apart and then rise again. He wanted her to see that in him tonight. To know that if she ever took a chance on him, he would fight for her the same way.

The next snap came. The offensive line held. Noah dropped back, eyes scanning the field. A defender surged through the gap, and Cade's throat closed. But then Noah spun to the right with the ball cradled tight against his chest. He pumped once, drawing the secondary forward, then let it fly.

The spiral cut through the night, arcing higher than any pass Cade had seen from the kid. The whole stadium seemed to hold its breath as the ball dropped perfectly into the waiting hands of a receiver streaking down the sideline.

Caught.

The boy never broke stride. He tore past the thirty, the twenty, the ten. Touchdown.

The stands went wild, and for the first time since kickoff, Jackson's face split into a wide grin. He glanced at Cade, and they exchanged a look. This was it. This was the moment the boys proved themselves, the moment all those long nights and brutal drills finally paid off. The scoreboard glowed like a promise, and the roar of the crowd pressed down around them. Cade couldn't hear his own thoughts, but it didn't matter. He knew. He knew what this meant.

The boys swarmed Noah in the end zone, helmets slapping against helmets, voices breaking with triumph. Cade jogged downfield, caught between restraint and the swell of pride that threatened to undo him. He reached Noah at the edge of the celebration, his hand landing firm on the boy's shoulder.

"You did it," he said. No fanfare or victory dance, just the plain, solid truth between coach and player.

Noah's grin was all teeth and disbelief. "*We* did it, Coach."

Cade nodded, his jaw tight. Yes. They had.

The final seconds ticked away, and when the whistle blew for the last time, the scoreboard blazed in triumph: Bulldogs 42, Roosters 35. The touchdown and the easy kick afterward for the extra point had sealed it, leaving no chance for Rustwood to catch up.

The field exploded into chaos. Students, parents, boosters and teachers surged from the stands, flooding the turf. Kids clambered over the railings, helmets bob-bing in the sea of humanity. Cade stood at the center of it, letting the noise wash over him. This was victory, hard-fought and hard-earned, and it felt good.

But even as the celebration raged, his eyes kept drifting upward. It was instinct by now—searching the stands, always searching. He wanted to see Bailey's face lit by the glow of the scoreboard, wanted to know if she felt even a fraction of the pride that burned in his chest. He wanted her to know that this win wasn't just about football. It was about proving that they could build some-thing new, something worth holding on to.

Through the swirling mass of fans and tiny bits of green and white paper that burst from the pep squad's confetti cannon, his gaze swept the stands. But the seat between Calla and Dr. Dunne was empty.

Bailey was gone.

The realization cut sharper than he expected. She'd been right there. He'd felt her presence just as keenly as he'd seen it. She was there, and now, she wasn't. Just like that. Just like last night, when she'd told him to leave.

He swallowed hard against the burn rising in his throat. Around him, the team lifted Noah onto their shoulders, their laughter spilling into the night air. But all Cade could see was the empty stretch of bleachers where Bailey should've been.

He stood in the middle of the jubilant chaos, the taste of victory still on his tongue, and the hollow ache of her absence pressing against his heart.

The boys didn't want to leave the field. No one did. From where Cade stood, just left of the forty, it looked like half the stands had spilled onto the turf. Parents snapped pictures, students high-fived each other and even the rest of the coaches couldn't quite bring themselves to herd the players toward the locker room. Jackson was still grinning from ear to ear. A few minutes ago, Cade had even seen him *hug* Earl Whitaker.

This was a night that would go down in Bulldogs history, no question. The town would be talking about it for years—how the boys rose up, how they shut down Bob Simmons and his hotshot quarterback, how Bishop Falls proved they weren't anyone's underdog.

By all accounts, Cade should have been soaring. He'd done it. He was the new assistant coach of the Bulldogs. The promotion was his, and with it, the stability he'd been chasing for so long. All the pieces of his life had finally clicked into place. His problems should've been solved.

And yet…

Cade rubbed his thumb over the bare place on his finger, tender with memory where his championship ring used to sit. The cheers around him rang hollow, bouncing off the emptiness in his chest. Because no matter how sweet the victory, it wasn't the thing he wanted most. Not anymore.

Where had Bailey gone?

"Lose something?"

He turned. Calla stood a few yards away, her blond waves spilling out from under one of Jackson's Bulldogs caps. She held something in her hand, the shape of it instantly familiar.

His state championship ring.

"I found this earlier," Calla said as she pressed it into

his palm. "I was down on the field before kickoff, snapping a few pictures for the *Gazette*. I knew it had to be yours the second I spotted it. And I knew exactly what finding it there meant."

Cade curled his fingers around it, a sting rising in his chest. "Yes, it's mine."

She lifted an accusatory eyebrow. "You left it there on purpose, didn't you?"

He really didn't have it in him to argue with Calla about this. Why couldn't she have just left the ring there where it belonged?

He cleared his throat. "Look, Calla. Thanks for returning it to me. I appreciate the gesture, but I don't want this ring anymore. It should've been Ethan's, not mine."

Calla's expression softened. "You've got to stop thinking that way. You earned this, Cade. You've carried this team."

He shook his head, jaw tight, but before he could answer, she tilted her chin, studying him with the same sharpness she'd had since they were kids.

"We're not just talking about the ring, are we?"

Cade stilled.

Calla's smile was sad, but sure. "I've seen the way you look at her. And I've seen the way she looks back. You've been trying to keep it quiet, but you can't hide something like that—not from me."

Heat rushed to Cade's neck. He thought they'd been careful.

She paused, her eyes flickering with the kind of protectiveness Cade had always admired in her. "You love her, don't you?"

He could've deflected. He could've dodged or made a

joke. But he was too tired, too raw, too *done*. He didn't want to lie to the people closest to him anymore. Besides, she'd already guessed the truth, and there wasn't a thing he could say to convince her otherwise. Calla was as stubborn as Bishop.

He nodded once. "Yeah. I do."

"Then what are you doing, standing here all alone? Fight for her, Cade."

"It's not that simple." He shook his head, the roar of the crowd swelling around them like it belonged to someone else's victory. "I think she feels the same, but I don't want to push her. She's just not ready."

Calla tilted her head, a spark in her eye. "Cade Montgomery, you've spent years of your life waiting on Bailey Davis. Maybe it's time to let her tell you herself whether or not she's ready."

Cade looked at her, uncertain. What was she talking about? His voice came out low, wary. "Calla—"

"Let's just say I think you might be surprised," Calla interrupted, her grin widening.

Before he could answer, she tugged his sleeve, pulling him toward the fifty-yard line. "Come on."

"Where?"

"Exactly where you belong," she said, her tone bright with confidence. "Trust me, Coach. Just this once, stop calling plays and let someone else run one for you."

The Bulldogs were still scattered across the field, helmets dangling from their hands, jerseys streaked with sweat and turf stains, when Jackson barked an order. Somehow, above the noise of the band and the chatter of the crowd, the boys heard him.

"Line it up, Bulldogs!"

They didn't even hesitate. They fell into formation, two neat rows stretching from the thirty to the fifty, their grins splitting wide as they realized what they were being asked to do. A victory tunnel—one they usually saved for big games, not spring scrimmages. The boys stomped their cleats, whooped and slapped their palms together overhead, forming an arch of green and white.

Cade blinked, thrown. "What in the world—"

"Just wait," Calla murmured at his side, her hand still hooked through his sleeve. Her eyes were dancing.

And then he saw her.

Bailey.

She stood at the far mouth of the tunnel, dark hair loose around her shoulders, her Bulldog sweatshirt swallowed up by the sea of players on either side of her. Her hands gripped a giant poster board, the marker lettering bold and uneven, probably scrawled in a rush.

This is My Hail Mary
Will You Be Mine, Coach?

Cade's breath hitched. His heart slammed once, hard, against his ribs.

The boys caught sight of the words and roared their approval, the sound building with the pounding of their cleats.

Someone started a chant. "Bailey! Bailey! Bailey!"

For a second, Cade wondered if she might change her mind, tuck the sign against her chest and bolt for the exit. No one in Bishop Falls missed a football game. *Literally* nobody. Every person who lived in a one-hundred-mile radius was here, plus more than a few out-of-towners and the greater population of Rustwood.

As far as promposals went, this was a lot—a production on par with a whole herd of goats and enough glitter to blind the Western hemisphere. But she didn't turn around. Her chin lifted, shoulders squaring with a courage that belonged to someone who'd chosen this moment, this field, this man. The poster rattled in her hands, but her eyes were steady. She was nervous—who wouldn't be, with half the county watching?—yet there was no hesitation whatsoever in her face.

And that was the thing that knocked the wind out of Cade's chest.

He'd wanted to go public, but he'd never imagined it like this. Not with his entire team thundering approval behind him. Not with the cheerleaders bouncing in sync to the chant of Bailey's name. Not with the entire town of Bishop Falls watching like it was the fourth quarter, and the game was on the line.

Still, it was perfect. Because it was her. Because she wasn't hiding anymore.

Cade's throat went tight, pride and awe tangling in a way that nearly undid him. He'd thought he was ready to step out of the shadows, but Bailey had just proved she was braver than he was. She wasn't asking for permission. She was telling the whole world.

And he loved her all the more for it.

Bailey lifted the poster high in the air and ran. The players whooped as she darted beneath their raised arms, the tunnel shaking with celebration. Hands clapped her shoulders as she passed, the sound of her name echoing in the stadium. All the while, Cade stood rooted to the fifty-yard line with his pulse hammering.

Bailey burst through the end of the tunnel and stopped just in front of him, her chest rising and falling with uneven breaths. She still held the poster, though her grip on it had loosened. Her big doe eyes locked on his, wide with both awe and certainty.

For a moment, the crowd noise seemed to fall away.

"It's you," she said, her voice soft but carrying, steady enough that Cade knew half the stadium had heard her. "It's you now. It's *only* you. I'm in love with you, Cade. To be honest, I've loved you for quite a while now."

The team cheered as the victory tunnel dissolved into a rowdy celebration, but Cade barely noticed. All he saw was Bailey, standing in the middle of the most crowded spot in Bishop Falls, telling him she loved him.

A rush of adrenaline surged through him, carrying him closer. One step, then another, until he stood directly in front of her. Slowly, he reached out, tugging the poster down so he could fully see her beautiful face.

"Are you sure about this?" he asked, the question aching in his throat.

Bailey nodded without a flicker of doubt. "I've never been more sure of anything in my life."

What had felt impossible an hour ago now seemed inevitable, fated…*right.* Cade caught her around the waist, pulled her close and planted a kiss on her lips that silenced even the rowdiest of his players.

For all of half a second.

A fresh round of cheers went up from the crowd, along with a few earsplitting whistles and bursts from the air horn that Earl Whitaker blasted without mercy every time the Bulldogs scored a touchdown.

Cade finally broke away, a crooked smile tugging at his mouth as he cradled Bailey's face in his hands. "Do you get the feeling," he murmured with a grin, "that maybe our little secret wasn't so secret, after all?"

"Apparently everyone knew… Everyone but us." Bailey laughed, and her cheeks flushed pink. "Now, I do, though. You, Cade Montgomery, are my best friend as well as the man that I love, and I can't decide which side of you I enjoy the most."

Something about the way she said it made him pause. He tipped his head, squinting down at her. "Hold on. Why does that sound so much like a line from *The Notebook*?"

She waggled her eyebrows. "Because it is. Maybe not word for word, but awfully close."

Cade narrowed his eyes at her. "I thought you hadn't seen that movie."

"I hadn't." She shrugged one slender shoulder. "Until today."

"Today?"

She nodded. "I went to see Mayor Pearl this morning. She told me you'd been there, right before she told me I could keep Bluebell." Bailey's eyes glistened with a shimmer of happy tears threatening to spill. "Afterward, I took my cat home, and we watched the movie. Then we watched three more romances, back-to-back-to-back."

Her confession made him chuckle. "Did you, now?"

She gave a little shrug, her grin blooming. "I think I might be a fan of happy endings, after all."

Cade's chest squeezed like he'd just clawed his way

to victory in the final play of a nail-biter of a game. The stadium lights shimmered against the sky, forming a soft halo around Bailey's dark hair. She looked just like she had at Miller's Bluff, when the world had fallen away and the night belonged only to them and the fireflies.

"Good," he said, his hand cupping her cheek. "Because this one's ours. And I promise you, Bailey Bear, our happy ending is just getting started."

* * * * *

Get up to 4 Free Books!

We'll send you 2 free books from each series you try
PLUS a free Mystery Gift.

FREE
Value Over
$25

Both the **Harlequin® Special Edition** and **Harlequin® Heartwarming™** series feature compelling novels filled with stories of love and strength where the bonds of friendship, family and community unite.

YES! Please send me 2 FREE novels from the Harlequin Special Edition or Harlequin Heartwarming series and my FREE Gift (gift is worth about $10 retail). I may cancel anytime by emailing ReaderServiceInfo@Harlequin.com or by calling 1-800-873-8635. If I don't cancel, I will receive 6 brand-new Harlequin Special Edition books every month and be billed just $6.39 each in the U.S. or $7.19 each in Canada, or 4 brand-new Harlequin Heartwarming Larger-Print books every month and be billed just $7.19 each in the U.S. or $7.99 each in Canada, a savings of 20% off the cover price. It's quite a bargain! Shipping and handling is just 75¢ per book in the U.S. and $1.75 per book in Canada.* I understand that accepting the free books and gift places me under no obligation to buy anything—they are mine to keep for free no matter what I decide.

Choose one: ☐ **Harlequin Special Edition**
(235/335 BPA G3CD)

☐ **Harlequin Heartwarming Larger-Print**
(161/361 BPA G3CD)

☐ **Or Try Both!**
(235/335 & 161/361 BPA G3CE)

Name (please print)

Address   Apt. #

City   State/Province   Zip/Postal Code

Email: Please check this box ☐ if you would like to receive newsletters and promotional emails from Harlequin Enterprises ULC and its affiliates. You can unsubscribe anytime.

Mail to the **Harlequin Reader Service:**
IN U.S.A.: P.O. Box 1341, Buffalo, NY 14240-8531
IN CANADA: P.O. Box 603, Fort Erie, Ontario L2A 5X3

Want to explore our other series or interested in ebooks? Visit www.ReaderService.com or call 1-800-873-8635.

---

*Terms and prices subject to change without notice. Prices do not include sales taxes, which will be charged (if applicable) based on your state or country of residence. Canadian residents will be charged applicable taxes. Offer not valid in Quebec. This offer is limited to one order per household. Books received may not be as shown. Not valid for current subscribers to the Harlequin Special Edition or Harlequin Heartwarming series. All orders subject to approval. Credit or debit balances in a customer's account(s) may be offset by any other outstanding balance owed by or to the customer. Please allow 4 to 6 weeks for delivery. Offer available while quantities last.

Your Privacy — Your information is being collected by Harlequin Enterprises ULC, operating as Harlequin Reader Service. For a complete summary of the information we collect, how we use this information and to whom it is disclosed, please visit our privacy notice located at https://corporate.harlequin.com/privacy-notice. Notice to California Residents—Under California law, you have specific rights to control and access your data. For more information on these rights and how to exercise them, visit https://corporate.harlequin.com/california-privacy. For additional information for residents of other U.S. states that provide their residents with certain rights with respect to personal data, visit https://corporate.harlequin.com/other-state-residents-privacy-rights.

HSEHW2603